# GONE TO GROUND

## A DCI BOYD THRILLER

## ALEX SCARROW

GrrBooks

Published by GrrBooks

*To Jake, my son, my mate... and God help me
competition one day, I fear :)*

# PROLOGUE

B oyd watched the coffin slowly edging forward into the crematorium oven, the squeaking rollers audible above the sound of Cockney Rebel's 'Come Up and See Me'. That track apparently had been one of his favourites. Okeke had told Boyd it was the most played track on his iPhone. 'Ordinary Day' by Duran Duran had been a close second.

He looked to his left, to where she was sitting. He'd learned over the last year that his good friend and colleague preferred to keep displays of emotion to herself, often hiding her feelings behind a façade of caustic banter.

For Samantha Okeke, tears were for bereaved mothers and favourite aunts. Snotty tears for scrotes in the dock who wanted to appear contrite. They were for family liaison officers to mop up in hospital waiting rooms or for a parent sitting on the end of a dead child's unmade bed.

Tears were not for her. No, sir.

But this morning, as he waited for the coffin to slowly disappear behind the curtain, Boyd glimpsed – for the first time – a tear rolling down her cheek...

# BEFORE

TWO WEEKS EARLIER

# 1

Murray Schofield had always had big *plans* – Life Plans. Ever since he'd watched the first season of *The X Factor* as a kid, he'd known that not only did he have the talent to become the next Ed Sheeran but also the drive, the voice, the looks. Of course, with shows like *X Factor* and platforms like YouTube and TikTok, he had many possible winding avenues down which to reach his goal.

And he really had given it his best shot. But... as the years had passed by, Murray had allowed his Life Plan to downscale by degrees. Okay, so maybe not Ed Sheeran then, but some level of success, any level that could be considered a career in showbiz.

A stage-school course had helped him to finally get a job aboard a cruise ship, but he'd only enjoyed a few months of that particular career before it had all come to an end with the arrival of Covid.

The furlough payments had sustained him for a while, but with no restaurants or bars open for cash gigs, it wasn't long before reality placed its crushing size 10 boot on his throat and squeezed the life out of his dreams.

And that's how Murray had ended up in his new career as a bin man.

Ironically, the other guys on his shift called him 'Ed' or 'Eddie' as in Ed Sheeran because he preferred to sing while he worked – his headphones on, accompanying various stage musical classics. You never knew when an audition opportunity might crop up and he wanted to keep his voice limbered up and ready, just in case.

January, he'd quickly realised, was a shit month to do this job. The wheelie bins were choked and overflowing with Christmas tat, upended threadbare pine trees, wrapping paper and the like. Plus... getting up at ridiculous o'clock and going out to work in midnight darkness wasn't much fun.

And it was bastardly cold as well at this time of year, which was why he had large furry earmuffs over his woollen beanie and earphones (to the amusement of the rest of 'the lads') and those muffs were probably the reason he didn't hear the shouting until it was too late.

Murray was vaguely aware of Gazza frantically waving his arms at him as he hurried across Milward Road towards the back of the truck, trying to get Murray's attention.

Instinctively he had pressed the compactor button the moment the wheelie bin was returned to the ground, and he had just started pushing the bin back to where he'd collected it when he saw Gazza sprinting. From the expression on his face, something ghastly had just happened, or was about to.

Murray pulled off his muffs and earphones. 'What's...?'

'There was someone in there!' Gazza yelled as he hurried past and slammed his gloved fist against the EMERGENCY STOP button.

The sound of the compactor's motor ceased immediately, but the pneumatic hinges of Jaws – their name for the gaping serrated maw of the compactor – still had momentum left in them and a half-compression cycle played out with the sound of glass bottles shattering, tin cans clanking... and a crack that sounded like a dry branch under a clumsy foot.

'Oh God! Oh Jesus!' Gazza rasped. His beetroot-red cheeks and dark beard were topped with two cue balls of horror.

Murray left his wheelie bin where it was in the middle of the road and hurried over to join him.

And immediately wished he hadn't.

# 2

Boyd had switched back to an old habit from his uniform days, which was setting his alarm an hour earlier than necessary so that the waking-dressing-making breakfast conveyor belt of getting up and out wasn't so rushed. There was something to be said for allowing oneself an extra ten minutes to wake up properly before kicking off the covers and beginning the grind of another day.

Ozzie was in no rush either apparently, displaying the perfect Spaniel Sprawl... flat on his back in the middle of the bed, arse-end pointing towards Boyd, legs spread like a hussy and snoring like a trucker.

Boyd mentally catalogued the work sitting in his in-tray; there was a shopping list of items the CPS's barrister wanted from him now that they'd started work on the Stephen Knight case. The trial would be six months from now. Boyd hoped that Knight would be sentenced heavily for the innocent lives he'd taken. Boyd, and Warren too, would almost certainly be called in by Knight's defence council to testify. There was also spill-over work from DCI Flack's ongoing operation – picking up on the paperwork and gopher jobs that Flack's team were, apparently, far too busy with *Important Things* to deal with.

He switched gears to matters that were non-work related. Namely Charlotte. The incident at the Martello tower had only been five weeks ago, which was no time at all when it came to processing such a traumatic experience. She'd been taken there by her ex-husband as a hostage and had thought he was going to stab her to death. Processing that level of visceral terror was going to be a years-long, probably decades-long endeavour for her. He needed to remind himself that it wasn't anything personal, her need to get away for a while. She'd gone to visit her parents and was planning to stay with them for a few weeks to try to build a mental firewall between the past and the present.

The last thing she'd said to him before departing was that she wanted them to stay close, to stay in touch, that she wanted, *needed* him in her life. But she'd said it in a way that could easily be interpreted as a 'friends only' sense. It was all too easy to *mis*interpret the inflection of a voice, the flicker of a smile. Given the horror she'd been through with her abusive ex-husband, Boyd couldn't blame her for wanting to park whatever it was they had between them, for a little sanity check.

Ozzie's splayed rear paws kicked in the air at invisible rabbits or cats, catching Boyd on his jaw.

'Ouch! Come on, you lazy lummox,' he said, nudging him. 'Time to get up.'

The dog's membranous inner eyelids slowly rolled back as he stirred from his slumber, and then a single clear thought had him leaping off the bed onto the wooden floor. He let out a volley of barks.

'That's right, me old sunshine,' grunted Boyd. 'Breakfast.'

BOYD PARKED HIS CAPTUR, grabbed his lunchbox and thermos flask from the passenger seat and opened the driver-side door, only for it to clunk against the vehicle next to him as he got out.

'Shit.'

It was Okeke's brown Datsun. He ducked down to see if she was inside. And she was – glaring out at him from behind her steering wheel, phone glued to her ear in one hand, cigarette in the other.

He mouthed an apology through the window and she shook her head in response, ended the call and climbed out. She hurried around to the passenger side of the car.

'Oh, for fu– you clumsy ape,' she said, inspecting the small mark.

'Sorry about that... I parked too close.'

She rubbed at it with her finger. 'No shit, Sherlock. You've put a bloody dent in it.'

'How can you tell?' replied Boyd. He wasn't actually being facetious; her car looked as though it had already had more than its fair share of encounters with shopping trolleys and bollards.

She sucked air between her teeth as she ran her finger along the small groove he'd added to the collection. 'Bloody idiot... *sir.*'

'All right, all right,' Boyd said. 'I've said I'm sorry. C'mon – I'll buy, upstairs. To make it up. How's that?'

'It's your round anyway,' she huffed.

He led Okeke into the lobby and they waggled their lanyards at the desk sergeant who buzzed them through to the stairwell.

'Thank God it's Friday, eh?' he said. 'Unless you're in tomorrow?'

She looked deadpan at him. Clearly she was.

'Right,' he replied, then grinned. 'Sorry.'

'I'll be filling in Team Flack's bloody paperwork tomorrow,' she grumbled. 'Yay, me. What I wouldn't give for a nice juicy crime of our own to deal with right now. Where are all the bloody scrotes when you want one?' She held her hand out to him. 'I'll dump your stuff if you're going up to the canteen.'

He handed her his thermos and lunchbox. 'Black, no sugar?'

'And a fried egg roll,' she groused. 'For the dent in my car.'

Boyd arrived back downstairs at his desk twenty minutes later with a frothy cappuccino for himself and Okeke's peace offering in a greasy paper bag. He placed the coffees and bag on his desk, shucked off his winter coat and took Okeke's breakfast over. She was on the phone again...

'OK. Thanks. We'll be right over.' She hung up and grinned at him. 'We've got a body in a wheelie bin, guv.'

## 3
---

This time of year – January into February – was supposedly the high-tide mark for suicides. He'd read that somewhere. The months directly after the faux goodwill of Christmas and the misplaced hope of a new year. Bizarrely, in the same article, the suicide peak day had been calculated by someone (armed with a spreadsheet and too much time on their hands) to a very specific date and time – 16 February, 3 a.m.

Boyd looked up at the grey sky and the mean-spirited drizzle tickling his face. The slate roof of the terraced houses on either side of the narrow road were slick with moisture and at least half a dozen windows were still filled with tired-looking decorations and spray snow, which looked, in his opinion, like white snot.

*Yup...* January into February, that made sense.

He let Okeke do the legwork, tapping details into her phone as she spoke to the bin men, while Boyd paced slowly around the truck sipping his still-hot cappuccino. The rubbish collection truck took up the width of the narrow street and he could see a pair of uniformed officers dealing with an irate bloke whose parked car was blocked in, leaving him unable to drive to work. The heated exchange involved a lot of hand-waving and finger-pointing.

Boyd rounded the far side of the truck and saw that an inner perimeter of tape had been set up around the rear of the vehicle. And of course, just like a wasp hovering above an open Coke can, Sully was there in his bunny suit with one of his team, both of them leaning over to peer into the back of the truck.

Boyd ducked under the tape and joined them. 'Morning.'

Sully stood up straight and turned round. 'Ah, morning Boyd.' He sounded cheerful behind his paper mask. 'This is Karen Magnusson. She's my new deputy. Karen, this is DCI Boyd.'

Boyd nodded politely. 'Welcome aboard, Karen.'

He realised that for once he was addressing someone taller than him. She offered him an elbow and he replied with a gentle bump – a Covid habit that had lingered for kitted-up SOCOs. The only part of her face he could see were two bulging eyes behind a pair of rimless glasses. 'Thank you, sir.'

'Oh, God, don't "sir" him, Karen,' said Sully. 'Only the plain-clothes and uniformed Neanderthals have to do that.'

Boyd craned his neck to look past Magnusson into the rear of the rubbish truck.

'Err... hold on, Boyd,' said Sully. 'You might not want to –'

Curiosity compelled him. He got a glimpse of its interior and immediately regretted it. He stepped back and took a moment to shrug off the wave of nausea that raced in from nowhere.

'Jesus Christ,' he uttered. 'That's a mess.'

'That's what eight tons psi of hydraulic compression will do to you if you pick a fight with it,' said Sully. He shrugged. 'I did try to warn you.'

Boyd nodded. 'Bit earlier and more emphatic next time maybe, Sully?'

Sully turned to look back in the rear of the truck. 'I think we need to have this truck taken back to the station, empty its contents into a skip and pick our way through it,' he said to his deputy.

'Sounds good,' she said a little too eagerly. 'It'll be like a lucky dip.'

*Christ*, thought Boyd, *There's two of them now.*

Sully looked back at Boyd. 'I'm afraid this time we're going to be handing Ellessey Forensics a John Doe in kit form.' He was smiling beneath his mask. 'That's going to be one hell of a fun puzzle... determining cause of death.'

Boyd left the CSIs to it and continued his walk around the perimeter of the rubbish truck. Okeke was sitting on the kerb, beside a young man wearing a high-vis vest; his head was dangling between his knees. She waved Boyd over.

'This is Murray Schofield,' she said. 'The one who tipped the body into the back.'

Boyd squatted down. 'You all right there, Murray?' he asked.

'Not really, no,' Murray replied. He was as white as a sheet.

Boyd patted his arm gently. 'I can't say I blame you. I just caught a glimpse too.'

'I told him we have PTSD aftercare resources,' Okeke said, tapping on her phone. 'There,' she said to Murray. 'I've just texted you the link.'

Murray nodded a thank you, then lifted his head to look at Boyd. 'He's dead, isn't he? The guy in the ...'

Boyd nodded. 'Yes. Very. Look... Something like this is pretty hard to blot out. DC Okeke's right. You should make sure you see someone about it, all right?'

Murray nodded again.

'And, for God's sake, don't go down the rabbit hole of

blaming yourself,' he added. 'That's not going to do you any favours.'

'It's not the first time something like this has happened,' offered Okeke. 'And it won't be the last. During the cold winter months, you're gonna get –'

'I know, I know,' said Murray. 'We had the advisory. I should have figured the bin was too heavy when I wheeled it over.' He looked up at Boyd. 'Will I need to come into the station? To give a statement?'

Boyd nodded. 'At some point, lad, yes. But certainly not today. We'll be in touch when we're ready.' He turned to Okeke. 'Do we know which wheelie –?'

'Already on it,' she replied, nodding at a green one that was smothered in Sully's 'hands off' stickers and surrounded by three cones with crime-scene tape strung out between them. The number 22 was scrawled in white paint across it.

'And, yes, Number Twenty-Two is next on my list,' she added. She gave the young man's shoulder a squeeze, then got up and headed over towards the terraced house in question.

'I'm going to take the pool car back and get the log set up,' he called out after her. 'You going to grab a lift back with Sully?'

She lifted a thumb in response before knocking on the front door.

Boyd held out his paper cup to Murray. 'Need some coffee?' It was still surprisingly warm.

Murray nodded, and Boyd handed it to him. 'It's all yours, mate.'

# 4

**B**oyd found Detective Superintendent Sutherland in the CID kitchenette.

'Ah, there you are, sir.'

Sutherland's hand jerked away from the open tin of Quality Street and shot to the kettle.

'How's the diet going?' Boyd asked.

Sutherland nodded vigorously. 'Splendid. Splendid. I maintained discipline over Christmas and haven't put any weight on.'

'Wish I could say the same,' replied Boyd, tapping his muffin-top waistline.

Sutherland stirred his coffee. 'We haven't really spoken much since the CID piss-up, Boyd. Did you have a nice Christmas?'

'We had a quiet one,' Boyd replied. He'd invited Charlotte and her dog, Mia, to join him, Emma and Ozzie on Christmas Day. He'd spent New Year's Eve alone with Ozzie. Emma had had to work and Charlotte had been nursing a shitty cold. 'You?' he asked.

'We had the grandkids over,' said Sutherland, his round

potato-head splitting with a wide grin. 'I spent the whole of Boxing Day on the floor with them building a Lego Hogwarts.'

Boyd felt a small prickle of envy. Noah would have been well into his Lego phase by now. If things had gone differently. He flipped the subject. 'Have you heard about the –'

'Body in a wheelie bin?' Sutherland finished. 'Yes. I was just coming to find you, to discuss allocations.'

'Your office in five, sir?' suggested Boyd. 'I need to nip to the gents, then grab myself a coffee.'

BOYD RAPPED his knuckles on the door and stepped into Sutherland's goldfish bowl of an office. It had glass walls on three of the four sides; the only peace it offered was respite from the general hubbub and noise on the main floor.

He walked over to the seat in front of Sutherland's desk and sat down, clocking a Lego Dumbledore sitting beneath the monitor. He sipped his coffee. 'It's a bit of a messy one this one,' he began.

'So I heard,' replied Sutherland. 'He ended up in the *compactor*?'

Boyd wasn't entirely clear as to how everyone could be so certain the body was male. From the brief glimpse he'd caught, it wasn't at all obvious that the mangled form was even human.

'Yup,' Boyd said. 'The poor young man who tipped him in is pretty messed up by it. He's going to need some counselling.' He winced at the image sitting in his own head. 'So am I for that matter.'

Sutherland sighed. 'It happens this time every year. It's the cold, you see. An empty wheelie bin's a more enticing prospect than sleeping out in the open on a damp piece of cardboard.'

Boyd nodded along to the obvious.

'Maybe everyone should start having padlocks on their

bins, or PIN numbers,' Sutherland muttered. 'My bloody neighbour keeps dropping his bloody recycling surplus into mine. All through Christmas... wrapping paper, Amazon boxes, bottles of –'

'Anyway...' Boyd nudged the Detective Superintendent back onto the subject at hand. 'You're right. It's more than likely a homeless person, or maybe...'

'Another McKeague?' Sutherland supplied.

Boyd nodded. Not that it had ever been confirmed that Corrie McKeague had ended up that way. The poor young airman had never been recovered.

'Well. We're in agreement,' Sutherland said. 'You should hand this down to a DC, Boyd. I'm not wasting my only free DCI on it.'

'Suits me,' Boyd said.

'You've got Knight's case to prep for the CPS and –'

'Yes, I'm well aware of that, sir. I've got Flack's mountain of paperwork to shuffle through too.' Boyd was wondering when Operation Rosper was going to deliver anything at all to merit the budget that had been splurged on it. 'Is there any progress on that front, sir?'

Sutherland actually harrumphed. 'They've collared a few low-level dealers recently but nothing substantial yet. All that's really been achieved so far is to push the drug dealing down the coast towards Bexhill.'

'Right.' Boyd filed that piece of information for later. From the way Flack had reported it, it was as though he'd just smashed some Colombian cartel.

'Anyway, I shouldn't really comment on his operation,' Sutherland said.

'No, of course.'

'So, one DC, Boyd. Take your pick from the litter. I need you and Minter in-office until my bloody budget's renewed.'

'And after that?' Boyd asked.

'That all depends on Her Madge,' Sutherland huffed. 'She seems adamant that half my money's going on Rosper until Hastings is a drug-free haven.'

'Which will never happen.'

'You tell her that.' Sutherland rolled his eyes. Then, realising he'd maybe gone a little too far, he cleared his throat and needlessly adjusted his monitor. 'But that's my concern, not yours.'

BOYD RETURNED to his desk to see Okeke's bag hanging on the back of her chair, but no sign of her. He picked out Warren and Minter standing either side of the photocopier, staring at it dull-eyed as it spat out printed sheets of paper.

'Morning, gents.'

'Morning, boss,' Minter replied.

'Do either of you know where Okeke is? I know she's back.'

'She's having a fag outside,' said Warren. He began to pat the side of his jacket for his own pack of cigarettes.

'Whoa now, Warren – hold on,' moaned Minter. 'You've just had a fag break, haven't you? Seriously! You total up the minutes in the day that you flipping smokers get to slope off work and...'

Boyd left them to it, crossed the floor, pushed the double doors into the hallway and took the stairs down to the lobby. He found Okeke outside, sheltering from the drizzle beneath the entrance portico and puffing away.

'Hey.'

'Guv.'

'You ever thought of taking up vaping?' he asked.

'What's the point?' she replied, taking another drag. 'I've still got to stand outside to do it.'

She had a fair point. 'What's the latest?' he asked.

Okeke tapped the cigarette ash away. 'I had a chat with the sweet little old lady at Number Twenty-Two: Mrs Martin. She was understandably mortified that her green bin had contained a rough sleeper last night.'

'I can imagine.'

'And Sully's had the rubbish-collection truck driven over to Vehicle Maintenance to have its contents emptied out.'

Boyd had wondered what that vaguely cheesy smell was when he'd stepped outside. Vehicle Maintenance was at the rear of the station a short distance away from the main building, but evidently not quite far enough.

'Lovely job,' he said, wrinkling his nose at the unpleasant scent.

Okeke grimaced in agreement.

'You're on your own with this one,' said Boyd. 'Sutherland wants to keep me office-bound. There are too few bodies on the main floor to keep it warm.' In truth, with Flack's man-power drain and seasonal sickness, the CID floor was beginning to look like a ghost town.

'*Oh, happy days*,' she sing-songed.

'Oh, lucky you,' he agreed. 'You might want to start by checking Milward Road for CCTVs.'

'Already have, guv,' she replied. 'Obviously there are no municipal cameras; it's just a residential street. But there were several private ones that overlook where Number Twenty-Two's bins are lined up. I'm going to sift through the footage from those this morning.' She pulled on her cigarette. 'In fact, as soon as I've finished this.'

'Good,' Boyd said, turning to leave.

'How's things with you and Charlotte?' Okeke asked. 'She's finding it tough, isn't she? She's definitely not the same party girl we all witnessed last summer.'

Over the Christmas week, he and Charlotte had joined Okeke and her boyfriend, Jay, for a pint and a burger in the old town. Charlotte had been noticeably subdued. 'That incident with her ex...' Boyd began, 'it's hit her harder than I realised. She's spending some time with her folks.'

Okeke nodded. 'I can understand that. Do you think she'll be back?'

Boyd nodded. 'Of course she will. She's got a house and a job here,' he replied with more certainty than he felt. Facing imminent death had a habit of flipping the card table over, so to speak, scattering one's plans and priorities.

*I hope so.*

Okeke finished her fag and crushed it underfoot. 'By the way, Jay says Emma's doing really well behind the bar.'

His daughter had switched jobs from the Lansdowne to the nightclub where Jay worked on the doors. She'd started the week before Christmas and slogged through New Year's Eve as well. Every time Boyd caught sight of her – usually the two or three hours that they overlapped in the early evening – she looked knackered. The hours were playing hell with her body clock, but so far she always seemed keen to get off to work. More so than she had when she'd been working at the hotel in the aftermath of Patrick-gate.

'Jay said, if she keeps on doing as well as she is now, she'll be bar manager in no time,' Okeke said.

'Bar manager. A girl's got to dream, I guess,' Boyd said, pleased nonetheless that Emma was doing well.

'Don't knock it,' replied Okeke. 'Bar manager today... maybe nightclub manager tomorrow?'

'We'll see,' Boyd said. He held the door open for her as they went back inside. 'Come on then, you idle slacker – go and get some bloody work done.'

# 5

The rubbish-collection truck's contents had been dumped on to a vinyl sheet inside the maintenance depot's main workshop to shield it from the weather. It was a giant compressed turd of waste, ranging from festering cartons of unfinished takeaways to broken lamp-stands, soiled nappies and soggy cardboard packets of cat litter.

And, of course, the various mangled pieces of the poor bastard who'd been tipped into the compactor earlier that morning.

Sully finished his coffee and ginger Hobnob and tucked the packet of biscuits back into his lunchbox. 'Okey-dokey then, Magnusson – ready to get started?'

His deputy capped her bottle of elderflower-flavoured spring water and pulled on a fresh pair of nitrile gloves. 'Great. So how are we doing this?'

'I'll start at one end and you can start at the other. We toss everything that *isn't* part of a person there –' Sully nodded, indicating a sheet of green tarp laid out on the floor – 'and we'll gather the rest in this body bag.' He unrolled a second black plastic sheet onto the floor, next to the one containing the torso, and spread it out.

'Right you are,' she said cheerily, pulling her mask up and squatting down beside the mound of rubbish. 'Let's be 'avin' *you* for starters, mister,' she said as she reached across for a foot, still in a black leather shoe and ending with the frayed end of a mashed shin bone.

Sully nodded approvingly, got down a few feet away from her and began tugging at a messy tangle of Tesco's carrier bags.

~

OKEKE STARTED with the private CCTV camera that had been located on the opposite side of the street to Number 22. The grainy black-and-white footage showed the property's small front yard and gate, beyond which was Milward Road, the residents' bins all lined up and ready for collection in the morning. On the far side of the road, she could see the two bins belonging to Mrs Martin parked just beyond her gate.

The footage had come in one big file that was a series of disjointed timestamped clips as the security camera was triggered by a motion sensor. Okeke scrubbed through the video until the timestamps showed eight p.m. She reasoned that if the unfortunate victim had been looking to bed down for the night, or a drunk staggering home from the pub, it was likely to be later in the evening, rather than earlier.

The next clip showed a couple of young lads with jauntily tilted-back baseball caps striding past the gate; one of them stopped, lifted the lid on the green recycling bin and tossed in a can of something.

She smiled. *Good boy...* And then chuckled at the thought that her own neighbour, Mrs Patton, would have been out in her dressing gown and waggling a rolling pin at them for daring to be so cheeky as to use *her* bin.

The next clip was triggered by a cat. And the next. She sighed and wondered how many millions of hours of motion-sensitive security camera footage pointlessly documented cats twatting around every night of the week.

The clips kept coming: more cats, a few cars passing or parking, the occasional person walking past. Milward Road, she knew, was a quiet one. It wasn't a shortcut to anywhere and therefore wasn't plagued by cars rat-running through and setting the cameras off. Which was, at least, something.

She managed to slog through until the midnight timestamp before deciding to take a late lunch break and grab something from the pier café.

SHE FOUND Warren puffing away outside. 'You all right there, Boy Wonder?' she asked, elbowing him in the ribs.

The nickname had stuck, as they'd all known it would. The CID owed a great debt of gratitude to the Ricky Harris case for coming up with that zinger.

'Uh-huh.' Warren was done with lunch; he was holding an empty chip carton and now having his obligatory post-lunch smoke. 'I heard you got your own case?' he said.

Okeke nodded. 'Berk in a bin.'

'Not a dumped body, then?' he asked.

She shrugged. 'Could be. But I reckon it's more likely that some unlucky drunken sod found an empty bin and climbed in for a kip.'

Warren looked at her. 'Do you know how hard it is to do that without toppling it over... when you're drunk?'

Okeke shook her head. 'Please tell me that isn't from personal experience.'

'It is, actually. Not to sleep in one... I was...' He shrugged and shucked out a laugh. 'I was out with O'Neal. Pub-crawling.'

'And what? Don't say he dared you to climb in one?'

Warren nodded. 'Well... basically, yeah.'

'You're an idiot.' She shook her head. 'Haven't I warned you about hanging around with the big bad boys?'

'Oh, haha. Very funny.' Warren scrunched up his chip carton and stubbed out his cigarette. 'So having this case all to yourself... does that make you the SIO?'

Okeke sighed. 'The IO, more like.'

He frowned.

'Work it out, genius,' she said, and headed off to get her lunch.

AN HOUR LATER, trawling through what felt like endless cat footage, Okeke finally struck gold. The CCTV timestamp had reached 3 a.m. and the triggering events for the last half-dozen clips had been urban foxes.

The segment started with a man walking into shot, smoking a cigarette and looking at his phone. He didn't seem drunk, and he didn't have the appearance of some unfortunate rough sleeper at his wits end for somewhere warm to curl up. He was walking past the wheelie bins of Number 22 when a second figure suddenly lurched into view. She paused the clip immediately and noted the timestamp on her pad before doing anything else.

The frozen image showed the second figure as a blur. Which meant he was running. Sprinting even. She took a deep breath and continued the playback.

What happened next occurred in no more than a heartbeat, or at least that's what it felt like to Okeke watching the scene play out. The man on his phone had heard nothing, no pounding of footsteps behind him – he must have been wearing headphones. The second figure appeared to hit him half a dozen times from behind and the man with the phone collapsed to his knees.

The attacker caught him before he went all the way down, flipped open the lid of the wheelie bin, hefted him up and over the lip, and closed the lid.

'Shit,' Okeke gasped, eyes widening.

The assailant seemed to hesitate for a moment, then lifted the lid, looked down into the bin and reached in.

*What's he doing now? Checking he's dead? Checking for a pulse? Fucking hell.*

Then he closed the lid again and calmly walked back out of shot, the way he'd come.

'You all right, Okeke?'

She looked up and saw Boyd had cleared the stack of forms he'd been working his way through and was staring pointedly at her. 'Okeke? You look like you've just found a tenner.'

She paused the video again. 'That wheelie-bin case you handed me, guv...'

'Yup?'

'It's a murder.'

# 6

He stared out at Hastings' seafront. *Such a quaint little seaside town.*

At this time of year, evenings seemed to begin at four. The street lights in every city and town winked on in unison and bathed the night in a sickly chemical orange.

He leant against the railings of his balcony and gazed down at the pier, almost directly below him. There was a café there and, halfway down its broad and empty length, what appeared to be a bar or a pub. He watched the inviting lights flickering and the silhouettes of late-afternoon patrons moving around inside.

He smiled. *I actually did it. I actually killed someone.*

Those few words set his shoulders and arms trembling uncontrollably again. It wasn't the cold, even though he was standing out here on the balcony in just a T-shirt. It was... *the rush*, the exhilaration, an almost equal mix of what-the-fuck-did-I-do fear and elation.

'I did it,' he whispered to himself.

It was like losing his virginity. The first blooding of a young fox hunter. The first-ever taste of Armand de Brignac champagne. He remembered being nine years old and whispering with Marcel in the dormitory bed next to his about what it would feel like to kill another human being.

Marcel hadn't been interested. Marcel was into rare stamps.

Well, now... he finally knew. Fucking great was how it felt. Better than sex or champagne. Better than drugs even. He shuddered and let out a soft whoop of adrenaline-fuelled delight.

It felt like permission... permission to be what he was always to meant to be. The King. And this little seaside town spread out below him like a toy town was going to be his personal fiefdom very soon.

'The killing was an unfortunate necessity, Father...' he voiced aloud. At some point he was going to have to explain it. Better to get the words straight now...

# 7

Okeke brought two pints of lager over to where Jay sat. He'd picked a table by the rear window that looked out onto the pier's decking, deserted this time of year and treacherously slick with drizzle.

'Here you go, love,' she said, setting the drinks down.

'Cheers, baby,' he said, immediately reaching for his. 'So why the early finish today?'

'Cashing in on my overtime hours,' she replied. 'Since the D-Sup isn't signing off on any overtime any more, he said I could take a little flexitime.'

'Well, that's decent of him,' Jay said, giving her a smile. 'Cheers.'

Okeke watched her boyfriend chug down a quarter of his pint in one go. 'Steady, Jay. It's only four.'

'Ah... It's okay, love. I'm not on tonight until ten,' Jay replied.

She looked up at him. 'You're *working tonight*?'

'Yeah.' He wiped the beer foam from his lips.

'I thought you said you'd swapped shifts with Louie?'

'Couldn't get hold of him to confirm it.' Jay tapped his

phone to wake it up. 'Nah, still no answer from the bugger. I *have* to be on the doors tonight, babes. I'm sorry.'

Okeke frowned. 'Great. I was hoping we could both get rat-arsed, grab a Chinese on the way home and have drunk sex later.'

'Sorry,' he said again. 'I can't just *assume* Louie's covering for me on the door tonight. I've got to go in.'

She flicked his arm.

'Ow!' he mock-yelped, rubbing it.

'I desperately need to get pissed,' she muttered. 'Arsehole.'

'Aren't you on shift tomorrow?' he asked, checking his phone again.

'I am... but I fancied a fun night.'

'Any particular reason?' he asked, putting his phone back down once more.

'I just lost my case.'

'Huh?'

'It's a murder case now. Above my pay grade, apparently. Boyd's got it.'

Jay perked up at the mention of the name. 'How is the guv? I haven't seen him since before Christmas.'

'Fine. The same old six-foot-five ugly block of wood.'

'How's his girlfriend?' Jay frowned for a moment. 'Charlotte?'

Okeke sucked air between her teeth. 'Apparently "girl-friend" isn't the correct term to use, according to him.'

He laughed. 'Friend with benefits, then?'

'Also not that. They're just "good friends".' She sipped her beer. 'She's taking time away. Because of all that shit that happened. The tower stuff.'

Jay raised a finger. 'Ah, right. Yeah. That.' He nodded. 'You know... I do worry about him, the guv.'

Okeke snorted. 'Um, excuse me... he's *my* workmate, not

*yours.* If there's any worrying about a colleague to be done, that's my job.'

'What he needs is a bird, Sam,' Jay said, ignoring her. 'Yeah... a good solid woman. That'll sort him out.'

'Bird? And which decade have you just crawled out from?'

'Huh?'

She shook her head. Although he had a lovely soul, he wasn't the sharpest tool in the box. For Jay, life's various dilemmas and their answers boiled down to certain-shaped pegs that could be banged into certain-shaped holes.

'He's a man who lost his wife and son three years ago,' she reminded him. 'That's not a thing you can wallpaper over with... a new "bird". Or are you going to tell me he'd be better off getting back on the bike...?' She paused. 'Seventies analogy aside.'

Jay laughed. 'Yeah, maybe you're right.'

She changed subject. 'Speaking of Boyd, how's Emma settling in behind the bar?'

'FINE,' replied Emma. She bent down and, in the fading light, managed to locate and scoop up Ozzie's offering off the pebbles with the poop bag. 'Not gonna lie, Dad – the shifts seem to whizz by. Which is great. I hate clock-watching.'

Boyd nodded. It was good to hear her say that. 'There's nothing worse than a job that drags.' He let Ozzie run the extendable lead out to its max as he pursued another cowardly wave back off *his* beach.

'It definitely doesn't drag,' she replied.

'You enjoying it, Ems?'

She looked at him. 'Mostly... except when you get dirty old creeps trying to hit on you across the bar.'

'What do you say to them?'

She laughed. 'Usually stuff they can't hear. It gets too noisy to talk when the girls come on.'

'Girls?'

'Uh-huh, the dancers.'

Boyd stopped walking. 'Hold up... Ems.' Okeke and Jay had said nothing to him about girls dancing when they mentioned there was a bar job going if Emma wanted it.

'Relax.' She turned to look at him. '*They're* doing the dancing, Dad, not me. I'm just serving ridiculously overpriced drinks to a bunch of dirty old men. It's fine. And the tips are good.'

'Emma... *tips*?!' He wondered what Julia would make of her daughter working in a place like CuffLinks.

'Jesus, Dad! Nothing dodgy! "Keep the change" kind of tips, okay?' She took a step back and grabbed his arm to get him walking again. 'The idiots that come in there are loaded with cash and they like to splash it around. You know?'

He was well aware of that particular kind of idiot – rich, ruddy-faced plonkers who'd hit the mid-life-crisis speed bump and were all about buying themselves a young piece of arse.

He could picture the inside of the club and the types of men that went there. He'd seen enough of them in his time at the Met. They were sad places, really.

'Just be careful, Emma,' he found himself saying.

'I am,' she replied. 'Plus... I've got Jay watching over me.'

*Right.* Much as he liked the big guy... and Okeke too, he was going to have words with her about not even hinting that Cuff-Links was, he strongly suspected, nothing more than a strip club.

'This is me,' she said, letting go of his arm. They were a hundred yards short of the pier and the White Rock Theatre across the road.

'You want me to wait up?' he asked. 'I can give you a lift home...'

'Dad?' she said, her voice rising at the end. A gentle admonishment. 'I can call an Uber. It's not like I can't afford it.'

She walked up the shingle towards the promenade, looking back to wave one last time. He watched her cross the road, then turned to gaze out to sea and the horizon, almost indistinguishable now as Friday night descended obscenely early.

He heard someone whoop from one of the penthouse flats overlooking the pier and smiled. Someone was obviously very happy the weekend was finally here.

*Lucky them.*

# 8

'I presume the reason it's you here. DC Okeke, and not DCI Boyd is that... what? He doesn't do weekend shifts?'

Okeke laughed, sensing that Dr Palmer was having a now-familiar dig at Boyd's weak stomach.

'I think we both know why he's not here,' she replied. She was tempted to declare out loud that he was a big wuss, but from the look on Palmer's face that would have been redundant; she was clearly thinking the same thing.

The guv had actually come in early this morning: an attempt to get ahead of the in-tray full of paperwork he needed to either clear or redirect. She'd popped in to log on, before going straight out again and over to Ellessey Forensics.

'He's working this morning,' said Okeke. 'He was rather impressed that you Ellessey folks work weekends, too.'

'I don't usually,' Palmer said with a sigh. 'But I've got some catch-up work to do, so here I am. And then of course there's this...' She pulled up a stool beside the examination table. 'I'm going to sit if you don't mind. My back's killing me.'

Okeke drew up beside the table to study the twisted, broken cadaver laid out upon it. The body had the look of a lazily stuffed Guy Fawkes, arms and legs bulbous and formless; the torso had been compressed around the waist to a narrow fold, causing the skin to burst around the navel. Most of the organs of his lower abdomen hung outside his skin, like toothpaste squeezed out of an old, wrinkled tube.

There was no recognisable head to speak of. Where the neck ended was an intact portion of jaw and teeth, but the rest of it was a flattened mush of bone, brains, skin and hair.

'Well, now...' Palmer began, 'this one's a bit of a mess. I hear he came out of a garbage compactor?'

Okeke nodded. 'He'd been tipped in by accident. We're keen to know if he was dead before he got mangled.' She was well aware that there was a young man who really needed to know the answer to that as soon as possible.

'Oh, yes,' Palmer replied. 'He would have died several hours before, I think.' She lifted one shoulder up carefully and Okeke heard the crackle of shattered bones grinding. 'Come and look at this,' she said.

Okeke rounded the table to Palmer's side. The pathologist pointed out five incisions at the top of the back and between the shoulders.

'He was stabbed with a large knife. And these are all deep; this was done with force and at least one of them punctured his heart. These wounds are what I would consider "frenzied" incisions. As in, the whole blade was fully inserted... right up to the handle.'

Okeke nodded. What she was looking at matched the security camera footage she'd watched yesterday. Frenzied was a good word for it.

'You get stab wounds like this with fights... The adrenaline's in full flow, punches flying, lots of kinetic energy.'

'But not in the back, surely?' said Okeke.

'Not in a fight, no. But I'm talking about the energy behind these penetrations. There's also this...' Palmer placed the shoulder back down gently and pointed to the neck, just beneath what remained of the man's jaw. 'The killer also had a go at cutting his throat. It's not an effective attempt, to be fair. On its own it wouldn't have been fatal. It missed the carotid.' Palmer looked at Okeke. 'But that would seem like someone wanting to make absolutely sure he was dead.'

Okeke nodded.

Dr Palmer settled back on her stool. 'I would say this was a very deliberate and very determined attempt to end a life.'

'Are there any identifying marks on the body?' Okeke asked.

Palmer turned over the left forearm to reveal a tattoo: a grinning skull with a red beret and an eagle's wings spread out behind it. 'At a guess, I'd say our Doe is an ex-para.'

~

BOYD TOOK the call as he watched Sully and Magnusson do a final pick-through of what was left of their pile of rubbish. The stench inside the vehicle maintenance workshop was almost unbearable. He was relieved to have an excuse to back out of it, into the fresh air.

It was Okeke on the phone. 'All right, guv?' she inquired.

'Better now I'm outside,' he admitted. 'We've managed to completely stink out the maintenance depot.' He had a feeling it was going to linger for days, if not weeks, and would well and truly piss off the mechanics who had to work in there. 'What have you got for me, Okeke?'

'Our guy was dead hours before he was tipped into the truck. Dr Palmer said cause of death was several deep penetrations to the back, which pierced the heart. He was attacked from behind, as we saw on the footage from the security cam. Oh... and there was an attempt to cut his throat for good measure.'

'Christ. That was what he was doing when he reached into the bin, then.'

'Right,' said Okeke. 'Not your average fist fight after closing.'

*To say the least.* 'Anything that's going to help us ID him?' Boyd asked.

'He's got a para tattoo.'

'Parrot?'

'Para!' Okeke repeated. 'As in... he's probably ex-paratrooper regiment.'

'Ah, right, got you. And nothing else? No wallet, car keys? Parking ticket? What about his phone?'

'No, nothing.'

'Great.' Boyd sighed. 'All right, then. Better get yourself back here and we can start brainstorming our next steps.'

He hung up and lingered outside the open doors of the workshop, preferring the cold damp aerosol-like rain to the pungent aroma inside. It was unlikely that anyone at Hastings would have opened a missing persons file just yet. A call from a concerned loved one might have been made, but since the victim was an adult male, there'd have been the usual 'give him twenty-four hours' advice from Control, followed by a 'you'll see, love... he'll be back with an apology and a bunch of flowers, later today'.

All the same, it might be worth checking on LEDS.

'WE SHOULD MOBILIZE some boots on the ground,' said Boyd. 'Get them pounding the pavements. The guy's mobile phone could have been tossed into any of those front yards along Milward Road.'

'Or the killer could have it,' said Okeke.

Boyd leaned back in his chair and stretched. 'He'd have to be a complete moron to hang on to it.'

Okeke threw a paperclip at his gut.

'What the –?'

'Your belly's showing,' she replied.

He looked down and spotted a shirt button undone. He fumbled hastily to do it up. 'He may well have tossed it into another bin further down the road.'

'Which could mean it's sitting in Sully's garbage pile,' said Okeke.

'Or in one of the bins that wasn't emptied,' mused Boyd. 'Either way, it would be helpful to get our hands on it to ID the victim.'

Okeke sat forward. 'You think we should –'

'Go and rummage in some bins?' Boyd pulled a face. 'No, I definitely don't. We can get the uniforms checking those at the same time as they're checking the gardens. There won't be another collection until Thursday. If it's there, it's not going anywhere.'

Okeke clicked through the security camera footage, stepping through it absently, frame by frame. 'Do you think they knew each other?'

Boyd sat forward again and played with his copy of the footage on his screen. 'Possibly.' The sudden and overwhelming violence of the attack suggested a motive driven by hate. 'Revenge?' he idled aloud.

'Crime of passion?' added Okeke.

'Or booze-fuelled testosterone.'

'What? *'Ere, mate, you spilt my bloody pint?*' Okeke said with her best pub-bloke voice.

Boyd shrugged. 'Or... *'Ere, mate, you tried chattin' up me girl.*' He scrubbed back to the start of the clip and watched the attack again. It seemed too ferocious, too desperate to be the result of some squabble in a club. 'The attacker's bloody manic. That kind of rage, it –'

'Oh, Boyd-eey!' The piercing high-pitched sing-song voice rang out across the floor.

He turned to see Sully approaching, with Magnusson, head and shoulders taller, following in his wake. Sully was holding a plastic in-tray in both hands as though it was a candle-lit birthday cake. 'You're going to be very happeee!' he sing-songed again.

Sully set the tray down on Boyd's desk. It held a large clear plastic evidence bag with a number of items inside. 'One blood-spattered set of house keys; no address on the fob unfortunately. One Fitbit watch in good working order... and one tie clip with the word "CuffLinks" on it.'

Okeke got up from her desk and hurried over to look down at the evidence. 'Shit. That's Jay's club.'

# 9

There was something about rubbing stained beeswax into old, thirsty wood that he found strangely satisfying. Sensual even. Maybe it was because it felt a little like he was massaging Sam, gently easing the wax into the grain like oil into the pores of her skin.

Not that he'd ever tell her that, he cautioned himself. She'd take the piss out of him relentlessly for getting horny over old oak furniture. But... ooh, that gentle circling motion with the cloth that brought up the whorls of wood grain to a rich, dark, shiny lustre was really quite something.

Jay reached out for his can of Black Label and took a generous slug. Saturday morning was his Man-Cave Time – a pass to do whatever he wanted whether Sam was at work or not. No judging. No guilt trip. It was also workshop time for him and Louie. Sam loved to tease him about his Saturday mornings, saying the 'boys' were playing *Repair Shop* together in the garage.

'*If sitting in your lock-up, stroking old furniture with a rag and drinking beer is your thing – have fun, guys.*'

His phone buzzed on the work bench.

'One moment, my lovely,' he said to the La Rochelle-styled antique armchair he was working on. He crossed the floor of his small workshop to see that it was Sam calling. He picked his phone up.

'Hey, baby,' he said, adopting his Barry White voice. 'I was just thinking about –'

'Not now, Jay,' cut in Okeke. 'I'm at work. Have you heard back from Louie yet?'

'No, not yet,' Jay replied. 'I was expecting him over this morning. We've got Mrs Patton's chair to finish... Why?'

'No reason – I just wondered what was going on,' Okeke said.

'I'll give him another nudge. See if he's okay.'

'All right. Let me know if he comes over to play.'

'Righto. Call you back, babes.' Jay hung up, then he checked his messages. The last few chat bubbles were all Jay's. In fact, Louie hadn't been in touch since Thursday night. Missing a shift was unlike Louie. Missing their Saturday morning workshop session was unheard of. Jay rubbed his fingers down his grubby work boiler suit and began to tap the screen.

Oi! Numbnuts... you doing the shift tonight or what?

He waited a few moments for the dancing ellipses to appear below. But nothing appeared.

Need to know asap, mate, if I'm covering the door tonight. Also... no workshop this morning?

Still nothing. With a sigh of irritation, he dialled Louie's number. If the single buzz of a message wasn't going to rouse him, then a phone call might. He hung on until the call finally went to voicemail.

'It's Jay, you big knob. Pick up the phone!' He ended the call, then set the phone down on the work bench, waiting for it to come buzzing back to life.

Louie was usually a hundred per cent reliable. Jay had known him since school. Louie and Jay had been the two gentle giants of Year Seven who'd lumbered around in each other's company and earned the shared nickname of Dumb and Dumber until their lives took different directions. Louie got an apprenticeship as a plumber for a couple of years, then signed up, joined the paras and was off all over the world.

While Jay – boring old Jay – remained in Hastings.

He picked up his phone and tried Louie again. Once again, it flipped over to voicemail.

'C'mon, Louie. Call me, you big bastard. I need to know if I'm going in tonight.'

He put the phone down again and this time it buzzed once in response.

That you, man? Can't talk. Not feeling great. In bed. You're going to have to cover for me tonight, that okay?

Jay stared at the message on his screen and let out a deep, long and puzzled *hmmm*. Everything about that message was wrong. Louie never used the word 'man'. Not like that anyway. It was too idiotically American for him. What's more, Louie was rarely, if ever, sick – and, on the rare occasions that he felt a little under the weather, he wasn't the type to just abandon his post and leave a mate in the lurch.

Jay's big thumbs pecked out another message.

Not like you, mate. Everything okay there?

He waited a couple of minutes for a response, but he got nothing. He tried one more time.

Louie, mate. You okay?

'Shit.'

The first prickle of concern tickled the hairs on the back of his neck. Something was up with his friend. He knew that Louie – tough bastard though he was – occasionally suffered from 'low spells'. That's what Louie called them anyway. He wouldn't ever call it 'depression', the term embarrassed him. Despite all the mental health awareness campaigns of recent years, Louie was one of a dwindling number of stubborn bastards who insisted that PTSD was a thing that could be dealt with by getting on with life. By 'manning up'.

Louie was prepared to admit that '*yeah, I saw some heavy shit over there...*' but he'd always cap that off by assuring Jay it was *shite* that he'd left behind him long ago.

'*I'm good, mate. Don't ever need to worry about me.*'

But Jay did. Louie was as close to being a brother as one could get without shared blood.

He peeled off his grubby boiler suit and tossed it onto the back of the armchair he'd just been fondling. Louie's flat was only a short walk from his lock-up, and some heavy pounding on his front door might stir the bugger out of this odd mood.

LOUIE'S PLACE was a ten-minute walk through the centre of town, past the Priory Meadow shopping centre, up Queens Road, a cut-through to Milward Road and onto Milward Crescent. He had the ground-floor flat of Number 38.

Jay took the half dozen steps up from the street to the front door and peered into the bay window of Louie's front room. Louie spent most of his time in the front room – that was where his TV, Xbox, sofa and his weights lived. If he was in, he'd be visible. Jay leaned in close and scanned the room through the window. It looked as it usually did: a bit grubby but essentially tidy. He could see the console controller sitting on the low coffee table beside the remote control and an empty mug. There was no sign of Louie, though.

Jay rang the bell. Louie was either in his bedroom or on the crapper at the back of his flat. He dutifully waited for his friend's lumbering shape to appear in the frosted glass of the front door, but again nothing.

He rang the bell once more and after another minute, now becoming increasingly anxious about his friend, he pulled his phone out and called him. Louie tended to leave his phone on and turned up to the max because he had a tendency to lose the bloody thing. Milward Crescent was a quiet road, quiet enough that Jay was pretty certain he'd be able to hear its annoying *Family Guy* ringtone through the single pane of Louie's bay window.

From his own phone he heard the gentle trill of Louie's phone ringing, but there was nothing coming through the glass.

*But he said he was in bed. Sick.* Jay's concern ticked up another notch. He did what he normally did when he'd run out of ideas. He called Okeke. She answered after the first ring.

'Have you spoken with him yet, Jay?'

'No,' he replied. 'Well... we've texted, not spoken. I'm at his place right now. He said he was in bed, sick, but he's not answering the door.'

'He texted you?'

'Yeah. But...'

'But what?'

'It didn't sound like him.' He heard her breath catch. 'Sam? What is it?'

'I'm... not gonna lie, love. We're a little concerned for his welfare,' she replied.

'We?'

'The police.'

The prickling sensation at the back of his neck suddenly rolled upwards and across his cropped scalp. 'What's happened?'

She hesitated. Then... 'A body was found on Milward Road yesterday. Friday morning.'

That was all he heard. He ended the call, tucked his phone away and kicked the front door open, stepping over a couple of takeaway menus. He marched up the short hall to Louie's door and did the same thing again. The door rattled inwards and he

44

strode into the compact flat, calling his name in the hope there'd be a pissed-off voice barking back a 'What the fuck?'

He jogged down the narrow hallway to the bathroom at the back and swung the door open, hoping to find his friend compromised and roosting on the toilet. But it was empty.

'Louie?' he called out loudly, his voice beginning to waver with concern as he hurried back up the hallway and pushed open the door to the bedroom.

Louie's bed was empty and made, flawless army style. His Oxfords were lined up in pairs at the end. The only concession to a slovenly civilian life in his bedroom was an empty plastic Huel porridge pot on his bedside table – he sometimes let his guard down and treated himself to breakfast in bed.

Jay backed out and peered into the kitchenette, then finally made his way into the front room he'd surveyed through the bay window, clutching at one last hope that maybe his old buddy was sparked out on the floor behind the end of the sofa. But... no.

'Oh, shit... shit... Louie, mate.' His voice had collapsed from a bark to an unguarded whisper as he slumped down onto the sofa's arm. 'Just be okay, you bastard...?'

# 10

Police Sergeant Bambridge and PC Gyton pulled up outside Number 38 Milward Crescent.

'There – that's the one,' said Bambridge. She tapped the radio mic on her tac vest. 'Police unit Tango-Echo-Two-Five attending welfare check at 38 Milward Crescent for one Louie Collins.' She looked up the steps to the front door. 'The door to the property appears to have been forced open.'

'We, uh... going in, are we, sarge?' asked Gyton. He looked up hesitantly at the damaged door and the jagged splinters of the door frame.

Bambridge scowled at him. '*Sergeant*. And yes – of course we bloody are. Come on.' She climbed out of the patrol car and tapped her vest cam on. She strode up the steps, calling out loudly, 'Police! Anyone inside... show yourself, please!'

She shoved the door fully open, stepped into the hallway and saw that the ground floor flat's front door had also been forced in.

'Police!' she barked again, then, more cautiously, she pushed the door wide open. Gyton crept up behind her, fumbling distractedly with something on his tac vest.

She sighed. 'What the fuck is the problem now?'

'Can't get my cam to come on, sarge.'

She rolled her eyes. That would be a form to fill in later. Marvellous. 'Just leave it for now,' she hissed. She took a step into the apartment. 'Police! If there's anyone in here show yourself, please!'

Bambridge entered the front room and found a large, muscular man with a shaved head slumped on a couch.

'Are you Louie Collins?' she asked, then an immediate follow-up: 'Is this *your* flat?'

The man slowly lifted his head to look up at her. 'No.'

PC Gyton squeezed into the front room and did a double take at the size of the man. There was no way the pair of them were going to be wrestling him into cuffs if he decided to kick off. He took a step back behind his sergeant.

'If this isn't your place, what're you doing here?' demanded PS Bambridge.

'I broke in,' he mumbled.

'I can see that. That was you, was it?'

He nodded. 'I... I was looking for Louie...'

The man's voice sounded faintly slurred. She leant in a little closer and could smell beer. 'All right then, sunshine... what's your name?'

'Jason Turner.'

He looked distressed. A little agitated. He smelled of beer, but he might also have taken something. Which could mean trouble given the size of him. She toyed with the idea of calling for backup in case he decided to get pissy but decided to try the softly-softly approach first.

She squatted down in front of him. 'You okay, Jason?' she asked.

'Not really,' he muttered. 'I think something's happened to Louie.'

'Mr Collins?'

Jay nodded.

PS Bambridge glanced over at PC Gyton, who shrugged. 'Okay, look, Mr Turner,' she said. 'I'm afraid I'm going to have to bring you in to the station to take a statement...'

~

BOYD LED the way into the interview room. 'All right, Jay,' he said. 'How're you doing?'

The big man offered him a beaten smile. 'Hey there, guv.'

Okeke entered the small room. 'Hey, love – you okay?' she asked.

Jay looked pitifully relieved to see her and got up. 'Babe.'

Okeke made her way to him and wrapped her arms around him. Boyd looked away to give them a moment or two of privacy, then pulled out a chair and sat down.

Okeke had briefed him as soon as they heard that Jay was coming in. The dead man, Louie Collins, wasn't only Jay's work colleague at *CuffLinks* – he was Jay's oldest and best friend. '*I mean... they're really, really, close. Like brothers. Closer even than his actual brother.*'

So far they had been light on what they had shared with Jay. Boyd was not looking forward to filling in the details.

'So, Jay,' he began, 'as you know, on Friday morning a body was found on Milward Road and we now believe the body is that of your friend Louie Collins.'

Jay looked up from the floor. 'Believe? Is it not definite?'

'I'm afraid, we're pretty certain,' replied Boyd. 'More so now that we know that he's not been home.' He opened a folder with some notes and a printed image taken from the security camera opposite Number 22.

'This was taken on Milward Road... He'd have walked down there to get home, wouldn't he?'

Jay nodded.

'And this image was taken at four minutes past three in the morning.' Boyd placed the image on the table in front of Jay. 'Does that look like Louie?'

Jay leant forward and studied the grainy image for a moment. 'Uh-huh.' He nodded. 'It could be.'

Boyd had a couple of other screen grabs printed in his folder, both showing the blurred attack. The second figure was just a grainy smear. Nothing that was going to help ID him. 'Louie was attacked from behind on Milward Road at about three a.m. on Friday morning,' Boyd continued. 'It appears to be unprovoked.'

Jay shook his head in disbelief. 'Attacked?'

'He was stabbed several times in the back,' said Okeke, as she reached across the table and grabbed one of his hands. 'I'm so sorry, love.'

'He worked at CuffLinks?' asked Boyd. 'With you?'

Jay nodded, wiping his nose on the back of his free hand. 'Doorman. We were both on Thursday night.'

'So at 3 a.m....?'

'We'd finished. He'd have been walking home from work,' Jay said, nodding. 'Weekdays we close a little earlier. Friday and Saturday, the shift ends at five.'

'Would he always take the same route home?' asked Boyd.

Jay nodded again. 'It was the quickest way back. So yeah.'

Boyd noted that down. He looked back at Jay. 'So, as you can see, we have the attack caught on someone's security camera.'

'Jesus,' Jay whispered.

*This really is shit*, thought Boyd, looking at the distraught figure opposite him. Both an interview and breaking the news in one sitting. What should have been two very different conversations. He glanced at Okeke – at least they'd been allowed to do it.

'Jay... It's not easy viewing, mate. It was sudden and brutal. Over in seconds. Normally we wouldn't ask you to look at it...'

Jay nodded gratefully.

'But...' Boyd continued, 'the thing is that the attack looks premeditated, as though someone had planned it.' He pulled out a printed image that showed the attack in progress. The frame he'd selected was the clearest one they had, which wasn't saying much. He placed the blurred image in front of Jay.

'God,' he whispered.

'Okeke tells me you two were close friends.'

Jay nodded. 'Since school. I used to go round his house for tea most nights when we were kids.'

'Jay was fostered. Bounced around a bit,' explained Okeke. 'Not a great childhood and Louie's family were there.'

Boyd nodded. 'Okay.' He returned the picture to his folder. 'Can you think of a reason why anyone would want to kill him?'

Jay sat back in his seat; it creaked softly beneath his weight. 'No. Not really.'

'Not really?'

He shrugged. 'You get arseholes we have to escort off the premises every now and then. But...' Jay shook his head. 'No, Louie's a decent bloke, guv. He was ex-military, you know? So, totally, like, straight... if you know what I mean.'

Boyd nodded and jotted that down.

'Jay, hu...' said Okeke. She squeezed his hand again. 'Just Boyd is fine. He's not your guv.'

'Right.' Jay replied, trying to smile.

'Were there any incidents you can think of that happened during the run-up to that particular night?' asked Boyd. 'Any difficult customers? Fights? Anyone you had to turn away at the door maybe?'

'Not fights,' replied Jay. 'Rarely *fights*. It's not that kind of place. It's more exclusive. It's members only. And if you're not a member, there's, like, a really steep guest fee.'

Boyd smiled. 'To keep the riff-raff out?'

Jay nodded. 'Right. Yeah. It's classy. Basically for rich bastards, not regular lads on, say, a stag do.'

*Classy.* Boyd wondered where Emma's dancing girls and sleazy old men fitted into the conventional definition of 'classy'.

'So nothing out of the ordinary happened that night at the club that you can remember?' Boyd prompted.

'Let me have a think.' Jay took in a long breath and closed his eyes.

Boyd sat back slowly in his seat so as not to disturb him. The gentle giant sitting opposite him looked broken and lost. There were friends and then there were *lifelong friends.* Collins and Jay had clearly been very close.

'Yeah, actually.' Jay opened his eyes and sat forward. 'There was kind of an incident outside.'

'What happened?' Boyd asked.

'Me and Louie were having a fag down the side of the club,' Jay began. 'It was a quiet part of the shift, you see...'

'Right.'

'And we overheard some bloke on the phone. Sounded like a dodgy call.'

'What do you mean by "dodgy"?'

Jay shrugged. 'Something, you know... dodgy. Illegal. I wasn't really paying attention.'

'Okay.'

'Louie walked out and said something to the guy, like, "Watch what you say out loud, mate – you never know who might be listening." Then the guy went into the club.'

'What did this man look like?' asked Okeke.

'Did you get a good look at his face? Could you describe him?' pressed Boyd.

'I only got a quick look. Wavy light, sandy hair, maybe blond. Kind of wimpy-looking. Skinny.'

'Age?'

Jay pursed his lips. 'Young, young-looking. Under thirty

maybe? He was well dressed. But then they all are. But he was *expensively* dressed, if you get my meaning. Like designer stuff.'

'Did he say anything threatening to Louie?' asked Okeke.

'He didn't say anything.'

'And then he went into CuffLinks?'

Jay nodded.

'What time was this?' asked Boyd.

Jay shook his head again. 'I can't remember. But the lobby cam will tell you.'

Boyd made a note of that. 'Right.'

Jay looked at Okeke. 'Is this shit for real? Louie's really dead?'

She nodded. 'I'm so sorry, baby.'

## 11

CuffLinks manager Luigi DeSantis was either an incredibly helpful bloke, or, Boyd suspected, just keen to get them in, out and away from his club as quickly as possible.

He bundled Boyd, Okeke and Jay through the bar area, where Boyd spotted Emma restocking bottles, and into a back office with security camera monitors lined up above a desk along one wall.

'What's this about?' asked DeSantis. 'We don't have fights or dealers here. This is an exclusive members-only –'

'Louie's dead,' said Jay flatly. 'Some bastard jumped him from behind and stabbed him to death while he walked home.'

'Oh my God!' DeSantis sat down hard on the nearest chair. 'Dead? Actually *dead*?!'

Boyd nodded. 'We believe the assailant was in the club earlier in the evening.'

DeSantis eyes bulged. 'Really? This is not that kind of a place. We don't have fights... or...'

'We have reason to believe something – an interaction –

occurred between Louie and one of your members,' Okeke explained.

'What... sort of interaction?' DeSantis asked.

'Jay says you've got a security cam in the lobby?' Boyd said, ignoring DeSantis's question.

DeSantis nodded. 'But this is a private club, Mr Boyd. Privacy for my clients is, well, it's very important...'

'We're not here to embarrass anyone,' Boyd assured him. 'We've got a pretty decent description from Jay. We just want to see if we can grab a half-decent image of the bloke coming in.'

DeSantis looked up at the row of monitors. 'So you want to view the CCTV?' He spread his hands at the desk. Be my guests.' He stood up. 'Can I get any of you a coffee or something?' Then he shook his head. 'Bloody hell.'

'I'll have a coffee,' said Okeke. 'Black please. Jay'll take a white. Guv?'

'Same,' Boyd said. 'I'll let you two get started.' He turned to DeSantis. 'Do you mind if I go and say hello to Emma?'

'Emma on the bar?' DeSantis had a pair Groucho Marx-like brows that bounced up. 'You know her?'

'She's my daughter,' Boyd said, smiling. 'Emma *Boyd*?'

'Ahhh.' DeSantis nodded. 'She's a good girl. Very hard worker. She'll do well here.'

'That's good to hear,' Boyd said. 'Just mind you keep an eye on her for me. All right?'

DeSantis backed out of the office to make the coffees, and Boyd ambled over towards the bar. The club was every tacky cliché he'd been expecting: leather and chrome, poles on mirrored podiums, couches around drinks tables tucked into discreet nooks, and several roped-off premium VIP areas with curtains that could be drawn for extra privacy.

Emma spotted him approaching and her mouth dropped open. 'Dad? What the hell are you doing here?'

Boyd pulled up a stool and sat down. 'So it *is* a bloody strip club. I knew it!'

Emma carried on restocking a shelf with bottles of tonic water. 'It's a VIP club.'

Boyd turned to nod at the dance poles. 'With strippers?'

'Pole dancers,' she countered. 'There's a difference.'

'Same thing, really, isn't it? Jiggling flesh to be ogled.'

'All right, Wokey McWokeface'

He laughed dryly. 'Just... given all the left-leaning, feminist, bra-burning spiel I've had from you in the past... I'm surprised that you're okay working in a place like this.'

'The pay's way better than the hotel,' she replied. 'And I'm constantly busy. It goes fast.'

'And what do you think your mum would have to say about this?' he asked.

'The exploitation of young women?'

Boyd nodded.

Emma stopped shelving the bottles and stood up straight. 'I think she'd agree with me that it's the women who are exploiting the stupid older men with their big fat wallets.'

Boyd smiled and shook his head, but this was something they could debate another time. 'Do you know Louie Collins?' he asked.

She nodded. 'Jay's mate? Yeah. They both work on the door. He's a really nice guy. Why?'

There was no easy way to say it. 'I'm afraid he's dead, Ems,' he said, reaching over the counter to squeeze her arm. 'Someone stabbed him to death after his shift on Thursday.'

'What?!' Her jaw dangled. 'You're shitting me!'

'No. It's... it's very real. A murder case. My murder case.'

'Jesus, Dad,' she whispered, still reeling.

'Jay's reviewing the CCTV,' Boyd said. 'He thinks he can ID a potential suspect entering the club.'

'The guy came in *here*?!' Emma exclaimed.

Boyd nodded. He told her what Jay had said, about the incident outside. 'It could be something or nothing, Ems. We just want to ID him if we can.'

'Christ. Well, if he came in... maybe I served him. What does he look like?'

He gave her Jay's description of the guy.

Emma's jaw clenched. 'Oh, shit, yes! I remember *him*! He tried chatting me up!'

'You spoke to him?' Boyd clarified.

'Over the bar, yeah. He... lingered for a while. Kept asking me questions.'

'Like what?' Boyd asked.

She shrugged. 'The usual. *Do you like working here? What time do you get off?*' She paused for a moment. 'God. If that was the *same actual bloke...*?'

Boyd nodded. 'Right. It's a horrible feeling, eh?' He could see her forearms were goose-bumping.

She puffed out air. 'If it was that guy, he was creepy, Dad. Slimy.'

'Slimy? How do you mean?' Boyd asked.

'I mean... like, totally up himself. Entitled. You know? Like that *Game of Thrones* guy,' she explained.

Boyd shook his head. 'What?' Then: 'Do you mean the blond brat who got poisoned?'

'No, the other brat with *long* blonde hair, pimping out his little sister,' Emma said.

*Ah yes*, he remembered. 'The one who ended up with a crown of gold melted onto his sizzling head.'

Emma nodded.

'So he was young then?' Boyd said. 'Or looked young?'

'Oh, definitely young. I got the impression he wasn't that much older than me.'

'Guv?'

Boyd turned to see Okeke's head poking out of the back office. 'We've got something.'

'Okay. I'll be there in a sec.' He turned back to Emma. 'If it is that guy, we'll need to interview you too, Ems. You okay with that?'

'No fricking problem,' she said. 'I'll happily be interviewed if it helps catch the bastard.'

Boyd patted her hand and went to join the others. 'So what do you have for me?'

Jay was sitting at the desk, pointing at one of the screens. 'That's the man. I'm pretty sure.'

Boyd sat down beside him and leant forward to inspect the grainy image. It was from a high angle and aimed *into* the club's entrance. He could see Jay on one side of the doorway and Collins on the other.

The suspect's head was just within shot. He was lean with light wavy hair. He was wearing a pale suit jacket and a white collared shirt. 'Can you jump that back a few frames so we can get a full body shot?' asked Boyd.

Jay tapped on the keyboard and the footage stepped back through a number of frames, one at a time, until the man in question was in full view and about to walk past Collins.

'There,' said Boyd. 'Let's grab that frame.'

'Sam?' Jay looked up. 'How do I...?'

She leant over and hit a couple of keys to save the screenshot. Okeke pulled out a USB stick and plugged it in just as Luigi DeSantis came back into the room with a tray of coffees.

'How's it going?' he asked.

'We think we've got our man on the lobby cam,' replied Okeke.

Boyd stared at the frozen image. Emma's *Game of Thrones* comment seemed to fit with what he was looking at.

'Emma said she remembers speaking to this guy at the bar,' said Boyd. 'He was chatting her up.'

'There's a camera behind the bar too,' said Jay. 'It's a much clearer one, I think.'

'Right, well then, I suppose we'd better start sifting through that,' Boyd replied.

DeSantis set the tray down. 'Could you copy the camera's information and go through it back at the station?' He looked at his watch. The manager gave them an apologetic smile. 'We open in a couple of hours. I mean, it's Saturday evening... nearly. And – you know how it is – our members would feel awkward with –'

'The Old Bill hanging around,' Boyd finished.

He nodded. 'I hope you don't mind.'

'No, it's fine.' Boyd picked up his coffee and took a courtesy sip.

On their way out, Boyd stopped beside the bar. 'Ems?' he called.

Her head popped up. 'You off?' she asked.

'Yeah.' He hesitated for a moment, wondering how to pose the question he wanted to ask. She could be so stubborn.

'You want to give me a lift home after work, don't you?' she guessed.

Boyd sighed, then nodded. 'I just think with what's happened –'

'Yes please. I'll take it, Dad.' She smiled gratefully. 'Thank you.'

# 12

Sundays, Boyd mused, were for reading the papers in bed and late roast lunches. Well, they used to be anyway, back in his old life. There was certainly no bloody way he'd have donated a Sunday morning to work back then. Not even for a murder case.

Of course, take away the family unit, and Sunday mornings had become a void to fill. Emma tended to sleep until two or three and, once Ozzie had had his hour of pounding the beach, there was little left to do but remember how things used to be.

Which was why he'd decided to come into work this morning. That and he wanted to go through the remaining CCTV footage himself. He sat through several hours of Emma's shift. She was right; the job most definitely did keep her busy. He was impressed with her diligence and efficiency and kept reminding himself that the object of the exercise was not to indulge in proud daddy moments but to look out for the sleazy, young, blond-haired suspect trying to chat her up.

Three hours in, the video timestamp was showing 11.05 p.m. in the corner... and Okeke loomed over his monitor mouthing something at him. He paused the music he'd been listening to, as well as the CCTV video, and pulled his earphones out.

'I just said "morning",' she repeated. 'Nothing more interesting than that.'

'Oh, right.' Boyd frowned. 'What are you doing here? I didn't see you on the rota for today.'

'I'm not,' she replied. 'And neither are you if I recall correctly.'

Apart from the pair of them, there was only one other detective on the main floor this morning: one of Flack's boys shuffled out to cover a gap on the Sunday shift.

'I wanted to get a head start on the bar camera,' replied Boyd. They'd briefly played around with the fuzzy image from the lobby camera before calling it quits yesterday afternoon. He was hoping that the sharper higher-resolution camera behind the bar would give them something more useful for LEDS's face-recognition software to work on.

'Me too,' she said, wheeling her chair around his desk so that she could study his monitor as well. 'Jay's really been hit hard by this.'

Boyd knew Jay well enough to know that his muscular, somewhat threatening stature and Neanderthal-like brow belied a rather sensitive and gentle soul. They'd spent a fair bit of time together, what with the pre-Christmas meal, Friday night team sessions down at the pub, the notorious summer barbecue and of course... Jay's timely assistance at the campsite nearly a year ago. He had a lot of time for the big guy.

'Jay and Louie went back a long, long way,' said Okeke.

'Did you know him well?' Boyd asked.

She shrugged. 'Since I moved in with Jay, we've had him around for dinner a dozen or so times. I got to know him a bit. But yeah... I mean, they went to school together.'

'So as far as you know there's nothing about Collins that

might suggest a motive for his stabbing? An old vendetta? Something from his time in the paras?'

She shrugged. 'Nothing comes to mind. His interests were pretty bland. He supported the local rugby club, liked a pint; he and Jay were both into tarting up stuff in Jay's workshop. Jay and Louie... Both of them are into the whole *Repair Shop* thing, sanding and buffing things on Saturdays, sometimes Sunday mornings in his lock-up.' She let out a sad humourless huff. '*Were*... I should say.' She shook her head. 'They kept talking about going into business together.'

'Christ. Poor Jay. Let's make sure we catch this scumbag,' Boyd said, starting the video again.

'Nothing so far, then?' asked Okeke.

He shook his head. 'Most of the people coming up to the bar are women.'

'That's how it works. They're the girls who work there. They bat their eyelids and give it the old "buy me a drink, big boy?" routine, then go and place the order. Usually for something ridiculously expensive. They get commission on the drinks that they order. Yeah... CuffLinks really is a mug-magnet.' She sighed. 'I suppose it's just human nature. As long you men remain slaves to your own little winkies, you'll always be suckers for places like this.'

'Errm, not all of us,' Boyd said.

She elbowed his arm. 'Have you never...?' she asked.

'Never,' he replied adamantly. 'Sad fucking places.' Boyd shook his head and turned his eyes back to the screen, just in time to see a man – no, *the* man – he'd seen on the lobby cam.

'Shit. There!' Okeke barked. Boyd paused the video and scribbled the timestamp into his notebook. 02.29 a.m. Then he resumed play.

It was definitely the same man that Jay had ID'd from the lobby cam: wavy light-coloured, hair, pale skinned, fine-featured. He was wearing what Boyd liked to think of as 'Toff casual' – a pale suit jacket with a dark hanky poking out of the top breast pocket, a white collared shirt, undone to two buttons down.

'He looks *very* young,' said Okeke.

'But dresses old,' muttered Boyd. 'Like something out of, I dunno... *Casablanca.*'

'Retro,' she said. 'Vintage. It's a fashion thing, guv... but I wouldn't expect you to know that.' She smirked.

The blond-haired man was talking to Emma, presumably ordering a drink as she had stepped out of shot. Boyd could see him leaning forward on the bar to study his daughter as she worked, oblivious to the creep's eyes walking up and down her. He stopped the video and took a screen grab; the sleazy bastard was giving the clearest view of his face that they were probably going to get.

'Let's see what this throws out,' he said, opening LEDS's facial-recognition tools and selecting the image file. He clicked on the scan button and immediately the software got to work, identifying reference nodes on the face and placing pixel markers.

'Fancy a brew?' he said.

They returned from the top-floor canteen twenty minutes later to find the process had run its course and identified a dozen ID probables in descending order of likelihood. At the top of the list was someone named Roland Sebastian Octavian Hammond.

'Jesus, that's a mouthful.' Boyd looked at the mugshot and nodded. 'That's our boy.'

Okeke sat down on Boyd's chair.

'Oh, right, help yourself,' he muttered as she did exactly that. She positioned the mouse and clicked on the details.

'He's got a previous for drink-driving, but that's about it...' she said. 'Oh, and also a few points for speeding. Naughty boy.'

She scrolled down. 'He had a caution as a minor for possession of cannabis. But otherwise that's it for previous.'

'Date of birth...' Boyd pointed at the DOB listing. 'What does that make him now?'

She did the maths. 'Twenty-seven.'

Boyd tapped his cheek absently. 'Problem is, there's nothing there that screams *our suspect...*'

Okeke shook her head. 'He looks like a Hooray Henry.'

Boyd laughed. That wasn't an expression he'd heard in a while. 'You remember Harry Enfield?'

She shook her head.

'Comedian. He did some characters like Tim Nice-But-Dim and... that "Loadsamoney" song.' He did the Cockney voice and mimed flapping a wedge of notes around.

Okeke looked at him blankly.

'Well, yeah, anyway,' he continued, 'that's... oh, never mind.'

Okeke shook her head and turned back to the screen. 'There's no record of violence. Just a bit of dope, one instance of driving under the influence.' She tutted. 'You can't be that kind of hair-trigger violent and get to twenty-seven without something else popping up on your rap sheet.' She looked at him. 'Maybe he just snapped?'

'But he didn't just snap though, did he?' Boyd pulled one of the printed images out from the Milward Road security camera. 'He's wearing dark clothes. Which means... if this is our guy, he went home, changed clothes, came back out and waited until Collins finished his shift. Then he followed him across town and finally stabbed him to death a few hundred meters from his home. That's looking very premeditated to me, not a heat-of-the-moment thing.'

'Do you think he knew Louie? Or had some history with him?' Okeke asked.

'I don't know.' Boyd shrugged. 'But remember – Jay said something about them overhearing him on a phone call, didn't he? And then Collins advising him to keep his business private? Maybe Collins heard something he shouldn't have?'

Okeke clacked her tongue. 'A drug deal? A hit?'

'Who knows?' Boyd said. 'It looks as though it could have been something important enough to want to get rid of him.' He kicked the chair's stand, jostling Okeke. 'Right. Budge. My chair. My desk.'

She got up.

Boyd stared at the record on the screen, at the disappointing rap sheet and at the young man with the face of a choir boy. 'Let's get his whereabouts and give him a call to come in. At the very least so we can rule him out.'

# 13

Okeke found Jay exactly where she knew he'd be. In his workshop. She quietly opened the garage door to find him huddled over, his back to her as he worked on a chair, sanding down the wooden arms ready to stain and wax. He had his old boom box on and was listening to something by Westlife.

She went in, closed the door as quietly as before and sat down on a stool to watch him work. She noticed the way he gently stroked the wood – sanding to preserve, not obliterate the grooves and curls carved by someone a hundred or more years ago. In that moment, she realised all the reasons why she loved him. His gentleness, his care, his patience and devotion. The chair was *her*, and everyone and everything he cared about.

'How're you doing, hun'?' she asked.

He jumped and turned round. 'Oh, hey, babycakes. Didn't hear you come in.'

He was doing his brave-man thing: a fake smile, fake cheery voice. But he was playing his Boy Band Ballads playlist – his go-to playlist whenever he was down.

'How was work?' he asked.

'We've ID'd the guy in the nightclub,' Okeke replied, pulling out her packet of fags. 'We're interviewing him tomorrow morning.'

He nodded. Relieved. 'That's good.'

'It's just an interview, Jay. He's not being arrested.'

He stopped sanding. 'Why not?'

'Evidence. As in, we don't have enough for us to start the clock ticking.' She held a cigarette out for him and he took it. 'It's what we call an elimination interview. We're checking him out to see whether we're going down a blind alley or not.'

She lit their cigarettes and Jay sat down cross-legged on the floor. 'You've got him on video stabbing Louie to death,' he said.

'We've got *someone* on video,' she said. 'That's all.'

He clamped his teeth together, making his jaw muscle flex – one of the many things he did unconsciously that made him look so damned good.

'We've submitted a request for his phone records,' Okeke said. 'Hopefully the mobile-phone pings will put him in the right place for the attack and at the right time. Then, maybe, we can start to think about charging him.'

Jay nodded and took a pull on his cigarette. 'What's his name?' he asked.

'Ah, love, you know I can't tell you that,' she replied.

'Just a first name,' he asked. 'Just so I've got a name I can hate on.'

She shook her head. 'Sorry, Jay. I can't.'

Robbie Williams was singing 'Angels' now and the melancholic chords and melody weren't helping Jay in his battle to remain composed. 'I can't believe Louie's gone,' he croaked pitifully.

Okeke slid off the stool and knelt in front of him. 'Come here, you big bug.'

He leant forward and she wrapped her arms around him. He buried his face in her shoulder and let go.

'Shhh...' she said, stroking his shaved head. 'We're going to find and bang up whoever did this. I promise you. You have to trust me, Jay.'

She held him for a while until he gently pulled back, sniffing coarsely and letting out a sigh.

'I've been doing some... remembering,' he muttered, wiping his eyes.

'Oh, yeah?' she said.

'About what happened,' he said.

'Outside the club?'

Jay nodded.

Okeke got up and sat back on her stool. 'Tell me.'

'Well, I mean, I wasn't really paying attention. Louie took in more of it than I did...'

'You guys were having a spliff down the side of the club?' she said.

He nodded guiltily. 'Just the one.'

'Fine. So what did you hear, Jay?'

'Just...' He shook his head. 'Something about someone being dead soon. Like, killed, rather than... you know, naturally.'

'So you think you overheard this guy planning a murder?'

He nodded.

'You're sure about that?'

He nodded again.

'Anything else? Anything specific? A place? A name?'

Jay frowned as he tried to play back the memory of them standing in the dark of the alley. He'd just taken a pull and was feeling light-headed. The memory was foggy and jumbled.

'I think I heard "blue tea" or something',' he said. 'And... "do it slowly, do it carefully".' He looked up at her. 'I mean, I was off with the fairies, Sam... Louie heard more.'

'Do *what* carefully?'

'Kill someone... I think.'

Okeke took in a deep breath. 'And you're sure about that, Jay?'

'Louie was pretty sure,' he replied. 'He didn't say that he heard the exact word "kill" – only that that's what the conversation sounded like to him.'

'Could he hear both sides of the conversation?' Okeke asked.

'No. Just the bloke on the phone.'

'Right,' she said. 'Okay. Because you didn't mention this on Friday.'

'I've been doing my best to remember,' Jay replied. 'Trying to join little bits up. I didn't think about it at all after he went in, you know. It was just one of those snippets of conversation you catch when you're standing on the door, right?'

'And did this guy see you?' Okeke asked.

'No. I saw him as he walked past... but he only saw Louie.'

She stubbed her cigarette out and dropped it into an empty can of Red Bull. 'Will you be happy to come in again and tell this to the guv?'

He nodded eagerly. 'Shit, yeah. No problem. Anything I can do to help, Sam. I mean it... *anything.*'

## 14

Boyd saw Chief Superintendent Hatcher in the hallway on his way to the interview room. She had a steaming paper cup from the canteen upstairs in one hand and a greasy paper bag in the other. He thought he spied a cheese-topped croissant showing a bit of leg out of the top of the bag.

'Morning, Boyd,' she said, far too bright and cheerful for a Monday morning.

'Morning, ma'am.' They passed each other, then he stopped. 'Oh, ma'am?'

She turned to look back at him. 'Yes?'

'An FYI... we've ID'd the person of interest from the nightclub.'

She frowned for a moment as she tried to recall the job. 'Ah yes, the wheelie-bin body, right?'

'Yup. I'm actually just about to start interviewing our suspect now.'

With a crinkle of the paper bag, Hatcher gave him a thumbs-up. 'That was quick work, Boyd. Well done.' She winked. 'Nail the bastard if you can.'

He nodded. 'I'll do my very best.'

∼

BOYD LET himself into interview room four and switched on the lights and the heater in the corner. Then he set his coffee and notes down on the table. Okeke entered a moment later.

'Guv, Roland Hammond's arrived. He's on his way up, and he's brought a solicitor with him.'

Boyd let his head droop slightly. 'Great. So a one-sided conversation it is, then,' he said.

'Also…' She closed the door. 'A quick word?'

He looked at his watch to indicate that it had better be.

'I spoke with Jay last night. He's remembered a bit more of what was overheard outside the club.'

'And?' Boyd asked.

'He said that what he overheard sounded like a murder being planned.' She raised her brows. 'You were right: Louie must have heard too much of something.' She sat down next to him. 'Do you think we should mention any of this to…' She indicated the empty seat opposite.

Boyd pulled a face. 'It's all a bit vague, isn't it? Plus, if he's bringing a solicitor, I doubt we'll get anything useful out of him at this point.'

'But we might get a reaction?' she pointed out.

'Or we might just put him on his guard.' Boyd stroked his beard. 'No. Let's make this feel like a box-ticking exercise. Just a few questions to rule him out so we can stop wasting both our time.'

There was knock on the door and a silver-haired, uniformed sergeant poked his head in. 'Mr Hammond plus solicitor for you, sir,' he said, stepping back to allow them into the small room.

Roland Hammond entered first – boldly, even chirpily. He offered Boyd his hand. 'Ah, you must be the plod I spoke to yesterday?'

Boyd ignored the outstretched hand. 'I'm DCI Boyd. And this is DC Samantha Okeke.'

Hammond shrugged and dropped his arm. 'And this is my very expensive legal rottweiler, Mr Karovic. Relax,' he said with a grin. 'He's not a biter.'

Mr Karovic stepped in behind Hammond. He looked like a highly polished concierge. Two rows of breast buttons rode up an expensive grey pinstriped suit, and he presented an impassive, creased and lean face, topped with a buzz cut of Yeltsin-white hair.

'Take a seat, gents,' said Boyd to both of them, then pulled up his own chair and sat down. 'This is just an informal interview, Mr Hammond. We want to clear a few things up so that we're not wasting our time going down an investigative dead end.'

'Well, that sounds perfectly sensible,' Hammond replied with a broad, congenial smile as he settled in on the far side of the table beside Mr Karovic. 'Hopefully this won't take too long. I'm a very busy man.'

'What do you do?' asked Okeke politely.

'Business,' replied Hammond. 'Property acquisition mainly. Big deals with lots of zeroes involved,' he added. 'And my time is money wasted that you can't even imagine.'

'My client,' cut in Karovic, 'has attended this meeting voluntarily. This is to be noted and acknowledged please.' His accent was harsh, with vowels clipped short. His 'please' sounded like 'pliss'.

Roland Hammond was wearing jeans, a blazer with a boating club emblem on it, and a pale blue shirt with a burgundy tie. The dress equivalent, Boyd thought with a smile, of a mullet: business on top, party down below. He nodded. 'Yes, well, thanks for *volunteering* to come in. Much appreciated, Roland.'

The young man stiffened. 'Mr Hammond will do, thanks.'

'Do you have any objections to our recording this interview?' Boyd asked.

'Since my client has not been charged, and since this is a goodwill appearance,' cut in Karovic, 'there will be no recording.'

'Fair enough.' Boyd pulled his biro and flipped open his notepad. 'Old-school ink and paper it is then.'

'Don't we get a coffee too?' said Hammond, eyeing the cups on the table. 'And perhaps a pastry or something?' He turned to Karovic. 'Miko? Do you want anything?'

Karovic shook his head, slightly irritably, Boyd thought.

Hammond glanced Okeke's way. 'I'll have coffee, white... sugar,' he oozed. 'And no vending-machine shit please. I'd like the good stuff.'

Boyd could feel fury boiling off Okeke in thermal waves. But, God bless her, she smiled and played along. 'One white coffee with sugar coming up.' She got up and left the room.

'I'll start by asking whether you're aware, Mr Hammond, that a doorman to CuffLinks nightclub was murdered in the early hours of Friday morning. A club that you attended that night?'

'Did I?' he replied casually. Karovic leant in to mutter some legal advice. 'Oh, for God's sake,' snapped Hammond. 'Yes, yes... all right!' He turned back to Boyd and sighed. 'I'm advised to say "no comment" to every single question you ask, so...' He sighed theatrically. 'So... *no comment*.'

'For your information, this is an informal interview – you're not being cautioned.' Boyd spread his hands and smiled disarmingly. 'It's just a chat. We're going through the club members we managed to identify in order to rule them out.'

'I'm not a member, just a passing guest,' Hammond replied. He smirked. 'It looked interesting so I thought I'd pop inside for a drink.'

Karovic tapped his finger irritably on the table.

Hammond laughed. 'Sorry...' He sighed again. 'Noooo comment.'

'How was my client identified?' asked Karovic.

'CCTV in the club's entrance,' replied Boyd. 'Not a particularly brilliant image, but enough for our facial-recognition software to bring your name up as a probable.'

Hammond pursed his lips and nodded. 'Big Brother, eh?'

Karovic tapped his finger again. 'You said *probable* ID, detective. So this does not confirm Mr Hammond was in this club.'

Boyd shrugged. 'No... but...' He looked at Hammond. 'Since Mr Hammond has very kindly clarified that he "popped in", can we take it that he *was* there?'

Karovic glared at Hammond.

'Hey, relax, Miko.' Hammond turned back to Boyd. 'Yes, I was. I popped in for a quick drink. It looked like a fun place. And I was at a loose end.'

'So, obviously, we ran your ID through our system, Mr Hammond. You've been a bit of naughty boy in the past, haven't you? Drink-driving, possession of cannabis...'

The younger man's face suddenly turned a blotchy pink. 'That was five bloody years ago. I was still at uni!'

Karovic tutted.

'I've grown up since then,' Hammond huffed irritably. 'No bloody comment.'

There was a knock on the door and Boyd turned, surprised that Okeke was back so soon. Except it was Chief Superintendent Hatcher that he could see through the gap in the door. She beckoned him to step outside.

'Ma'am? What is it?' he asked.

'Now!' she hissed.

Boyd turned back to Hammond and his attack dog: Karovic remained stony-faced, but Hammond was grinning as he said, 'Off you trot, little man.'

Boyd got up, stepped outside and closed the door to the interview room. 'What's up, ma'am?'

Hatcher's face was stony. Boyd noticed she had her coat draped over one arm.

'What's going on?'

'We're going outside to get some fresh air,' she said briskly. 'Come...'

## 15

Her Madge led Boyd down the stairwell, through the foyer and out through the double doors of the station.

'Okay,' said Boyd. 'Now we have some fresh air, what's going on?'

'Not yet,' she said, crossing the car park and beckoning him to keep up. She turned out of the station's entrance onto Bohemia Road and began to head downhill towards the seafront.

'Ma'am, with all due respect... I'm in the middle of an interview. What the hell's going on?'

She kept going in silence for another minute before eventually stopping beside a low brick wall. She looked around – an almost comical am-dram performance – before speaking. 'Let's see your phone, Boyd.'

'What?'

'Get it out!' she snapped.

Boyd fished out his work phone.

'And your personal phone please.'

He held them both out and she took them, placed them on the brick wall and placed hers beside them. She then strode another few yards along the wall, stopped and turned to face him.

'The young man you have in that interview room is...' She paused for a moment. 'God, I need a cigarette,' she muttered. 'You don't have one on you, do you?'

Boyd shook his head impatiently. 'Who've I got in there?' he asked.

She looked around nervously. 'Rovshan Salikov's son.'

It took Boyd a couple of seconds to parse the words she'd just whispered.

'Salikov?' he repeated. 'The Georgian maf–'

'Georgian mafia. The big man! Yes!'

Boyd needed a moment to switch mental gears. The Salikov connection with Hastings was something he'd begun to hope had been a passing thing. It had been his very first case down in East Sussex. Gerald Nix, a dim-witted financial expert had got in way too deep with them and their murky dealings, which had resulted in him murdering Salikov's daughter and, consequently, invoking the old man's brutal revenge.

Boyd had been assuming – hoping – that Rovshan Salikov had moved on to bigger, better and shinier things in London, since that's where all the dirty Russian money tended to gravitate.

'What the fuck?' is all he could think to say, despite the fact that he had a perfectly legitimate queue of questions building up in his head.

'Roland Hammond... is Rovshan Salikov's son with Letitia Hammond-Bowles,' Hatcher explained.

That meant absolutely nothing to Boyd, as his bewildered expression clearly showed.

'She's the daughter of Lord Bowles. A socialite – a royal

hanger-on. She's a regular face in the gossip mags. A Russian billionaire's upper-crust, well-connected WAG.'

'Shit.'

'Exactly!' she muttered. 'I just had a call from a Mr Karovic...'

'He's the legal ankle-biter Hammond just brought in with him,' Boyd said. 'I didn't see him make a –'

'He must have called me on the way up the stairs.' She waved that away. 'It doesn't matter when he called. You need to release Roland Hammond right now. And you need to apologise for wasting his time. Smooth things over.'

'Are you serious? And why would I do that?' Boyd snapped. *This was fucking ridiculous.*

Hatcher took a step closer to him. 'Because he called me ten minutes ago and said so. That's why!'

Boyd was a beat away from telling her he would do no such bloody thing.

'Boyd, you and I are stuck in their web, whether you like it or not,' she reminded him. 'We're both little insects and they would happily squash us and our families without a second thought.'

'I haven't had anything to do with them since the Nix case,' he replied. 'I haven't heard a thing.'

She closed her eyes. 'That really doesn't matter. The fact is they know that you know about them. About what they've been doing. And they know that I know...'

'Laundering a shit ton of money, you mean?' Boyd muttered.

Hatcher winced. 'We... are firmly on their radar. Which, frankly, is a very uncomfortable place to be. These people, Boyd, they don't mess around. There's a hello that basically means 'We know where you live and if we need your help, we'll "ask".' She took a deep breath. 'And it's more of a warning than a hello. I had mine delivered last year.'

Boyd did too. A cardboard box with a wedge of blood-spattered money and a severed ear. He wondered what hers had contained.

She looked at him and slowly nodded. 'You too? I suspected as much.'

'An ear,' replied Boyd. 'And money. In a delivered box.'

'Poor Mr Nix. One ear each, then.' She blew out a cloud of breath. 'Jesus.'

'I've kept mine,' said Boyd. 'As evidence... if it's ever needed.'

'I threw mine away.' She laughed dryly. A little desperately. 'I have a son. I... didn't want...'

'And I've got a daughter,' Boyd said. 'So we're in the same fix.'

She nodded. 'Boyd, listen... These people do things brutally. They only "ask" once. There's no second time – you do understand that, don't you?'

'I'm well aware of what the Salikovs are like, ma'am,' he said.

'So... you're going to walk back up this hill to the station, go into that interview room, and tell Hammond and his solicitor that you're sorry for wasting their time and thanks for coming in.'

'The problem is, we're pretty sure he's...' Boyd began.

'There's *no problem* – is that clear, Boyd? Just do it!'

His hesitation pushed Hatcher further. 'Dammit! I mean it!' There was a brittle edge to her voice now. 'If you piss them off, Boyd... if you... I'll have no choice.'

'No choice? What does *that* mean?'

She shook her head angrily. 'Use your bloody imagination.' She turned away from him, collected her phone and began walking back up the hill towards the station.

Boyd RETURNED to the interview room to find Okeke waiting patiently on her side of the table and Hammond and his solicitor on the other. Hammond was gently stirring brown sugar sachets into his frothy coffee.

'Right...' Boyd had rehearsed what he was going to say three different ways while walking back into the station and none of them sat well with him. 'We're all done here,' he said.

Okeke straightened in her seat. 'What?!'

'We're done,' repeated Boyd more firmly. 'Thanks for your time, Mr Hammond,' he added. He was damned if he was going to apologise to the supercilious bastard, though.

'Guv?' Okeke looked totally confused.

Karovic stood up, but Hammond remained seated. 'Let me at least try my coffee,' he said with a smile. He slowly lifted the coffee cup, pinkie finger stretched out for effect, pursed his lips and slurped at the froth noisily. 'Hmmm...' He turned to Okeke. 'Want a bit of feedback, my lovely?'

She glared at him.

'Be a bit quicker next time,' he said, smirking. 'It's tepid.' He set the cup down noisily and got up. Karovic steered him towards the door, but Hammond stopped in front of Boyd. He leant forward. 'Now you know exactly *who I am*,' he whispered softly, 'be a good dog and don't ever waste my time like that again.'

'This way, Mr Hammond,' coaxed Karovic. 'Please?'

Hammond remained where he was, his blue-grey eyes locked on Boyd's. 'I'm really very good at remembering names and faces.' He winked. 'I've got yours in my head now.'

'This way,' insisted Karovic. The two men stepped past Boyd, out into the hallway and towards the swing doors at the end.

'What. The. Actual. Fuck?' complained Okeke, still sitting at the table.

'Not now,' Boyd snapped.

'Guv? Why the fu–'

'I said, *not now!*' he growled, heading out of the door and leaving Okeke, alone and utterly bewildered in the interview room.

# 16

'I don't understand why, Jay. I really don't.'

He stared at the doner kebab on his work bench; his appetite had suddenly abandoned him. In fact, he actually felt sick. 'But... that bastard did it!' he replied. We know it was him!'

'To be fair, love, we don't really have anything solid on him,' Okeke said. 'We have him at CuffLinks on the same night, but that's all.'

'*What about what I told you!?*' Jay snapped angrily.

Okeke got up off the stool and reached out for him. 'Honey...'

'I'm sorry,' he mumbled. 'I didn't mean to shout. I... I just...'

'I know.' She reached up and stroked the back of his neck. 'Listen, there's not a lot we can do right now to progress this,' she said. 'If something else turns up, some evidence that ties him in, then...'

'Who is he?' asked Jay.

She shook her head. 'You know I can't.'

'Is he super-fucking rich? Is that it? Did he just bribe someone?'

She stopped stroking his neck and let her arm fall to her side. A gentle admonishment. 'That's not how things work, babe. Not here in Sussex. This isn't some sort of gangster movie we're in.'

He moved away from her. 'What does the guv think?'

'He's frustrated too,' she replied. But, to be entirely honest, she had no idea what was going through Boyd's head. Before she'd been dismissed by Hammond to fetch his coffee, Boyd had been all for questioning him – albeit gently. When he came back from wherever he'd been, he'd been unapproachable, with a face like a smacked arse, and it had remained that way for the rest of the day.

'It's just not right,' Jay said. 'What's going on? Is he some chief inspector's son or something? Or a... a... a politician's nephew or...'

'Jay, I don't know anything. And if I did, I couldn't tell you. Look... I know Louie thought he overheard something, but listen, it's –'

'He overheard a fucking *murder* being arranged!' Jay spat.

In their two years together, she'd heard Jay raise his voice only a handful of times. And on those occasions it had been directed at work tools or pieces of split timber. Never people. He didn't do angry. He didn't need to. His imposing muscular frame did most of the talking for him.

'Jay, baby,' she spoke softly. 'Is it possible you and Louie misheard? Or misinterpreted what you heard?'

Jay frowned. 'No. It's not.' He looked at his watch and started to tidy away the tools spread out across his work bench. 'I got to get ready for work.'

She watched him brush the curls of wood shavings onto the floor and slot his carpentry tools into their correct pigeonholes. She wanted to share with him that everything about Hammond's smug behaviour during interview, and the fact that he'd felt the need to bring legal counsel in with him, suggested to her that he had something to hide. But that would only add fuel to Jay's fire.

Jay picked up the doner kebab and held it out to her. She shook her head.

'Louie and me may be doormen... but that doesn't mean we're complete idiots,' he grumbled as he left the garage to get ready for work.

～

BOYD OPENED the safe in his study; it was the kind you could buy in a B&Q for fifty quid and supposed to be secured to a wall – otherwise, it was basically just a heavy box with a 'nick me' flag on it. It was another odd job that he'd not got around to doing after more than a year of living in the house.

Inside the safe he kept his and Emma's passports – not that they'd ever been used in the last five years, and of course... his 'gift' from the Salikovs. He pulled the small cardboard box out, opened the flaps and stared down at the contents.

The polystyrene packing chips were still in there, as was the bundle of blood-stained fifty-pound notes. And the scrawled note.

*Boyd*
*Nix – no more. Stay away. Stay Silence.*

NIX'S severed ear was now preserved in a sealed and otherwise-empty jar of Tesco's own-brand stuffed olives, floating in a cloudy bath of Bombay Sapphire gin. That had been the only bit of tampering Boyd had done – in a DIY bid to preserve it.

*For what? For a day like this?*

Money and an ear. If it had been just the ear in the box, he'd have felt a lot easier about things. The message could be interpreted simply as 'keep your mouth shut or it'll be *your* ear next'. But the bundle of money added an unsettling caveat.

*We may call on your services one day.*

'One day', it seemed, had just arrived.

Boyd turned back to his PC and carried on reading. It seemed that Her Madge was correct. Rovshan Salikov had had a second relationship with Letitia Hammond-Bowles. Not a marriage... nothing so overt and attention-grabbing. She was his British trophy mistress, thirty years younger than him. In the mid-nineties she'd been an It Girl, stumbling out of places like Tramps alongside minor royalty, hedge-fund playboys and various face-of-the-week musicians; her tanned face had been a regular one in the 'Who's Been Out and About' section of various supermarket glossies.

She'd had a thing with the Big Man himself... and given him a son, Roland, and only recently – finally – married him. All part of the rehabilitation, the white-washing of his reputation.

'Christ,' he muttered. He topped up his glass of wine and took another long glug.

So what the fuck was Roland Hammond doing down in Hastings? Surely, if arsing about in VIP strip clubs was his thing, there was a far wider choice of places like that up in London for him to throw his money around. And then there was what Okeke had shared with him this morning... that Louie might have overheard something he shouldn't have. More to the point, if Hammond was innocent of Louie's stabbing, why the hell had a call been made to Hatcher to drop the case?

'Oh shit,' he whispered to Ozzie, who was stretching up to the desk to sniff the side of the small box, scenting the old, dried blood inside. A part of Boyd was tempted to open the jar, toss Ozzie a pickled snack, and burn all the money. But... a 'gift' like this wasn't one you could destroy and forget about. It was a calling card.

~

JAY HEARD the man's voice before he saw him; it was a voice in a slightly higher register than average and the kind of accent that he associated with the experts on *Antiques Roadshow* – all plummy vowels and present-and-correct consonants. He turned to see the bastard approaching from the same direction as last time.

He was on his phone again, talking business with someone as he waggled a guest-membership pass at Jay and Gary before breezing into the club.

Jay turned to watch him stride down the lobby and through the inner doors.

'What's up, Jay?' asked Gary. 'Is he famous or what? Is he off *Made in Chelsea*?'

Gary, ironically given Jay's recent conversation with Sam, *was* a dumb doorman.

'Nope,' Jay said, heart pumping. 'Just sounds like a bit of a twat.'

Gary chuckled. 'They all do, mate. They all do.'

The conversation returned to the subject du jour – Louie's death. Gary was canvassing Jay on whether or not it was an insensitive time to discuss a pay rise with Luigi DeSantis. If there was an actual risk of death doing this job, surely they deserved better than £13.50 an hour?

Jay gave Gary's grumblings the minimum of attention while his mind was focused elsewhere – on that murdering DFL bastard who'd just waltzed back into the club as if nothing had happened. It had taken every ounce of restraint not to knock that phone out of his hand and pin him up against the lobby wall.

*Then what, you big ape?*

The little head-gremlin who'd voiced that wasn't Sam. Her advice nuggets came more tenderly and were delivered more gently. This gremlin was Karl. His younger brother.

*You just smack him? Are you really THAT stupid?*

There was a reason why Jay worked with wood and Karl worked with code. Karl was the uber-smart one. Sam had also advised restraint if the same man came back to the club. She'd reminded Jay that there was no firm evidence, despite what he and Louie thought they'd heard him say.

Karl's whispered voice was a little more circumspect. *Seriously, bro, if you want to get even... you need to think smarter.*

Jay spent the rest of his shift pondering just that – smart ways to exercise some justice when an opportunity presented itself.

'Hey, you... big man – call me a cab.'

Jay turned round in the doorway to see the bastard emerging into the lobby, with one of the club's escort girls clinging to his arm.

'Where to?' asked Gary, pulling out his mobile.

'Sea View Apartments. Opposite the pier.'

'Name?'

'Roland Hammond,' the man replied. Then: 'And ask the fellow how long, would you?'

Gary raised a finger as the call connected. He spoke briefly with the despatcher, then ended the call. 'Five minutes, sir.'

Hammond nodded and led the girl out onto the pavement. Jay did his best not to notice them as they waited. Did his best not to notice the man grasping at the girl's arse, teasing her short skirt up as she wrestled it back down with a gently scolding 'Wait!' while he whispered what he was going to do to her in his penthouse.

The cab arrived, Hammond bundled her quickly into the back, and then they were gone.

*Think smart*, Jay reminded himself.

# 17

'So, let me guess. You've dragged me all the way out here to apologise for being so ratty with me yesterday?' said Okeke.

'Umm... not really,' replied Boyd.

She eyed the deserted beach. 'Well, you're going to have to start with that, guv, or I'm going back into the warm –'

'I'm sorry,' he replied quickly.

'Is that it?'

He wasn't in the mood to fence with her this morning. 'Roland Hammond is Rovshan Salikov's son,' he said.

He watched several stages of comprehension slide across her face until she finally settled on: 'Oh fuck.'

'He's his only son,' added Boyd. 'He lost his eldest son, Revaz, five months ago. And of course we know what happened to his daughter, Zophia.'

'Hold up,' cut in Okeke. 'How the hell is that chinless preppie, Hammond, a Russian gangster?'

Boyd explained what he'd dug up last night about Rovshan and his blue-blooded trophy mistress from the Shires. 'Shagging Letitia Hammond-Bowles and producing that piece of shit was either bad luck or some pretty advanced forward planning.'

Okeke's expression was still set on 'oh fuck'. He was concerned a strong wind would leave her face stuck like that forever.

'I suspect she and her son were part of his long-term plan to migrate to the UK,' Boyd continued. 'He's after a "respectable" new start over here.'

'Christ. Do you think he'll end up buying a football team?'

Boyd laughed. 'Who knows.' He bent down and scooped up a stone to throw for Ozzie to chase into the surf – and promptly dropped it, realising that Oz would be curled up on the sofa at home. 'Force of habit,' he explained automatically.

Okeke was still running the information through her head. 'So… what's his son doing hanging around Hastings murdering people?' she asked.

'Another good question,' he replied. 'I was hoping he's here for a seaside jolly, but I suspect it may be something longer term.'

'Looking out for investment opportunities for Dad?' she wondered.

Boyd pulled a face and did air quotes with his fingers. 'Yeah, "investment" opportunities.'

'Laundering opportunities,' Okeke clarified.

'Exactly.'

'And where's his dad? In Georgia still?'

'No. Rovshan Salikov's in London now, with Letitia Hammond-Bowles. He recently bought a big old town house in Belgravia and he's in the process of gutting and redecorating it.'

He'd found that little nugget in a *Canary* article about London property prices holding out post-Brexit. It had listed a number of 'dubious new arrivals': several Saudi princes ousted by King Salman, a Colombian security minister with blood money on his hands… and of course a fair number of Russian 'businessmen', all looking to move their fortunes to all-new, no-questions-asked Brexit Britain.

'Gerald Nix was just one of many laundering routes into this country,' he continued. 'I think that's become something of a cottage industry in recent years.' He sipped his coffee. 'Point is, it looks like Salikov's got a significant chunk of his dirty money in and now he wants to clean it.'

Okeke shook her head in disbelief. 'In Hastings, though?!'

Boyd shrugged. 'Maybe. I don't know. That's *a* theory for why Roland Hammond's down here. I'm open to other suggestions.'

'But *Hastings*?' she said again and laughed. 'It's not exactly Las Vegas.' She paused for a moment, then: 'So, about yesterday? When I went to get him his bloody coffee... something was said, right?'

Boyd sighed. He trusted Okeke and he'd thought long and hard about what he was going to tell her.

'Hatcher pulled me out of the room,' he said carefully. 'She actually walked me right out of the station. His legal counsel, Karovic, gave her a call on the way in and told her to drop this.'

'You're shitting me!' Okeke shook her head, her eyes were out on stalks.

Boyd shook his head. 'And, for your information, we had a *very* candid talk outside.'

'About?'

'About the fact that she's been asked, very politely, to make this stop... and about the fact that she's not going to give them any opportunities to "ask" again.'

Okeke's jaw hung open. 'Tell me you're joking?'

Boyd shook his head. 'By the way, this is obviously between me and you only. Don't even tell Jay. Do you understand?'

She rolled her eyes. 'So this is where we're parked right now, is it? We're supposed to let this case quietly grow cold and step away from it...'

'If we don't, we'll be kicking a hornet's nest,' Boyd said.

Okeke tugged the collar of her leather jacket up against the needling cold wind and fumbled in her pockets for her cigarettes.

'I'll be honest with you...' began Boyd. He could feel an echo of the terror that had come off Gerald Nix in waves as he'd talked about the Salikovs. *They won't simply kill me if they find me, Boyd... they'll take their fucking time!* For sure, Boyd understood. The Georgian Mafia, the Russian Mafia, they were all big on 'messages'. And the best way to transmit what they wanted to say was with the grisly mess of a corpse that they left behind in a ditch or propped in a doorway.

'I'm not after a medal for bravery here, Sam.'

Okeke found her smokes, lit one up and blew out a cloud that was quickly whisked away. 'What about Louie? What about what Jay heard? What if there is a murder... a hit being planned?'

'Then hopefully it isn't on our patch.'

She turned to him. 'Seriously?'

'What?'

'What if Hammond *is* doing Daddy's dirty work. Clearing up the laundry trail? Planning a hit on another Gerald Nix in the area?'

'That's a big *if*... Sam. It's easy to get the wrong end of the stick with only half of an overheard conversation.'

'*If*...' she agreed. 'But what then? What if there's another murder here that links to the Salikovs?'

He knew what he'd like to say. *Fucking go after them, of course.* But that answer would have had to come from a different Boyd in a different world in which he'd lost his *entire* family in a crumpled car. Not this one where he still had a daughter at home.

'They know where I live,' he said.

'So we're not playing Caped Crusaders again?'

He sucked in a deep breath and let it out slowly. 'Last time we had no bloody idea what we were stepping into. This time we do.' He shook his head. 'So it's a flat no. Not on your life.'

*Not on Emma's life, anyway.*

'You know, Jay's really cut up about this,' said Okeke. 'Louie and him go way back. I've never seen him so...'

'I know. I know. And I'm really sorry about that. Jay's a good guy with a big heart. But –'

'He thinks Hammond bribed his way out of the station,' Okeke cut in. 'He just wants to get his hands on him.'

'Well, he needs to quickly unthink that,' replied Boyd. 'Seriously, Sam... these are not people that Jay wants to go and pick a fight with. You need to sell him on the we-don't-have-enough-to-charge-him angle. Which we really don't, by the way.'

Okeke nodded, her face creasing into a worried frown. 'I've tried that already.'

'And?'

'I just hope he doesn't accidentally bump into Hammond in the street.'

Boyd closed his eyes and let out a deep sigh. 'Is there any chance you could keep him sedated and locked in a box for a few months?'

# 18

Jay had barely slept since coming in from his shift. He'd made a go of it, crawling into bed beside Sam – who was snoring like a diesel generator – and trying his best to switch his buzzing brain off. He must have got *some* sleep, he reasoned, because Sam had gone and a coffee was cooling on his bedside table.

He lectured himself over his bowl of Rice Krispies that he needed to work on the La Rochelle armchair this morning. It really did need to be finished up and taken over to Mrs Patton's and unveiled *Repair Shop*-style before her today.

He reminded himself, as he pulled on his scruffy workshop roughs, that if he wanted to grow this fledgling upcycling and repair business – to drag his and Louie's dream into reality – he needed to deliver on time, as promised and not get distracted. By anything. As he got into his van and turned out of Crescent Garden Road, he repeated Sam's assurances that if something 'firm' came up linking the bastard to Louie's death, they'd march Hammond straight back into the station.

But, despite all the muttered promises in his head, Jay found himself parked up on the seafront road and peering up at the penthouse balcony of Sea View Apartments. He wasn't entirely sure why he was sitting there or what his plan of action was. If he had to be honest with himself, there wasn't actually a plan. None at all. He desperately *wanted* to put one of his big hands around that scrawny little twat's throat and explain to him at length how Louie was worth ten million of him no matter how fucking rich he was. He also *wanted* to put the fear of God into him... to tell him that the police had info on him and they'd inevitably be coming for him sooner or later.

*Roland Hammond.* Even the name sounded contemptible and entitled.

*Think smarter, bro.* There it was again, Karl's voice.

'What the fuck am I doing?' he muttered. 'You're right, Karl... this is totally stupid. Think smart, Jay. Think smart.'

He was just about to drive off when a DPD delivery van pulled up right outside the apartment block's entrance foyer.

Before he could even think about what he was doing, he jumped out of his own van and crossed the road. He climbed the six steps up from the pavement to the main entrance, which was hidden under a greened-bronze portico, and made a show of patting himself down for keys. A moment later the driver was standing beside him with a parcel and buzzed for Apartment 3.

'I'd let you in if I could find my...' mumbled Jay apologetically to the driver.

The intercom crackled with a female voice. 'Hello?'

'DPD for Maureen Webb?' the driver said.

'That's me,' she answered.

The door buzzed and the DPD driver pushed it open. He glanced at Jay. 'Coming in, mate?'

Jay nodded and smiled. 'Cheers.' He stepped in with the DPD guy. 'Is that for Maureen?'

The driver nodded.

'I'm going up,' replied Jay. 'I'll put it outside her door. Save you the stairs.' He realised, belatedly, that he hadn't needed to do that – he was already inside the building.

'Ah, cheers, man.' The driver handed him the box and took a quick photo of the parcel in Jay's hands. 'Your surname?'

'Statham.'

The DPD looked at him. 'Like the actor?'

Jay gave him a smile. 'Yeah.'

The driver tapped it into his phone, waved a 'thanks' and was gone, hurrying back outside, the front door swinging shut behind him.

Jay looked at the lift, then the stairs, and opted for the latter. He now had a frigging parcel to deliver first. 'Great.'

He made his way up the two flights of stairs, with Sam sitting on one shoulder, scolding him for being a bloody idiot, and Karl on the other, saying if he wanted to get even, this was a pretty stupid way of going about it. He emerged onto the landing, spotted the front door for Apartment 3 and gently placed the parcel at the foot of the door.

'*Now, go home, babes,*' Sam whispered in his ear.

'*She's right,*' added Karl. '*Another time, another day, bro, eh?*'

He paused as he stood looking at the stairs, one flight leading down to common sense; the other, up and a chance to get even for Louie. He paused. He knew his mate would be saying the same thing as the others. '*He's not fucking worth it, Jay.*'

He took the stairs leading upwards.

The top-floor hallway was carpeted. Red carpet, of course. Just then the door opened and a young woman emerged. He recognised the escort Hammond had left the club with last night. Her hair looked dishevelled; her make-up smeared. She pulled the door shut behind her and headed towards the stairs, noticing Jay standing there at the last moment.

He stood stock still as she brushed past him, muttering to herself. 'Never again. Not worth it. Not worth it.'

Her heels clacked down the stairs and Jay watched her go, so desperate to get out of there that she wasn't bothering to wait for the lift. If his mind hadn't been a red mist of anger, he might have heeded her wise words.

Instead he approached the door. The only door on this floor. Apartment 6. The Penthouse.

OKEKE LIT up and took a quick pull on her fag. She waited until the two PCs emerging from their patrol car had crossed the forecourt and gone into the lobby, then she pulled her phone out and dialled Jay's number.

It rang, unbeknown to her, in the glove compartment of his van, eventually switching to voicemail.

'Jay, love... it's Sam. Listen, I know you're still messed up about Louie. I know you know it's this guy from the club. But look...' She paused for a moment, wondering how much to share with him right now. The mafia connection – if he was thinking clearly – would seriously give him pause for thought. If he was lying in bed still and fantasizing about roughing up Hammond next time he showed his face at CuffLinks, knowing that he'd be messing with the same people they'd faced nearly a year ago, would surely cool him down a little. Jay wasn't an idiot. But then...

'Jay, we've got this, all right? Me and the guv. We're going to bring the bastard back in again when we've got enough evidence to send him down. I promise you.' She pondered again whether or not to say anything more. Better in person, she decided. Phone messages were damning evidence-in-waiting and right now he was probably still sleeping.

'Love you, babe,' she added, and ended the call.

# 19

Jay knocked on the door and waited. He couldn't hear a thing from behind it. He tried again and finally heard a muffled voice muttering. A bolt snicked, the door opened wide and Roland Hammond appeared before him wearing a red silk kimono and nothing else.

'Fuck's sake, you silly bitch...what did you for–' he was saying as he jerked the door open, but he stopped mid-word, not out of shock or surprise – there wasn't the slightest glint of recognition in his eyes – but out of sheer irritation. 'Who are you?!'

Jay had hurriedly concocted some bullshit about maintenance on the apartment's heating to get him through the front door, but seeing Hammond standing there, looking up at Jay yet somehow managing to look down his nose at him at the same time, the balance tipped and the heating maintenance bullshit went out of the window.

Jay pushed Hammond roughly backwards and stepped into the apartment, slamming the door shut behind him.

Hammond began to scream. Which meant Jay had to shut him up quickly, a step he hadn't considered he'd need to take this soon. He charged forward and rugby-tackled him, landing on top of Hammond and knocking the wind out of him.

But the scrawny little kid – and he did look just like a kid, like some A-level student playing dress-up with Mummy's wardrobe – continued screaming. Jay slapped a big fist over his mouth.

'SHUT UP!' he hissed. 'Shut up, you little piece of arse-shit.'

Jay planted his knees on the man's spindly arms and sat on his bare chest. His bulk was more than enough to hold him in place, but the muted screaming was surely going to bring someone knocking soon. He looked up and saw that he was in the apartment's main lounge. French doors opened onto the grand balcony – and of course... they were bloody well wide open. Added to that, he could feel the little fucker was trying to get a purchase on his palm with his teeth. He scanned the room for something to gag him with and saw a balled-up sock within reach on the floor. He grabbed it and quickly forced the sock into Hammond's mouth before he could let rip with another ear-splitting scream. Then he tugged at the silk belt that dangled from the loops of his silk robe to get it free, flipped Hammond over onto his belly and hog-tied his wrists and his ankles behind his back.

'There.' Jay smacked Hammond's bare, bony arse hard and sat back, satisfied the scrawny whelp was constrained and muzzled for now. 'Hah. You look like a trussed-up turkey.'

Hammond's jaw was working on the sock. He was trying to push it out with his tongue.

'You spit that out... and I'll piss on it, then shove it right back in your mouth,' snarled Jay.

Hammond stopped immediately.

Jay took a few moments to get his breath back and gather his thoughts. The elephant in the room was blindingly obvious to him. *What the fuck do I do now?* He'd compiled a menu of options in his head as he'd climbed the stairs that ranged from harsh words to minor physical harm. He'd ruled out killing the little bastard because that *would* be dumb. It wouldn't bring back Louie and he wasn't prepared to serve time for this scumbag.

*Scare him.* That was probably the best way forward. *Scare the crap out of him.* Let him know that Jay *knew* he'd stabbed Louie and that justice was eventually going to catch up with him, no matter how fucking rich and powerful he thought he was.

Jay got up off the floor and sat down in a leather chair. 'I know you did it…' he began. 'I know you killed my mate.'

Hammond's eyes swivelled his way.

'Yeah, that's right. Recognise me now, do you?' Jay sat forward and clasped his hands together like he was getting ready to tell a bedtime story. 'See… it wasn't just Louie who heard you on the phone, you dickhead. I heard you too.'

The young man's eyes widened a little more.

'Oh, yeah.' Jay grinned. The fear on Hammond's face was going to be way more satisfying than planting a few bruises on it. The thing was… Jay didn't have much to play with. He and Louie had heard something about a *hit*. Possibly a poisoning.

*Keep it vague*, he told himself.

'I know…' he continued. 'We heard it all – we heard what you're planning, fuckwit. Every little bit, sunshine. And I'm sorely tempted to tell the cops. They're already on to you, aren't they? Or maybe… I dunno, I'll just plaster it all over social media. I've not decided yet.'

Hammond mumbled and rolled over onto his side. Jay noticed a little spurt of darkly coloured piss jetting out and couldn't help a chuckle of glee. 'Heh… that's right. You go piss yourself, little man. You probably should.'

This felt good. This felt right, actually. Not slapping him up, but just letting him know his Sam and her guv were on to him and no amount of bribe money was going to save his scrawny rich arse. No punching required.

'Yeah,' he said, still grinning. 'Everyone's going to know what you're up to, Hammond.'

*Keep it vague, bro.* But also... *Give it some convincing little detail, right?*

'Louie wrote it down. The name you mentioned. The stuff you're planning. The *blue tea*.' Jay tapped his head and pulled what he thought was a menacing grin. 'You're so fucked, mate.'

## 20

Boyd had been kept busy with all the to-ing and fro-ing on the Stephen Knight case with the CPS's case preparation contact, Lesley Lloyd. She had a comprehensive list of items for which she wanted guaranteed evidence-chain documentation, things that had been retrieved from Knight's house after the arrest. Knight had enough money to afford a decent defence barrister who was pretty hot on spotting police procedure gaffs.

Ms Lloyd wasn't leaving anything to chance.

He stopped work at midday to check his phone. There was a brief message from Charlotte and a selfie of her walking Mia with her elderly parents and their dogs. She looked relaxed and happy. He felt a mix of emotions. Pleased that she was reconnecting after being isolated from them for so long; pleased that the haunted look on her face had been erased, for the duration of the selfie at least. But he also felt a selfish prickle of concern that things would be different between them on her return.

Not that they'd stepped over any lines together – they were both still firmly planted in each other's 'just good friends' camp. But there'd been some tiptoeing going on, he thought. Tiptoeing to the very edge of that boundary.

He was mulling over the idea of taking himself up to the top floor to grab one of the canteen's notorious mega-bacon baps when Okeke arrived in front of him, blocking his view.

'Guv?'

'Uh?'

She dropped a printout on his desk. 'It's the ping data on Louie's missing phone.'

Boyd looked down at various road maps of Hastings and mobile-phone-mast radius markers all superimposed on top of one another. 'It was active for just over thirty hours after his stabbing.' She pointed at a cluster of ping-location pegs. 'It was bobbing around here for a while, just by the pier, before it went off for good.'

Boyd studied the location markers for a few moments.

Okeke bent over the desk. 'Roland Hammond recently rented the penthouse flat at Sea View Apartments.' She pointed to a spot on the map, her fingernail bang in the middle of the cluster of printed pegs.

Boyd's heart sank. He looked up at her and he could see her lips pressed firmly together, her brows raised like a drawn bow. 'The evidence all points his way, guv,' she said quietly.

He looked around the office. Warren was busy gophering up the details Lesley Lloyd had been badgering Boyd for. Minter had headphones on and was tapping away at his keyboard, and the half-dozen other misfits and rejects from Team Flack were all distracted with their own mundane tasks.

He pointed at the double doors. 'Pier? Chips?' he suggested.

~

'THE CHOICE, Okeke, is pretty stark. Hammond may well be our man,' said Boyd, 'but he's a Salikov.'

'And that's it?' She shrugged, then leant against the railing and blew a cloud of smoke out to sea. 'Is Hastings their turf now? Their stomping ground and they can do what the hell they want?'

He sighed. As usual, Okeke had cut straight to the point. There was little chance of fudging an answer and brushing her off.

'I had *hoped* they were just passing through,' he replied. 'Well, at least their money was. But I guess if Rovshan Salikov's son is setting up camp here... they've decided Hastings might be a good place to invest.'

'Invest?' She made a pffft sound. 'With all their black money? Drugs? Extortion? Refugee smuggling? And who knows what else?'

He tried to lighten the mood. 'At least it shows Hastings is moving up in the world, eh?'

She shook her head, in no mood for levity. 'Right. Awash with dirty Russian money. No thank you.'

'I'd like to think I'm one of the good coppers,' he said after a while. 'One of the reliable, steady ones. God knows, after the Met's recent years, there's a need for a few of those.'

'And you are,' she replied. 'I can see that.'

'A good cop, Okeke... as in not on the take. But...'

'But?' she repeated.

He looked at her. 'I'm also not a bloody idiot. The Salikovs have resources, deep pockets, and they've also made how they operate very clear.' He wondered whether he should share Hatcher's revelation with her. Why not? She knew most of it.

'Her Madge received the same message as I did. A blood-stained bribe and a threat.'

Okeke's jaw hung. 'You're shitting me!'

'She told me yesterday. She got the same delivery a year ago. And she's clearly terrified about us bringing in Hammond for questioning. And, I'll be honest with you, I'm a little wary too.' He sipped his takeaway coffee. 'Have you spoken with Jay yet?'

'No. I left a message on his phone to stay calm. To not do anything stupid. That we've got this. I told him we'd get something sooner or later on Hammond and bring him in again.'

Boyd let out a deep breath. 'Well, that's another thing you'll need to deal with, then. Managing Jay's expectations.'

'He isn't going to go *rogue*, guv. I've talked to him. I've explained the best way to seek justice for Louie is to let us do our job.'

He looked at her. 'But, you know, we can't do that this time?'

Her eyes narrowed. 'You're really just letting this go?'

'We got very lucky last year, Sam. We brushed up against an OCG that makes our local county-lines scrotes look like a bunch of clueless prats. We got a polite warning to back off.'

'Polite?'

'Trust me.' He gazed out at the seagulls a dozen yards out, dipping and rising on the stiff breeze yet otherwise motionless.

'So we're stalling on Hammond, then?'

'Afraid so,' he replied. 'You have to pick the right fights, mate. The ones you have at least a *chance* of winning.'

BOYD LEFT Okeke outside to have her post-lunch fag; it was too nippy to linger.

He dropped his coat on to the back of the chair and was about to go for a pee, when he saw Sutherland bowling out of his goldfish-bowl office towards him.

'Sir?'

'Hatcher,' Sutherland replied. Everything Boyd needed to know packaged up in one word.

'Is it urgent?' he asked. 'I just need a quick –'

'Now!' clarified Sutherland.

Boyd knocked on the door and opened it. He tried not to react as his eyes settled on

Miko Karovic and a man it took him a few seconds to recognise: Roland Hammond. Hammond had a medical dressing on his cheek, and the skin around one eye looked red and swollen.

'Boyd,' started Hatcher. 'Mr Hammond has just –'

'My client,' cut in Karovic, 'wishes to report that he was violently assaulted this morning at gunpoint.'

'Okay...' Boyd said.

Hatcher continued. 'Mr Hammond was at home when a man broke into his apartment, threatened to kill him and then assaulted him.' She looked as pale as ghost. 'Mr Hammond managed to – very bravely – fight back and the armed man fled the scene.'

'With his gun,' added Hammond.

'Right.' Shit. *You'd better respond how they want you to respond, Bill.* 'Right,' he repeated. 'Do we have a description to work with?'

'No need,' said Karovic. 'My client recognised him as one of the doormen at the nightclub called CuffLinks.' He looked down at his yellow legal notepad. 'The assailant's name is Jason Turner.'

'Jason Turner?' Boyd felt his heart sink. 'Are you sure?'

Karovic nodded. 'He accused Mr Hammond of murdering his colleague. And this act of vigilantism is a direct consequence of you bringing my client in to be questioned. You made him look like a suspect.'

Boyd looked at Hammond. 'You say he did this at *gunpoint*?'

'Yes. Yes, of course,' Hammond replied. 'I would have put up more of a fight otherwise.'

'What kind of gun?' Boyd asked.

Hammond hunched his shoulders. 'I'm not a ruddy expert,

Boyd... a handgun! Turner somehow got hold of my address. He would have killed me if I hadn't fought back!'

*Killed him?* None of this sounded like Jay. 'Are you certain?'

'It's true, dammit! Look at me!' he continued. 'Turner forced his way in, caught me off guard. Fuck's sake... I wasn't even dressed!'

'My client was able to fight back, forcing Mr Turner to abandon his ill-judged attempt at vigilantism.'

'Boyd...' Hatcher seemed eager to appear proactive in front of the other two. 'I've just issued a warrant and authorised an ARU to go to his address and arrest him.'

'An armed unit?! But...'

'Yes, of course an armed unit,' she replied quickly. 'They have a Mark One shoot order if they see him holding a gun. *You're* to be SIO on this, Boyd. If they bring him in, he's yours alone to interview, do you understand?'

'Uh, that's not –'

'On my orders, Boyd. You *alone* will interview him and make a record of it. He'll be charged and immediately placed on remand.' She leant forward, knuckles on her desk. '*We* want a police officer who's a *friendly* on this... is that perfectly clear?'

She was doing him a favour. *Do. This. Right. And. They'll. Leave. You. Alone.*

He nodded. 'Of course, ma'am.'

'Off you go, then. Bring him in.'

Hammond snorted dryly. 'Go fetch the ball, Boyd... There's a good dog.'

# 21

Boyd closed Hatcher's office door behind him. 'Fuck,' he whispered softly.

*Jay's a dead man.* Those words popped into his head with absolute certainty behind them. If he tried to bolt with anything in his hand that looked even remotely like a gun, he was going to get shot.

Mark One. Lethal force already authorised.

And if they brought Jay in alive and he was put on remand, the moment he entered the general prison population he would be a dead man walking. He'd be dead long before there was any kind of trial.

Boyd strode down the hallway with Hatcher's voice still in his ear. '*... authorised an ARU to go to his address and arrest him ...*'

*Shit. Shit. Shit.*

He picked up the pace as he hurried down the steps to the CID floor, then pushed through the double doors to scan the open-plan office for Okeke. There was no sign of her.

For a brief moment he considered texting her, but then that would be actionable evidence sitting right there on his phone, no matter how carefully he nuanced the warning.

Maybe she was still outside having her fag...

He hurried down the stairs, pushed through the security door, then the lobby door and stepped outside.

He was right. Okeke was there, on her phone and finishing her smoke. So was Warren; it looked like he'd just lit his.

'Warren,' said Boyd. 'Put it out.'

'But, sir, I just...'

'Out! And get back to work!'

The young DC looked like a scolded schoolboy caught smoking behind the bike shed.

'NOW!' snapped Boyd. Warren dropped his cig, toed it out and backed away, crimson-faced. He disappeared back inside the station.

Okeke was staring wide-eyed at him. 'What the fuck was *that* for?'

'Who're you on the phone to?' Boyd snapped.

'Jay,' she replied. 'Guv...'

'Where is he?' Boyd cut across her.

'He's in bed. What's –'

'Tell him to get out of the house!' He snatched the phone out of her hand. 'Jay? This is Boyd...'

'Hey there, boss!' Jay sounded dozy yet pleased to hear from him. 'How're you do–'

'Jay, just shut up and listen. You need to get out of your house right now! There's an armed response unit on their way over to arrest you for threatening Hammond with a gun. You need to move now!'

'What? Hey... I didn't –' Jay protested.

'There is no time for this, mate – get dressed and get out!'

'Guv?' cut in Okeke. 'What's going on?'

He ignored her. 'Jay, listen to me... Hammond is one of those "Russians". Remember them?'

There was a pause. He could hear Jay's breathing. Then: 'You mean those mafia dudes?'

'Yes! And you just assaulted the big boss's son!'

'Oh... shit.' Jay said as the penny finally dropped.

JAY DROPPED his phone on the bed and untangled himself from the duvet. He slid his feet into his flip-flops and staggered over to the door to pull Sam's fluffy pink dressing gown off its hook. *God, it's cold*, he thought as he tugged the too-small dressing gown around his torso, cinching the belt tight. Their gurgling radiator needed bleeding, a job he kept booting down the road.

*Russians?* That made absolutely no sense. Roland Hammond wasn't a bloody Russian. He didn't look like one or even sound like one. He was just a posh boy, a preppie DFL, a chinless fuckwit who...

*Who we caught out discussing a murder...*

That thought woke him up a little. That and the fact that the guv didn't seem like the kind of bloke who screamed 'get out' for no reason.

*Shit*, Jay thought, finally shaking himself awake. *Come to think of it, the guv had sounded panicked.* He'd better listen to him; he had to get dressed and get out.

His clothes were still in the bathroom. He'd had a long soak after scaring that brat to the point of wetting himself. After that, Jay'd gone back to bed to catch up on the sleep he'd missed out on last night.

Before he could reach the bathroom, tendrils of steam still escaping the slightly open door, he heard a loud knock on the front door. He glanced down the stairs and saw several dark rippling silhouettes through the frosted glass. 'ARMED POLICE!'

He froze. The guv had said *run*... but... running meant going downstairs right past the front door. They'd see him. He looked at the bathroom ahead of him and glanced at the little sash window that looked out onto their small backyard.

There was another heavy hammering from below. 'JASON TURNER, ARMED POLICE. OPEN THE DOOR. DO NOT HAVE ANYTHING IN YOUR HANDS!'

He hurried into the bathroom and locked the door behind him. He gathered up the clothes he'd scattered nonchalantly on the tiled floor earlier and he'd just loosened the dressing gown's belt when he heard the loud crash of the front door being rammed open, followed by thundering footsteps into his house and half a dozen voices barking 'POLICE' like kennel dogs.

He yanked the sash window open, hopped up onto the toilet seat and swung a leg over the sill and outside into the cold air. 'Oh, this is bloody nuts,' he muttered. The drop was about twelve feet onto uneven paving slabs and an obstacle course of wooden frames from old furniture and pallets he'd been in the process of breaking down. A stupid jump at the best of times, but in flip-flops?

A fist hammered against the bathroom door. 'TURNER! YOU IN THERE?'

He ducked his head under the window frame and lifted his other leg up, over the sill, to dangle outside.

'Get the BRK up here now! He's in the bathroom!'

He leant forward, bum shuffling towards the edge of the sill as he tried to calculate what precisely he was going to land on.

The voice on the other side of the door ordered him to unlock and open the door or stand the fuck back. Then a moment later it too crashed open. Jay lurched forward off the sill and plummeted downwards.

'He did *WHAT*?!'

'Beat up Hammond,' Boyd replied. 'Apparently he also threatened him with a gun.'

'A gun?! Well, that's bollocks! He doesn't have one. Nor does he know anyone who would!'

Boyd looked at her. 'Please tell me you didn't give him Hammond's name and details?'

Okeke shook her head. 'Of course I didn't!' Then her fist came up to her mouth as she added the pieces of the situation together. 'Oh, fuck... Oh, God! He's in danger, right?'

Boyd nodded. 'Big time. If he gets arrested, there'll be no bail – it'll be straight to pre-trial detention and straight into general prison circulation.'

The very thing that Gerald Nix had been terrified of. The price on his head in prison would have been a fraction of the price out on the street.

Okeke reached out and grabbed her phone out of Boyd's hand. 'I've got to call him!'

'No. Okeke. Stop! Any calls you make to him are going to make you look complicit.'

'I don't give a shit.' She thumbed his name and waited for a few moments.

'Okeke, you can't even leave a message. If you do, you'll –'

'Babes, it's me,' she said. 'Go to the chair... I'll come get you!'

Boyd's head dropped, as she hung up.

'What?' She shook her head with exasperation. 'My career or Jay's life? No fucking question!'

She turned away from him and hurried across the forecourt towards her car.

'For God's sake! Okeke! Stop!'

She turned to look at him. 'He's not good on his own. He needs me.'

'Okeke... you'll end up being a target too. Do you understand?'

'If this was Emma, what would you be doing?' she said, challenging him. 'Well?'

There really was no answer to that. He watched her go.

JAY LANDED ON HIS FEET – mercifully – on a paving slab, narrowly avoiding the jagged wooden slats of a pallet sitting next to it. His legs buckled under his weight and he rolled to the side. Above him he saw a policeman's head poking out of the bathroom's sash window.

'He's down! Backyard!'

Jay gathered the dressing gown around him and made for the garden fence, just in time to see a copper wrestling with the stiff bolt on the back door. It had a warped frame – another job that had been sitting on his backburner to-do list for far too long. He scrambled up the fence and was astride it at the very moment the back door was wrenched open and the armed officer spilled out of it, deftly dodging the bric-a-brac cluttering the ground. He managed to get his hands wrapped around Jay's left ankle before Jay could lift his other leg over.

Jay flailed his foot frantically to shake him off, the rough top of the fence slats digging into his bare arse and ball sack. 'Ahhh!' he bellowed. 'My bollocks!'

The copper grinned. 'Ooh, that's gotta hurt, eh, mate?'

Jay leant over and walloped the side of his head. The copper let go and staggered backwards into the mess of wood carcasses he'd managed to avoid in the first place. Jay swung his leg up and over, his left flip-flop flying off into the yard some-where, and dropped down into next door's garden, navigating around a child's netted-in trampoline, several discarded tricy-cles and a rusting oil-barrel barbecue.

At the next fence he repeated the ungainly manoeuvre, one leg over, bollocks and bum scraping painfully as he pivoted and swung the other leg over, dropping down into Mrs Patton's backyard. He could see the old lady in her kitchen, popping the kettle on. He opened the back door. She jumped at the sudden noise.

'Sorry, Mrs P,' he said, pulling the gown tightly around himself for decency.

She did a double take at the state of him. 'Are you all right there, poppet?'

'I errr... I locked myself out in the yard,' he explained.

She rolled her eyes. 'Oh, you're a wally, Jason. Do you want a cuppa? I've just put the kettle on.'

'No, that's... no thanks, Mrs P. Can I just come through and go out your side?'

She had a second back door off her utility room that opened onto a rat-run alleyway that divided the long row of terraced houses.

'Do you need to wait for Sam to come home? You can watch some telly in the front room if you –'

'No... I think I'll just... err... just go to my workshop,' he replied. 'I've got some overalls there.'

'Oooh!' Mrs Patton smiled. 'How's my armchair coming along?'

Jay turned to answer her as he stepped into her utility room. 'Good. Really good. I'll have it done by the weekend.' He pulled the door open. 'I promise.'

'Jason?' she called out.

He stopped again. 'Yeah?'

'You're missing a flip-flop, my dear.'

# 22

Chief Superintendent Hatcher looked only marginally less stressed out now that Hammond and the Salikov's family solicitor had departed the station.

Sutherland simply looked as though somebody had turned over two pages at once. 'Why the big priority on this assault?' His puzzled, rumpled forehead looked like a stack of poorly folded laundry. 'Surely the Collins stabbing is top of the list?'

'Sutherland,' Hatched said sternly, looking at him, 'are you aware who Roland Hammond is?'

He shrugged.

'He's the son of a billionaire. A Russian one. A well-connected Russian one.'

'I don't care if he's the King of Morocco! We've got a murder case to –'

'Ma'am,' Boyd interjected. 'There's an added complication with the assault case, which also applies to the murder case.'

'Which is?'

'Jason Turner is the partner of one of our detectives.'

Sutherland nodded. 'Of course! Bloody hell, yes. He's DC Okeke's other half, isn't he?'

'Yup. And Louie Collins was Jason Turner's close friend,' added Boyd. 'Jay attacked Hammond because he believed he was responsible for Collins' stabbing.'

She shot him a pointed watch-what-you-say look that Sutherland completely missed.

'There's absolutely no evidence for Turner's belief, as far as I'm aware,' said Hatcher. 'Whereas we have Hammond's account, facial injuries that verify his account and, according to Mr Karovic, there's CCTV footage from the apartment block of Turner forcing his way in.' Hatcher's gaze lingered on Boyd and it came with a clear-as-glass subtext.

*We are playing along. Understand?*

'Well, you can't have Okeke on your team,' said Sutherland. 'For obvious personal reasons. I know you prefer to work with her, Boyd, but... I'll have to go and explain to her that she's off the Collins case as of now.'

'Take anyone you need,' said Hatcher. 'Even off Flack's team if you need more manpower. Any uniformed resources you need as well. Just find Turner *as quickly as you can.*'

Sutherland shook his head and sighed at her resource-grabbing. 'All this for an assault?"

'Just get it done!' she snapped at him. She rose from her chair to signal that the meeting was over, and both Sutherland and Boyd got up and headed for the door.

Boyd lingered. 'Ma'am?'

She watched Sutherland head off down the hall, then turned her attention to Boyd. 'What is it?'

'Can we speak privately, ma'am?'

She ushered him back into her office and closed the door. 'We said everything we needed to say yesterday, Boyd. I don't want to repeat myself. Certainly not here. Or now.'

'Who are you in contact with? Directly? The family lawyer, Karovic?'

She didn't reply.

'The Salikovs themselves?'

She remained silent.

'Have they communicated with you?'

She held her hand out and he realised she was asking for his phones. He pulled them out and handed them to her. She briefly inspected each one, then powered them down and placed them in a glass display cabinet and slid the glass shut.

She turned round. 'This is the last time we do this.'

'Have they said what's going to happen to Turner?'

She spoke very softly. 'You don't need to know any more than that he needs to be found, very quickly, charged and then put on remand. That's what they've asked for. And that's what we need to give them.'

'They're going to get to him, aren't they? Wherever he's held?'

She hesitated for a moment, then nodded. 'They'll get to him on the inside, or they'll track him down on the outside and, I dare say, if it's the latter, they'll take their time with him.'

She pressed her lips together, producing a row of purse lines. 'This is not a hill I'm prepared to die on, Boyd. Do you understand? Turner picked the wrong man to go after.'

'Jesus, and that's it?'

'You don't do that to the son of a Russian mafia boss and just stroll away. This is a bloody nightmare that I do not intend to get sucked into. And nor will you, Boyd.' She slid the glass aside and reached for his phones.

'Just do your job, Boyd, and bloody well find him.'

She handed them back and nodded towards her door. The meeting was over.

## 23

'You idiot, Jay. You giant fricking idiot,' said Okeke. Then she flung her arms around him. He held her tightly for a moment, then let her go.

'I'm so sorry, Sam.'

She shook her head. 'Hammond said you had a gun.'

He spread his hands. 'What? No. I just... I was empty-handed.'

'And he said you assaulted him, that he fought you off and you fled.'

Jay snorted. 'Well, that's a load of crap. I rugby-tackled him. And then, okay, I tied his hands up and put a sock in his mouth. But I didn't hit him and I certainly didn't have a bloody gun!'

She clacked her tongue. 'So mostly his bullshit, then. But, Jesus, Jay... I told you to leave him to me and Boyd.'

'Don't get mad with me. I didn't know he was a Russian!' said Jay. 'He certainly didn't sound or look like one.'

'Oh, God help me...' She sighed. 'They don't all look like Dolph Lundgren in *Rocky*, you muppet.' She stood back and looked him over. He was wearing her pink dressing gown and little else. 'You're going to need some clothes.'

'And shoes,' he said, sitting back down and waggling a bare foot. 'I can't go back to the house?'

She shook her head. 'It won't take long before they realise you've got a workshop. So you can't hide out here, I'm afraid.'

'Oh.' He looked disappointed. 'That was my plan: bunk up here and wait for things to blow over.'

'It's not going to "blow over", love.'

Sitting in Mrs Patton's armchair in nothing but her bathrobe and a single flip-flop, Jay couldn't have looked less ready to face the shitshow he'd just kicked off.

'The police or the Salikovs *are* going to find you here, babe... you've got to find somewhere better than this to lay low.'

'How about round Gary's?'

'No. You work with him. They'll be knocking on his door soon enough.'

*Karl's.* That was the only other place she could think of: his half-brother's.

'Not Karl,' he said, reading her expression.

'*Yes*, Karl.'

'No. He already thinks I'm a loser. And you want me rocking up at his place begging for a place to stay?'

She grabbed his shoulders. 'Jay! This is serious! This is *your life* we're talking about!'

He pulled a dismissive smile. 'Oh, come on. They're just a bunch of dumb scrotes in shell suits, babe. We took 'em last time.'

'Jesus.' She wanted to slap that idiot grin off his face. 'Have you forgotten what actually happened last year? How close they came to killing you and Boyd?!'

'If I recall, we kicked *their* arses.'

'No, love. You didn't. You got away. That's it. You got away by the skin of your teeth. And the only reason you didn't wind up dead was that they had the person they were after.'

She realised there was a disconnect between what she knew

and what Jay knew about the whole situation. He'd turned up on the night to look big and scary in front of Nix. That was it. And, in the aftermath of that night, all she'd told him was that the men he'd come up against were low-level Russian thugs.

'Jay, listen to me carefully. You just roughed up the son of a Russian mafia boss,' she said.

'I didn't touch him! Not after I tied him up, anyway. I just wanted him to know that you and the guv were going to take him down for killing Louie. And I told him we both heard him plan a murder.' Jay smiled. 'Hammond *literally* peed himself when I mentioned that. I literally scared the piss out of him.'

Okeke took a deep breath and sat down on the stool. 'Jay, let me explain your situation... You need to listen to me now. Rovshan Salikov is the big boss. He runs the biggest organised crime group in Georgia. That's drug money, extortion, people smuggling, human slavery, torture, murder. He's brought that all over here. Now I don't know whether he's planning to start up a criminal empire in the UK, or simply looking to clean his money – either way, he's not the type to settle for you getting six months' suspended sentence and a hundred hours' community service for attacking his son.'

That stupid smirk had finally gone from Jay's face. 'Well... what if I just hand myself in, then?' he asked.

'No. No. No! You don't understand. Salikov's already got his grubby hands on...'

*Do I tell him?* She decided she *had* to. 'They've basically got a chokehold on the Chief Superintendent. And Boyd.'

'The guv?' Jay's jaw dropped.

'He's been threatened, yes. As in "you find Jay or you're next"!' Saying that out loud, the realisation finally slotted into place for her. She wasn't going to be able to trust Boyd this time round. They could threaten Emma. 'Listen, babe. I know you think Boyd's a great guy, but do you see...? He's got no choice. He has to bring you in, Jay. Do you understand?'

'But he wouldn't,' Jay replied. 'Not the guv.'

'What if they threaten Emma? Huh? What if they already have?'

His brows dropped to a troubled ridge.

'If it comes down to you or Emma... who do you think he's going to pick?'

'Bollocks,' he mumbled. 'Maybe you're right.'

She nodded. 'So... Karl's it is. You're going to get your arse over to Karl's and then we can work out what we do next.'

'What about you, Sam?' he asked.

'I'll be fine. I'm not wanted by anyone.'

'You could come with me?'

Okeke shook her head. 'If I'm at the station, I can help you to stay ahead of the manhunt.'

*Hopefully.* There was a good chance that Boyd wouldn't use her... or had already been told he couldn't use her. However, within the open CID floor, intel was pretty porous. She could possibly squeeze Warren for titbits outside during a ciggie break. Plus, she'd have access to LEDS.

'I'm going to get you some stuff to wear,' said Okeke. 'Then you need to go, baby. You need to go.'

# 24

The town house that Roland's father had bought was Number 17 Eaton Square. A magnificent five floors of whitewashed stone, balconies with gold-painted railings and a grand portico entrance with five marble steps leading up to it from a spotless pavement.

At any other time, Eaton Square would have been an oasis of suburban calm in the middle of Belgravia, London. But right now the pavements and road outside his house were cluttered with contractors' vans.

Roland hurried up the steps and paused to make way for a couple of workmen who were carrying out a large panel of dark oak. He let them pass and hurried into the entrance hall.

Inside the *Downton Abbey*-like décor was being ruthlessly stripped from the walls and floors to make way for a more contemporary look. The Old Man was getting on, but he made every effort to disguise his age. Not just in his personal appearance but in his choice of women, the environment he lived in and the cars he drove.

Mother had shown Roland the interior designer's renderings of the town house – how it would look when every last detail had finally been completed. To his eyes, it looked cold and very masculine. All chrome and slate, hard edges and ninety-degree angles. He much preferred the Regency-era look that was currently being brutally torn out of the house.

He spotted his mother's PA hurrying down the central stairs, clipboard in one hand and phone to her ear in the other.

'Gillian, where's Mummy?'

She paused to look at him. 'Are you okay?' she asked.

He ignored her and repeated, 'Where's Mother?'

'She's upstairs in the music room,' she replied.

He took the marble steps up, two at a time, stopping again for a pair of workmen carrying out a chaise longue between them. Roland had just got used to thinking of this place as home of sorts. Until Rovshan had announced he was stripping out the whole building and modernising it, stamping his gaudy, vulgar, Liberace-like notion of 'style' all over it. He'd started with the top floor and was working his way down-wards. The workmen – or clueless bloody vandals as Roland liked to think of them – had reached the third floor, and his bedroom. Accepting Rovshan's errand to take some time to scout out Hastings for some investment opportunities had turned out to be a merciful escape, rather that than watching these apes in overalls strip the gorgeous mahogany panelling from his walls.

He pushed the large French doors inwards and spotted his mother sitting in the bay window with a glass of something clear and sparkling in one hand while she puffed frantically on a cigarette. The open doors allowed the noise of hammering, grinding and sawing to invade her quiet space and she whirled irritably round in her seat. She beamed when she was it was her son who'd entered the room.

'Oh, Roland,' she gasped.

He closed the doors behind him, the sounds of the workmen muted once again, and hurried quickly across the wooden floor. He gave her a peck on the cheek and sat down. 'Where's the old man?' he asked.

'Somewhere upstairs,' Letitia said, gesturing at the ceiling. There were three more floors above them. 'Probably discussing what he can ruin next with his project manager and his bloody designer.'

'Mummy, we need to talk.'

'What happened to your face?' she asked, reaching out to touch it.

Roland shook his head. The *genuine* scrapes and bruises on his cheeks and temples were nothing compared to the cosmetically enhanced ones he'd walked into the police station with. It was amazing how a little rouge deployed around a slight graze could make it look like a significant injury.

'I got into a fight. It's nothing.'

'Rolly! A fight?!' He could hear her voice slurring. It was only 6 p.m. She must have started on her first gin at lunchtime.

'It was a misunderstanding, all right?' he said impatiently. 'Now listen – we really need to talk.'

Letitia Hammond-Bowles took another slurp from her glass.

'Oh, Rolly,' she slurred. 'I'm not in the mood for talking today.'

Roland grabbed the glass from her shaking hand and set it down on the drinks table next to her.

She began to cry. 'Rolly, I've had enough of this – I just want it all to stop.'

'Shhhhh...' He massaged her hand gently between his. 'It's okay. It's going to be okay, Mummy.'

Her shoulders began to lift and drop, lift and drop, as she eased back from the edge of a panic attack.

'Easy now. That's it. Easy,' he reassured her.

There was a loud crash from outside the double doors, followed by a shout and laughter from the workmen.

'I can't do this, Rolly!' she cried. 'I really can't do this any more.'

She took a pull on her cigarette and blew a cloud of smoke towards the dark window. The doll's-house buildings around Eaton Square were lit up like Harrods' display windows and provided her a Peeping Tom's paradise.

'Mummy, I really need to talk to you today,' Roland tried again.

'Oh, Rolly...' she whimpered. 'I wish we'd never started...'

He sighed. 'Listen, I'll take care of you, okay? All you've got to do is stay calm and keep doing what you're doing? All right?'

She managed a nod. 'Can I have my drink back please?'

'There's a good girl.' He kissed her hand and passed the glass to her. 'This'll all be over with soon enough. I promise.'

'God, I hope so,' she said, and took a gulp of her gin.

He smiled. 'I'm going to go up and try to have a chat with Daddy.'

## 25

The wind along the seafront was tugging at Boyd's coat like a bored child and forcing noisy frothy waves high up onto the shingle beach. Ozzie was, of course, incandescent with rage at the Channel for being so presumptuous.

'Sounds rough there,' said Charlotte. 'Are the waves up to the top?'

'Nearly,' he replied.

'It's a bit blowy here too. Dad's worried about an old elm that's swaying around above the conservatory. He's forbidden me and Mum from stepping in there today in case it comes down.' He heard her chuckle. 'It's not exactly the storm of the century.'

Boyd smiled. She sounded a little more like her old self. The time with her folks was healing time, catch-up time for all those years she'd stayed away from them.

'Are you okay?' she asked presently. 'You sound a tad... *pensive.*'

'Fine,' he replied, not really helping his case.

'Is it work?' she asked.

'Uh-huh.'

'As in too much?' she probed. 'Or a particularly difficult job?'

'More the second,' he replied.

'Is it anything you can talk about?'

Boyd sighed. He really wished he could let it all out for her to hear, and maybe if she was on the beach standing here with him, he might have. But not over the phone.

'I'm sorry, Charlotte, not really.'

She was silent for a moment.

He could hear the mournful wail of wind down the phone. 'It sounds like you're in a haunted house.'

'It's a draughty house,' she replied, 'that's for sure.'

'How's Mia getting on with your parents?' he asked.

'With my parents, fine. With their spaniels? Well... there've been a few harsh words exchanged between them. She's been a bit bossy.'

Boyd laughed. Charlotte's dog was a lot smaller than Ozzie, and very sweet, but she could hold her own. 'I can imagine. And you and your folks? How're you getting on?'

He heard her set a teacup down on its saucer. 'It's a bit strained every now and then. I mean, I've been a bit of a stranger to them for so long. In some ways, it's peculiar, Bill; it's like it was when I was eighteen.' She laughed. 'I'm actually in my old bedroom. It hasn't changed a bit. Would you believe there's still a poster of Kate Bush up on my wall?'

He laughed. The small talk about dogs, her parents, her childhood bedroom was the antidote he needed right now: a slice of normality. A piece of calm.

'Look, I'd better go,' he said reluctantly. 'I've got to get Ozzie back home and then I'm in at work.'

'Yes, of course,' Charlotte said. 'Give my love to Emma. And Ozzie.'

'I will.'

'And you can have some too,' she added.

He smiled. 'Same.' They said their goodbyes and she was gone. For the first time in a very long time he wanted to climb into his phone and escape to the other end. To where she was. Away from here.

He cast his eyes up and down the foaming beach. The only fools out down here in this weather seemed to be other spaniel owners. With a gnawing sensation in his gut, he turned his mind towards the day ahead. Towards the task ahead.

HE PARKED his Captur close to the station's main entrance. Close enough that he'd be able to spot and hopefully intercept Okeke in the car park before she stepped inside.

They needed to talk. Outside. Face to face and not over the phone. Perhaps he was being paranoid, perhaps not. If Hatcher had a suspicion about him, a doubt that he was on *exactly* the same page as her, then it wouldn't be beyond belief that she'd have obtained access to his work phone's call log.

With Okeke now excluded from the Incident Room and his team, he had no legitimate reason to talk to her, unless it was in an interview room, on the record and about the whereabouts of her missing boyfriend. Any phone record of them talking together would be a huge red flag.

And this morning one of the first things he was going to have to do was just that – interview her formally. Sutherland would be in the room with him, Hatcher no doubt listening in.

'Sam, I have to make it look like I'm giving this my A game,' he muttered. 'I have to make it look like I'm really doing everything possible to track down Jay. You understand that, right?'

That's how he was would begin the conversation and she was just going to have to trust him.

He caught sight of her Datsun pulling into the parking area.

Helpfully, she parked in the space right beside his car. He watched her through his side window. Oblivious to the fact he was sitting there and that she was being observed, she settled back in her seat, closed her eyes, puffed her cheeks and blew out a deep breath.

He let Okeke have her moment of decompression, then waved a hand. The motion caught her attention. He lowered his window, and after a moment's hesitation she lowered her passenger side one.

'All right?' he asked.

She nodded warily. 'Guv.'

'We need to talk,' he said. 'Is this okay with you?'

'What? Sitting in our cars?'

He nodded. She shuffled across, over the handbrake, until she was on the passenger seat. 'Shit. Has it really come down to this? All cloak and daggers?'

'As far as it goes with Hatcher, yes,' he replied. 'We have to start thinking of her as one of Them.'

'You're serious?'

'She's a nervous wreck... She's falling apart, Sam.'

'Sam? Is it?' She raised a brow. 'So I'm definitely not on the team?'

He shook his head. 'There's no way you could be,' he replied, 'even if the Russians weren't involved.'

Her eyes locked on his. 'So where does this put us, guv?'

'On the same side. We both want a way out for Jay,' he assured her.

'I spoke with him last night. There was no gun. Hammond made that shit up.'

Boyd nodded. 'I can believe that.'

'And there was no fight. No punches thrown. Jay said he rugby-tackled him to the ground, bound and gagged him, then gave him a talking to.'

Boyd laughed. 'And I can believe that too.'

128

'And he told Hammond about him and Louie hearing him plan a murder.'

Boyd sucked air in between his teeth. 'That's not so good. That's another reason they'll want him, Sam.'

'Want him *dead*,' she clarified.

He nodded. 'I want to find a way out for him.' He tapped his steering wheel. 'He saved my life.'

'Yes, he did.'

Boyd shrugged. 'So I owe him.'

She nodded. 'Yes, you do.' She looked around the car park to make sure they weren't being observed. 'So how are you going to do that?'

'You have to trust me, Sam. If I know where Jay is hiding, I know where *not* to direct the search.'

She offered him a wan smile. 'Which is all well and good until they threaten your Emma. Then tell me... what happens at that point? Do I keep trusting you?'

He'd wondered how quickly she'd come to that, and he didn't have an answer.

'Right.' She nodded at his silence. 'So, no offence intended, guv, but I *can't* completely trust you, can I?'

He couldn't lie to her.

'If they threatened Emma? Would you even tell me they had?'

He could see she knew the answer to that already.

'I know you want to find a way out for Jay... but I also know if they come knocking on your door, guv...'

'You're right,' he said, nodding. 'Then how about this? I make every effort. I pull the stops out to find him, but as long as he stays one step ahead of me...'

'It's Jason Turner we're talking about, guv.' She couldn't help smiling. 'Not Jason Bourne.'

Boyd returned a muted smile. 'So long as I'm seen to be leaving no stone unturned... I can throw you a steer or two.'

'Until at some point, they say find him now... or you're dead. Then what?' She shrugged.

'If it comes to that... I suppose me and Emma would have to do a runner as well,' he replied.

'You say that...'

Boyd glanced at his watch. 'Look, we'd better head in before we attract attention. And separately.'

She nodded. 'Right.'

'Once I've set up my team this morning, I'm going to be interviewing you, Sam. Get your head together. Get your story straight. You have no idea where he is. He's vanished.'

## 26

Jay was impressed with himself for deftly switching vehicles. He'd spent last night on the sofa at Howler's place. Greg Howler wasn't one of Sam's favourites when it came to his gym mates. In her words, he was an 'offensively sexist knuckle-dragger' who could barely manage a sentence without relying on the 'C-word. He was known by the lads as Howler the Prowler because, above getting trashed, he was always on the lookout for an opportunity to 'pull'.

Howler was well up for the idea of swapping Jay's Transit for his Bedford van for a 'try-out week'. Jay had dangled the prospect of a straight swap if they were both happy with each other's vehicles and Howler had leapt on the idea.

So, until the police caught up with that switcheroo, he was ANPR-proof.

Sam had drawn out £300 from her bank account and given Jay the cash, instructing him that the first thing he was going to do with that money was buy a cheap pre-paid *dumb* phone. His beloved iPhone was no doubt now sitting on someone's desk in Hastings police station, and they'd probably already gone through his photo roll. He hadn't dared mention to Sam there were still some candid pictures on there from when they'd first got together. She was going to hand him his arse for that once this situation was over.

He focused back on the present, and Karl. His half-brother was based in Brighton, down near the front, in Kemptown. Kemptown was, of course, the *coolest* part of Brighton, the LGBT, rainbow-hued, everything-is-awesome hub for the city of Brighton and Hove. The last address he had for Karl was Unit 17, Hamble House, Eastern Terrace Mews, which sounded like a workplace rather than a home address.

Without his iPhone to hand, he was going to have to figure his way there old-school-style: a paperback A–Z and a lot of asking of random strangers, each giving him a string of directions that he was going to forget thirty seconds later.

'Honey,' Sam had whispered to him as they'd parted. 'Please... please... *please*, be careful. These people are fucking dangerous. Stay low. Stay hidden.'

'Got it,' he assured her.

'And for God's sake be super nice to Karl. He doesn't *have* to help you out, you know?'

He was pretty sure Karl would. They might not have much, if anything, in common, but they had the same blood – well, a fifty-per-cent diluted version of blood – running through their veins.

Jay pulled off the A27 into the Lewes service station, primarily for a pee, but also to buy himself a Brighton and Hove A–Z – if such an antiquated thing was still sold in petrol stations. He parked the van away from the shop entrance. He'd watched enough episodes of *24 Hours in Police Custody* to know that there was always a camera deployed just inside and outside the glass doors. He grabbed the baseball cap that Okeke had insisted he take with him and pulled it down onto his head. He felt like a complete muppet wearing the damned thing, but she was absolutely right: he needed something to disguise his face. He pulled the peak down low and got out.

# 27

'Now listen, Sam...' began Sutherland.

*Okay, so everyone's calling me Sam all of a sudden, huh?* She wondered what that inferred – that she was now being treated as a civvy? That she was no longer one of them?

'This is off the record. It's just you, me and Boyd, all right?'

She nodded. 'Yes, sir.'

He steepled his fingers, then lightly rested his chin on them. 'Jason Turner... where is he?'

'I honestly don't know.' She shrugged. 'If I knew, obviously, I'd tell you, sir.'

Sutherland nodded sympathetically. 'You see, Sam, I'd like to have complete confidence in that answer but...'

'The problem, sir, is that Hammond was lying about Jay. He hasn't done anything. He's made that crap up.'

Sutherland tried to look understanding. 'Maybe not, Sam, but we have to take those allegations seriously and we also have to accept that Jason had a strong motive to harm Mr Hammond. Revenge. Righting an injustice... as *he* perceived it.'

'I get what you're saying, sir, and I'm also well aware that his going on the run doesn't look good.'

'No,' replied Sutherland. 'It really doesn't look good.'

'Look, he genuinely believes Hammond is Louie Collins' murderer. He was emotionally impacted by that. Louie and Jay go way back.'

Sutherland looked down at his notes. 'They were childhood friends, yes?'

'Exactly. Louie was the closest thing he had to family.'

Sutherland nodded. 'I understand. And he was very hurt. He was very angry –'

'Because we'd just let Roland Hammond walk free!'

Sutherland frowned. 'How did he know that, out of interest?'

She sighed. 'I might have mentioned something about our suspect walking free.'

The detective superintendent tutted and shook his head. 'Christ, Okeke.'

'But I didn't give him the suspect's name!' She turned to Boyd, hoping for a bit of support – even though she knew he couldn't give it. He had to *appear* to be on the same page as Sutherland.

'If you didn't tell him, then Jay must have gone and done some detective work,' Boyd said sternly. 'Identified him somehow and worked out where he was staying? Are you sure you didn't feed that information to him? Perhaps accidentally?'

'No. Absolutely not!' She genuinely didn't know how he'd found out. But somehow he'd managed. Maybe he was more savvy than he let on?

Jay studied himself in the grubby toilet mirror. Actually, with the baseball cap on and the peak pulled down low, he didn't look too bad. In fact, it kind of suited him. Made him look a bit like a hitman or, better still, Jack Reacher.

He washed his hands, wiped them on his jeans, pushed the gents' door open and stepped back into the petrol station's shop. He scanned the shelves near the till and finally found what he was looking for – a faded Brighton A–Z, which must have been shelf-squatting for years. He also picked up a Yorkie and a can of Red Bull.

*Gotta keep the ol' senses sharp.*

'Any fuel?' the girl at the counter asked.

'No gas, ma'am,' he replied, and realized for some daft reason he'd slipped into some kind of transatlantic accent. The girl gave him a second look. 'Hey. Are you American?'

The question jerked him out of his foolish role play. He was supposed to be incognito, attracting zero attention. He dipped his head and let the peak drop to cover his face. 'Uh. no... just... errr... from up north.'

'Oh, okay. Anyway, that's... seven pounds sixty please.'

He gave her a tenner, grabbed the change, turned and hastened back to the van.

'Okay, so... let's put your minor indiscretion aside,' continued Sutherland. 'Let's talk about where Jason could have gone. Any thoughts on that? Any other close friends? Family?'

Okeke sat back in her chair and made a big show of racking her brains. 'I... Jay and I've only been cohabiting for a bit, sir. It's not like we're, you know, a fully *entangled* couple.'

'So how much do you know about his past?' pressed Sutherland. 'Does he have a history of violence?'

'Jay?' She laughed at the idea of that. 'No. He's soft as anything.'

'But you've met his family?' asked Boyd.

'No.' She shook her head. 'Not really.'

'Not really?' Boyd pushed.

'He doesn't really have family. I mean, he's got a string of temporary foster parents from a while back... but he hasn't stayed in contact with any of them.'

That much she knew was true. Jay had been a care-home kid.

'Siblings?' asked Sutherland.

'One half-brother... I think.'

Sutherland glanced at Boyd with a hopeful look on his face. 'What's his name?'

'Marcus,' she replied. 'Or Mark.'

*That's it, Sam... you've now officially lied.* She'd stepped over that invisible line and, however this situation panned out, it was going to come back and bite her arse; she was sure of it. They would definitely uncover it – but it would hopefully take them a while.

'What about a surname?' asked Boyd. 'Turner as well?'

She shook her head. 'No. Not Turner. I don't know what it is, though.'

Sutherland looked over his glasses at her. 'You don't know the name of your boyfriend's only blood relative?'

She looked at him defiantly. 'No, sir.'

Boyd turned to Sutherland. 'We can probably dig that out of the system.' Then he leant forward, across the table and gave her his firm, no-messing-around-here face. 'Sam, we need to find him quickly. I don't want Jay to get himself into any deeper trouble.'

'That makes two of us,' she replied.

'So what about any friends, then?' asked Boyd. 'Any other mates he might have turned to for help?'

*He should be in Brighton by now. With Karl.* She decided a bum steer might slow them down a bit. 'The gym. He's got some work-out buddies at the gym.'

'Which gym?' asked Boyd.

She knew he knew. He was putting on a show for Sutherland. She hoped.

'The White Rock Gym. The same one Minter goes to, guv.'

'Any names for these friends?' Boyd asked.

She shook her head. 'Not proper ones. They've all got macho nicknames there.'

Sutherland shook his head. 'Of course they do.'

Again, she made a show of trying to remember. 'I dunno. Boff, I think. There's a Rocky.'

'Rocky? Does he box, by any chance?' tried Sutherland.

'No,' Okeke said. 'He's a regular there. White Rock – Rocky? See?'

'Ahhh... I see,' Sutherland said.

'There's a Blow-Joe... Growler... Jimbo...' She shook her head. 'That's all I've got.'

Boyd noted those down. 'All right. That's something for us to get cracking on.' He turned to Sutherland, glancing briefly at the camera and knowing Her Madge was almost certainly watching this interview in the other room.

'I suggest we get a team put together, asap.'

Sutherland nodded.

'And get an APB on Turner's van.' He looked at Okeke for the details.

'FP19 JHT,' she responded. 'It's a white Ford Transit.'

JAY FINALLY FOUND the bloody place – it was one of a row of cream-coloured townhouses that sported peeling paint and screamed 'faded grandeur', looking out across the seafront road onto Brighton Marina. What would once have been a row of rear gardens that regularly hosted tea parties and games of bridge was now a grubby parking area for the business premises that they'd become.

The parking was tight. Very tight. Jay found a spare spot marked for visitors but with no indication as to which business laid claim to it. He pulled the handbrake on, turned the engine off and climbed out. He walked along the row of townhouses looking for a plaque or a sign that would tell him which building was Unit 17.

He spotted a couple of gawky lads smoking on the step of one of the properties. Both were wearing slim-fitting jeans that made their skinny legs look comically thin and they were both on their phones.

'Hey, you two,' he called, approaching them. 'I'm looking for Unit Seventeen. But I can't see any bloody numbers along here.'

One of them looked up, doing an almost comical double-take at Jay's bulky body. 'Uh, bro... you found us. We're Unit Seventeen.'

'As in –' the other one looked up and did the exact same double take – 'as in, that's what the software company's called. Unit Seventeen. It's not a house number.'

'Ahhh.' Jay nodded slowly. 'Right. I got you.' He looked up at the building they were smoking outside. It was the grubbiest and least-loved town house in the row. 'Karl works with you, right?'

'Karl?' asked the first one. 'Yeah, he works here. You wanna see him?'

'Yeah,' Jay said.

The guy pinched his roll-up out and tucked what was left of it into the pocket of his hoodie. 'I'll see if he's in. Who're you, dude?'

'I'm his brother,' Jay said.

'His brother?!' The lad's eyes widened. 'You're shitting me.'

Jay was used to hearing that. They looked absolutely

nothing alike. Apart from having entirely different physiques, Jay was white and Karl was mixed race.

'No,' replied Jay. 'No, no shitting.'

The lad waved him in. 'Ah, you might as well come with... I'll take you up.'

# 28

Boyd looked at the crowded Incident Room. Hatcher had followed through on her promise to provide him with all the resources he'd need to get the job done. She'd got Sutherland to pull half of Flack's team off gazing-at-their-own-navel duty to help in the hunt for Jay. For the first time since joining Sussex Police, he was addressing a full room.

It was a hard-to-justify sell for Boyd. He had to tell this many detectives, all crammed into one room, that they were on the hunt for a single bloke who'd merely punched another. Sutherland stood beside him at the front for moral support, but Hatcher was there, right at the back by the door, watching his every move.

'Okay – settle down, everyone,' he began. 'This operation –' Sutherland handed him a printout with the name selected randomly by LEDS – 'Operation Flapjack is a manhunt. We're looking for a bloke called Jason Turner.' He pressed the Power-Point clicker and Jay's face appeared on the screen behind him. 'He's thirty-three years old and he's a doorman who works at CuffLinks nightclub. He's wanted for a home invasion and the violent assault of one Roland Hammond.'

Already he could see puzzled faces as the group before him looked around at the manpower assembled.

'Turner's a big guy,' he continued. *You've got to sell it, mate. She's watching you like a hawk.* 'He's got a violent disposition and a hair-trigger temper. And he's quite possibly suffering some kind of mental breakdown. Most importantly, boys and girls... it's possible he may be armed.'

That helped clear up a few of the confused expressions.

'He's done a runner and basically, folks, we need him back in custody before he beats the crap out of some other random person.'

'Or decides to use that gun,' added Sutherland.

'What kind of a gun, boss?' asked one of Flack's seconded team.

'Sorry, mate, you are?' asked Boyd.

'DI Shannon. Are we talking sawn-off shotgun, handgun, rifle?'

'A handgun,' Boyd answered. 'The victim wasn't able to identify what kind. Or whether it was even real.'

'But we have to assume it may be real,' cautioned Sutherland.

Boyd had to nod along. *Although*, he thought, *if Jay had access to a bloody gun, why the hell hadn't he brought it along when they could have done with one a year ago?*

'And we're going to have to move pretty quickly,' Boyd added. 'Hence the number of us crammed in here this morning. I'm not going to tie-up man-hours with a long brief now – we need to get moving.' Boyd picked out Minter. 'DS Minter's my second and action log gatekeeper.'

'Surely a DI –' called out Shannon.

'Minter's my second,' Boyd replied firmly, cutting him off with a glare. 'Now then, tasks... Warren, ANPR hits for Turner's van. White Ford Transit, Foxtrot-Papa-nineteen-Juliet-Hotel-Tango.'

'On it, guv.'

'We need a detailed bio on Jason Turner and we need to put out an All Forces Warning on him,' said Boyd. 'Check on LEDS for previous; check on socials for any family or friends he might have gone to. Apparently he has a half-brother called Marcus. DI Shannon, pick a pair from this litter to help you.'

Shannon nodded. 'Right.'

'Turner works out at the White Rock Gym and he has a few buddies up there...' Boyd checked his notepad. 'We're looking for some bulky lads who have nicknames: Jimbo, Growler and Rocky.' He paused to let the chuckles die down. 'Basically ask around for anybody who Turner worked out with regularly.' He picked out O'Neal. 'O'Neal, let's have you... and let's see... DC Fox, isn't it?'

'Yessir,' Fox replied.

'He also has a side business upcycling old furniture. There's a lock-up garage he uses at the end of Crescent Garden Road as his workshop. I want some bodies over there; he may have client phone numbers and contacts that could prove useful. Let's interview them. Finally, Sully? Where are you?'

A hand went up near the back. 'Over here!'

'Where are you with his phone?'

'Already cracked that particular nut open, Boyd.' He looked very pleased with himself. 'Passcode was Okeke's date of birth.'

*For crying out loud, Jay... really?*

Sully went on. 'I've got his contact list and access to his various social media apps, his photos, his Facebook friends. There's quite a dump of information to go through.'

'All right,' said Boyd. 'The rest of the team is on that, then. Let's see if we can get a few useful names and numbers. Okay.' Boyd clapped his hands together. 'Chop, chop, everyone.'

His eyes flickered across to Hatcher. She gave him a discrete nod – content, it seemed, that they were on the same page – then she quietly left the room.

# 29

Jay had been expecting something a little more swanky and corporate, given all the bragging Karl had done the last time they'd had a pint together. What with all his big talk about developing software and making big money through data-mining, Jay had been picturing a building composed of mirrored glass and chrome nestled in beautifully landscaped gardens.

Instead he'd walked into what looked like a condemned building full of teenage squatters. The narrow stairwell was all bare boards and flaky handrail, the walls a mottled patchwork of lingering faded wallpaper and bare plaster. On each floor, Jay got a glimpse into tall-ceilinged rooms with picture rails and fireplaces – rooms that once had been grand but were now cluttered with Ikea desks and cubicle partitions, twisting nests of network cables and computer monitors decorated with Post-it notes and action figures. They passed one room where camouflage netting had been attached to a hook in the ceiling and hung like the canvas of a circus tent.

Despite the chaotic interior, every floor was as quiet as a monastery, the only sound the sporadic clattering of computer keys and the *tsk-tsk-tsk* of music leaking from headphones.

At the top of the last flight of stairs, Jay's guide cut him loose. 'Karl's in there,' he said, pointing to an open door. Jay thanked him, rapped his knuckles on the door and peered in.

Karl sat with his back to the door and he was staring at several screens of multicoloured, indented gobbledygook computer code. He was wearing a big set of headphones – the kind musos call 'cans' – that made his gently bobbing head look comically tiny. Jay stepped into the room and lightly tapped him on the shoulder. Karl raised a finger to indicate he'd be a moment longer, then finally peeled his eyes from the screens and looked round.

'Fuck me!' he gasped, tearing his headphones off. 'What the hell are you doing here, Jay?!'

'Hey there, little bro,' Jay replied. 'I need some help.'

KARL'S EYES were already big, magnified by the thick lenses of his glasses, but now they bulged like some badly drawn manga character. 'Russian mafia??'

'Christ, mate!' hissed Jay. 'Keep it down, will you!'

Karl had taken him to a greasy-spoon American-style diner that looked out on to Marine Parade. Midday, mid-week, mid-winter, as it was, the place was virtually empty, and jazz music filled the void that would normally have been a hubbub of noisy conversations shouted over plates of fish and chips.

Karl's cheeks dimpled with a nervous smile. 'This is a wind-up, right?'

Jay shook his head. 'I didn't even hit him, Karl. I mean... I just tackled him really, but the little shit claims I nearly beat him to death at gunpoint.'

'Gun?' Karl whispered. 'You've got a gun?!'

'Have I arse,' Jay scowled. 'It's all bullshit. I'm being set up, aren't I?'

'By the Russian mafia?!'

'Crissake!' Jay hissed. 'Can you stop saying that out loud!' He looked around, half expecting a scrum of men in black suits and sunglasses to converge on him.

Karl swore under his breath. 'Crap, Jay... you're really in deep shit, man.'

'Yeah, well, thanks for nothing. I've managed to work that bit out.' He sipped his mug of tea. 'Sam said I should come and find you.'

Karl looked surprised. 'Are you guys still an item?'

'Yes,' Jay replied defensively. 'Why wouldn't we be?'

Karl shrugged. 'No reason, just...I mean, she's... you know, degree-level smart. And you're...'

Jay's brows rose. 'Go on...' he challenged.

'Not,' Karl finished lamely.

There was a pause and they both laughed.

'Okay,' Karl said. 'So what was Sam's thinking? You bunk down with me for a while?'

Jay nodded. 'Just for a bit. Until this mess settles down.'

'Bro, I'm no expert on OCGs but –'

'OCGs?' Jay asked, confused.

'Organised criminal groups – don't you watch *Line of Duty*, bro? There's a universal rule they all live by, which is that you're never allowed to lose face. If you roughed up the boss's son, there's only one way this can go... He'll make a messy example of you.'

'That's pretty much what Sam said.' Jay absently fiddled with the salt and pepper pots on the table.

'Well, you can't go back,' Karl said. 'This kind of thing doesn't just settle down. As soon as you're spotted back in Hastings... you'll be mincemeat.'

'She also said that.'

Karl shook his head. 'Why the hell did you assault a mafia boss's son in the first place?'

During the drive over this morning, Jay had pondered how much to share with his brother. He figured the Russians probably wouldn't be that bothered how much Karl knew if they found out that he was hiding him. He decided to tell him the lot – the full monty, including his first encounter with the Salikovs last January.

## 30

Roland Hammond took a deep breath to steady his nerves.

*I've got this. I've got this.* He repeated those words in his head like a shaman's chant as one of his father's lackeys – a snaggle-toothed, wiry old bastard – accompanied him in the lift to the top floor of the hotel. Rovshan had block-booked the penthouse suite and all the other rooms on that floor for a few weeks in a bid to get away from the noise and dust at his Eaton Square home.

The lift doors pinged and opened. The lackey – Gregor, or it might have been Gregori – led him along the carpeted hallway to the double doors at the end.

'You wait here,' he said. He cracked one door open, stepped inside and closed it gently behind him.

Since his father had moved from Georgia to London at the beginning of the year, it had been surprisingly difficult to get any face-to-face time with him. Roland's calls were diverted to the old man's *consiglieri*, Karovic, who assured him that his father would talk with him when he had more time.

*'Your father has many matters to attend to at the moment.'*

Roland could hear voices beyond the door, softly spoken ones. He didn't bother trying to lean in to hear what was being said as it would be in Georgian. During his prep-school years, Mother had paid for him to have private lessons, but Roland had only managed to pick up a few phrases. Languages just weren't his thing, and anyway she'd repeatedly told him over the years that, one day, his father intended to become a British citizen.

*So why learn, right?*

A door opened and Gregor stepped out. 'He will see you,' he said gruffly.

Roland straightened his tie, patted down his wavy hair and entered the room, the double doors clicking shut behind him.

The hotel suite was large and luxurious and decorated like a museum diorama celebrating Louis XVI-level extravagance. His father was stretched out on a chaise longue in a deep-blue silk house coat beside a crackling fire.

'Roland,' he called with a deep rasping voice. 'You come sit down with me.'

Roland's footsteps echoed on the marble floor, then suddenly hushed as he stepped onto a thick rug. The last time he'd actually spoken to his father had been three weeks ago when the old man had given him the task of scouting Hastings. He half suspected the old man had just wanted him out of the townhouse for a while. There was an awkwardness between them now that Rovshan had finally made the move to London. Father and son they may be, but they were essentially strangers.

The previous time before that, when Roland had spoken to him before the move, had been during the spring the year before in Tbilisi, Georgia. It had been at the wedding of Rovshan's other son, Revaz – his favourite son, Roland suspected. He had never been able to think of that foreign side as his family. The wedding had been a lavish and traditional celebration that had lasted for several days. If he was honest, it had been several intimidating days. His mother hadn't been invited, to avoid any awkwardness between Rovshan's ex-wife and her. But, as the blood of his father, Roland had no choice but to attend. His lack of Georgian had been embarrassing, more so because most of the Salikov family had at least a workable knowledge of the English language under their belts. He'd felt like an outsider. The village idiot. He'd been fairly certain that he'd been an object of ridicule to everyone there.

'Father,' said Roland, bending down and offering the old man a kiss on one cheek.

'Sit, boy, sit,' Rovshan said, gesturing at the armchair beside him.

His father looked like a pale shadow of the man he'd been last summer. He'd lost some weight; his hair was a little longer than Roland knew he liked. And, he noticed, beneath his housecoat Rovshan was wearing pyjamas.

The death of his daughter, Zophia, over a year ago, and the more recent death of Revaz, soon after his wedding, had taken its toll on the old man.

'How are you?' asked Roland.

Rovshan shrugged. 'Very busy. Also very tired.'

'I've seen the town house. It's going to be impressive when it's all complete.'

Rovshan nodded. 'This is the point. To make the impression. The Salikovs have come to UK to stay.'

'Right.' Roland smiled. 'How's the transition of... things going?'

His father ignored the question and adjusted the cushions behind his back, wheezing as he did so. 'Now... Roland... you and I must talk.'

'Yes, sir.'

Blue-grey eyes settled on his English son; he absently

pinched his lips in thought for a moment. 'Tell me, Roland, why did you kill this man in... Hastings?'

*I've got this. I've got this.*

'Father, now... you recall you gave me this job of looking for investment opportunities down there? And I found some very promising ones. Along the seafront. Cash-only businesses that we can use to filter your money. A lot of them are struggling and –'

'Enough,' interrupted Rovshan. 'Why did you kill this man?'

*I've got this.* Roland took a deep breath.

'I'm trying to tell you, Father. We had a problem. A local civil servant...we call them planning officers over here. Basically, he needs to approve the purchase of any businesses by vetting the source of the money. You know how it is these days.'

'So?' Rovshan shrugged. 'You bribe. You *convince.*'

'Which I tried and...' Roland puffed out air. 'It didn't go so well.'

'So you *killed him*?!'

'No... no! I didn't. But I... yes... I was looking into a way to... *remove him*. You know, cautiously, carefully.'

*Christ. Pull yourself together.* Every time he'd met his Georgian father had been a nerve-wracking experience; it was like being sent to the headmaster's study or, he almost chuckled, Darth Vader's private Sith temple. He took another deep breath. 'I was discussing this... situation... on the phone. And... a man happened to overhear me.'

'This man you killed?'

Roland pressed his lips together, then nodded.

The old man tutted and shook his head. 'You are careless. Very careless, boy.'

'I know. I know. I... knew it was stupid. But look – I had to do something quickly. He heard the p-planning officer's name. And if, you know, if something then happened to that chap then... You see? We would have had a bigger problem. I took a decision... I know it was a rash one but –'

'This is not Georgia,' cut in Rovshan. 'This is UK. We have to be much more careful!'

'I know. I know. I... know...' Roland could hear his voice wobble, making him sound weak – something he knew that his father would find off-putting. And disappointing. He steadied himself. 'I did what I thought was right. And I did it quickly,' he said firmly.

The old man said nothing for a while, then finally he nodded. 'This matter is over, then?'

God, if only he could say yes. If only that was the end of this.

'There is still a problem, sir.'

His father's eyes narrowed.

'He told what he'd heard to his friend. And this friend knows that I killed him. This man came to my place and attempted to blackmail me.' Roland really needed to get this next bit right. 'He said he knew I killed the man... said he knew why, and that he wanted some money. So – and I... I think this next bit was clever – this was a clever call...'

Rovshan Salikov waited patiently.

'So I set him up. I made it look like he attempted to kill me.'

Rovshan nodded slowly. 'This part I know about. Miko inform me you went to the police and claim the man attack you... with a gun?'

'Yes, sir.'

Roland studied his father's face, looking for a sign as to what he was thinking. The old man was either going to erupt with rage and berate him for his reckless stupidity or...

A mischievous smile slowly began to stretch across Rovshan's dry lips. 'This *was* clever,' he uttered.

Roland could feel the tension begin to slide away. The old bastard looked as though he approved. 'I mean, I banged myself a few times,' added Roland, pointing to the fading graze mark on his forehead. 'I had to make it look convincing. But, yes, then... I took it to the police and said he'd threatened me with a gun, that he wanted his revenge... That he was a dangerous man. Out of control.'

Rovshan reached out for a delicate porcelain cup of herbal tea. He gently sipped it, then set it back down on its saucer. 'Clever boy. Good decision.'

Roland grinned. 'I think so. I think it's worked out well. He's a fugitive now. He's on the run.'

'This is fine. The police in this town are *ours*,' said Rovshan. 'We will find him and deal with him.'

'But... one thing, sir?'

'What is it?' His irritated voice lacked the threatening, room-filling bark it'd had barely a year ago. However, though it now rustled like paper being screwed up, his voice was enough to command silence. Even the gentle crackling coming from the fireplace seemed to have quietened.

'It's best that he's not arrested,' continued Roland. 'We need him *dead*. He knows too much.'

Rovshan closed his eyes and spoke slowly. 'Listen to me, my boy... this is not Georgia. You cannot do here as we do at home. You must be –' he rubbed his thumb and index finger together as he hunted for the word– 'discreet.'

The old man opened his eyes again. 'Roland, you were careless. Foolish.' He sighed. 'I do not condemn my children for making mistake, but I do expect them to fix it. And to learn from it.'

'It's just this man, Turner,' Roland replied, 'then it'll all be fixed. I'll deal with the planning officer your way, Father, and we will have no more problems down in Hastings.'

Rovshan gave that a moment's consideration and nodded at last. 'No problems in Hastings. Good. I want this town to clean all the family silver. You understand this?'

Roland nodded.

The old man reached for his tea again. 'You can take Gregor. And he will take whoever else he needs. But –' he wagged a cautionary finger – 'leave me no problems, yes?'

Roland nodded eagerly. This could not have gone any better. 'Of course.'

# 31

'Okeke's been suspended?!'

Sutherland shook his head. 'Not suspended, Boyd. I put it down as sick leave.' He sighed. 'In other words, she's getting paid to do bugger all.'

Boyd looked across at her desk, almost expecting to see a sign hooked onto the back of her chair informing him that her workstation was 'closed for business'.

'But why? She can still work on the main floor,' he protested.

'Hatcher's orders,' Sutherland replied. 'There's a personal connection, Boyd. There's no way she can be wandering around CID while there's a manhunt going on for her boyfriend. You know that.'

To be honest, he'd known this might happen, although the fact that she'd been removed, rather than redeployed to a smaller station, smacked of Hatcher's growing panic. Her Madge clearly wanted Okeke well out of the way. Away from interacting with colleagues and most definitely away from interacting with LEDS.

Boyd opened the door to the Incident Room and immediately noticed the Chief Super sitting at the back of the crowded room, cradling a mug of coffee. Her eyes locked on to him.

'Ma'am,' he said, nodding at her, and made his way to the digital whiteboard at the front. Minter had a laptop plugged in and the action log open, ready for updates.

'Morning, everyone,' Boyd barked over the chatter. 'Let's crack on.' The room quickly quietened down. Hatcher remained perched at the back.

'Let's start by running through yesterday's action points. O'Neal, Fox? Anything on Turner's gym mates?'

'Yes, guv,' DC Fox answered. 'We got four names to look into. Everyone down in the weights section seems to know everyone else.' He looked at Minter and grinned. 'They all know you, sergeant. You're a bit of a superstar there apparently.'

There was a chuckling across the floor, while Minter tried to ignore them. The whole station knew about the modelling scout and the dubious-looking calling card.

'All right, that's enough, folks,' Boyd cut in. 'O'Neal?'

'We have several names – but there's a Greg Howler at the top of the list. Me and Foxy are going to door-knock him right after this.'

'Good. Okay. DI Shannon, how's it going with the background on Turner?'

'We've gone through all the socials on his phone, boss. He has a lot of casual mates, mostly gym mates, pub mates. Louie Collins and Greg Howler seem to be the ones he talked to most on WhatsApp and Messenger. There are no secret girlfriends, or –'

'Or Okeke would skin him alive,' Warren cut in.

There was another ripple of amusement.

'Yeah,' said Shannon. 'I mean... most of his messages, the lion's portion of it, are with DC Okeke. And that's mostly, you know, personal stuff which... errr...'

'Which is understandable,' Boyd interrupted. The room really didn't need to rake through Okeke and Jay's private exchanges. 'Right, so Greg Howler seems to be the next stop. What about search histories? Anything useful there? Any locations to focus on?'

'Nothing that stands out,' Shannon replied.

'Anything about guns? Getting hold of one? Owning one? Any sign of Tor or dark-web browsing?'

Shannon shook his head. 'But then he's going out with Okeke...' He shrugged, then grinned. 'I bet he has to hand his phone over to her to check every day.'

More laughter.

Boyd waited for the room to quieten down again. 'What about Turner's family?' he asked.

'We checked on LEDS. His mother died when he was ten. She had two kids with different partners; there's a younger sibling called Karl Craymore. The boys were fostered together for the first few years and then separated.'

'Why were they separated?'

'Jason Turner was a bit of a problem child; he ended up being bounced around from one place to another, whereas Karl found a foster home that worked for him and stayed put.'

'Right. So there's no other family?' Boyd asked.

'None.'

'Are they in touch?' interjected Hatcher. 'The brothers?' All heads swivelled to look back at her. 'That's something that should be checked immediately,' she added. 'People do reach out in later years.'

Boyd nodded. 'Yes, of course, ma'am. Shannon, you'd better look into that.'

'Yes, sir.'

'Okay, then... so what about ANPR hits on his van? Who's on that?'

'Me,' replied Warren. 'We've had a couple in and around Hastings yesterday and this morning at the Tesco in Ore.'

'Well, that doesn't sound like a man on the run,' said DI Abbott.

'He's obviously done a vehicle swap with someone, you muppet,' said DI Shannon.

Boyd nodded. 'It sounds like it. O'Neal, check that with this Greg Howler and the other gym mates. Check for the regs of their vehicles and check for Jay's van. Check garages too. Whether they want you to or not. Okay?'

'On it,' replied O'Neal.

Boyd looked down at his notepad. 'And who went to his workshop?'

A hand went up.

'DC Carmichael, sir. We pulled it apart. There's nothing useful. No address books, no invoices or accounts. His furniture business looks pretty ad hoc and informal. Probably cash-in-hand jobs.'

'Right,' Boyd said.

'I think we need to bring Okeke in, Boyd,' said Hatcher. 'I know she's one of us, but – let's be blunt here – Turner's her partner. It would be hard to believe that he hasn't tried contacting her from a payphone or another mobile.'

He nodded. 'Yes of course, ma'am.'

The meeting ended five minutes later and Boyd watched his team file out of the Incident Room to the main floor. Through the glass wall, he thought he caught a glimpse of Chief Superintendent Hatcher walking just behind O'Neal. He wouldn't have given it a second thought if it wasn't for the fact that O'Neal looked, even walking away from Boyd, incredibly uncomfortable.

*Is she asking him to keep an eye on me?*

That didn't sit well at all. If Hatcher was doing that, then she was having doubts about him. And if that was fed back to the Salikovs, he wondered how long it would be before one of them paid him a personal visit and reminded him that they liked their results fast.

# 32

Roland felt like Al Pacino. Like Tony Montana.

The SUV had tinted windows and a bulletproof windscreen. It was a proper mobster's motor. And Roland had his very own pet mobsters to command like minions. Driving the SUV was a thickset ape in his forties with a forest of hair on each forearm, a thick black beard and a perfectly round bald spot like a monk's tonsure on the top of his head. The man didn't speak a word of English.

In the front passenger seat was another, much younger, man with long wavy black hair pulled back into a man bun, and a tattoo of a snake that went up the side of his neck. He looked like an imported Premier League footballer wearing joggers, trainers and a Lacoste sweatshirt. And he didn't speak a word of English either.

Beside Roland sat Gregor: a scrawny little rat-like man with a buzzcut of silver hair, pockmarked skin and cold grey eyes. He looked old enough to have flown in Sputnik alongside Laika. He *did* speak English, but it was so heavily accented that Roland had to concentrate hard to get the gist of what he was saying. Sometimes he had to wait until the end of the man's short guttural outbursts to build enough context to decipher the intended meaning.

Gregor, then, was Roland's interface with the other two. Roland chuckled to himself 'Tony Soprano' was driving, and his sidekick was 'Cristiano Ronaldo', who was currently checking himself out in the window's reflection.

'So what is plan?' growled Gregor beside him.

'When we get our hands on the bastard, we will kill the bastard,' replied Roland. He was feeling good this morning, in control, and he liked how that had sounded coming out of his mouth: ruthless, cold, precise. No mealy-mouthed synonyms, just a plain-as-day command for his troops.

'The police will track him down for us.'

'You *trust* this police?'

Roland had got the woman's number from Karovic. The old fart had been extremely reluctant to hand it over, arguing that it was best practice for there to be an *indirect* link between the Salikovs and the Chief Superintendent. Roland had had to remind Karovic that Rovshan had given him carte blanche to fix this problem. More to the point, there was going to be a time, one day soon, when Rovshan wasn't going to be the Big Boss any more. It would be Roland himself.

Anyway, he now had a direct line to the top cop – one Margaret Hatcher – and as soon as the police had a location for Turner, she'd promised to make contact.

'We sit tight,' he told Gregor, 'until we get a call. You'd better tell those two what the plan is.'

Gregor spoke to the other two men in Georgian. Both of them laughed. He had a nagging suspicion that the laughter might be something to do with him.

'What did you just say?' he asked Gregor.

'I tell them plan,' he replied.

'And what was so bloody funny?'

Gregor looked at him and smiled. 'They like plan very much.'

~

KARL HAD GONE into work this morning and left Jay to his own devices with strict instructions not to mess around with his sound system and, even more importantly, not to go wandering around in the mews outside his place. He was meant to be in hiding, not on holiday.

His parting words had been ominous. 'I read up on this Rovshan Salikov last night. Bro, you have no idea how big a shit-splat you've stepped in, do you? We'll talk later.'

Until that point Jay had thought himself well aware. He'd threatened a Russian mobster's son and would have to lay low for a bit. That was it. He hadn't even hit him, he reasoned; he'd just given the little twat a piece of his mind.

It was a shitty note on which to leave him as he went to work. *'You're totally fucked, bro, but I'll explain in what way later.'*

Absently his thumb stroked the buttons of his cheap phone. He desperately wanted to talk to Sam, to check that she was all right and to ask her if she knew any more about these scary Russians he'd managed to piss off.

But he resisted the urge. The more information he shared with her, the greater danger he might be putting her in. At the very least, there would be damage to her career prospects if she was forced to lie about what knowledge she did and didn't have.

Karl had promised to be back at lunchtime to talk through Jay's options. Which were pretty stark and limited, according to him.

Jay pulled a beer from Karl's fridge and put on the TV, wondering, in a sudden fit of paranoia, if he'd made the local news yet, but there was nothing. He tried to calm himself down as he flicked through several other stations until *SpongeBob*

*SquarePants* appeared on the screen. It was a cartoon he happily watched with a beer or two after his shift at the nightclub. Clearly TV schedulers were aware that out there in Viewer Land there was an appetite for the show long after all the kids had gone to bed. An audience of mildly pissed people who identified with the persistent life-draining cynicism of Squidward and wished they had the inexhaustible life-affirming optimism of SpongeBob.

He watched a few episodes before getting up to explore Karl's open-plan apartment. He had the whole top floor of an old, perhaps Victorian-era, brewery. It had been restored and made fashionably modern while leaving exposed the old wooden beams of the roof and the austere weathered brick walls.

Karl had stamped his personality on the place with a few additions of his own: a large wooden mannequin with articulated limbs – for what reason, Jay could not fathom. He presumed it was Karl's nerdish idea of art. Jay amused himself for a while, posing the arms and raising the legs, before leaving it looking like it was getting ready to do a dump. He chuckled to himself and moved on. There was an archery target on a stand at one end of the floor and a crossbow hung on the wall beside it. He was sorely tempted to give that a go. And of course the inevitable recycled vintage jukebox, rescued from some old American diner.

He wandered down the metal stairway to the old brewery's ground floor and tried the light switch. Nothing happened. There was no feed down here. Faint daylight pierced a few shuttered windows and, from what he could see in the gloom, it was nothing more than a dust-covered, web-filled labyrinth of barrels, vats, pipes and discarded furniture.

Jay was back upstairs on the leather couch watching *SpongeBob* again when he heard the large front door open downstairs. He switched the TV off, rather than be caught watching a kids show, just as Karl emerged from the top of the stairs.

'I've cleared my in-tray for a few days,' Karl said. 'Maybe even a week.' He clocked the half-empty bottle of beer in Jay's fist. 'Good idea.'

He grabbed one from the fridge, popped it open, sat down on the beanbag sofa in front of his giant TV and took a long glug.

'Karl,' Jay asked. 'Are you going to tell me what kind of shit I'm in, then?'

# 33

'Is this some sort of disciplinary thing?' asked Okeke.

Boyd shook his head before Hatcher could say otherwise. 'You've done nothing wrong, Sam. We just need your help.'

Okeke eyed Her Madge suspiciously. 'Ma'am?'

'Agreed,' she replied. 'We need to find Mr Turner as soon as possible, before he does any harm to anyone else.'

Okeke looked around the interview room. It was the smallest one. There was no observation window – just a camera in the corner, which, she noted, showed no red light.

It was off.

'Jay isn't going to do any harm to anyone else,' she said, 'because he didn't do any harm to anyone in the first place.'

'Well, this is exactly why he needs to come in,' Hatcher replied, 'so that he can give his side of the story.'

'There's no side he needs to give!' Okeke said, her voice rising. 'He was set up by Hammond. We all know that.'

'Okeke,' said Hatcher softly, 'we want what's best for Jay. If you know where he is, the best way that you can help him is to let us know.'

'I *don't* know,' Okeke said. 'He made a run for it when armed police crashed into our place. And, honestly, I can't say I blame him.'

'And why would he run? If he had nothing to run for? If he was entirely innocent?' Hatcher pressed.

Okeke shrugged. 'I don't know. Maybe he thought he was in danger of being accidentally shot while resisting arrest? How's that for starters?'

She studied the Chief Super and could see that the knuckles of Her Madge's interlaced fingers bulged white. The woman looked as brittle as a bundle of dried twigs.

*She's going to lose it.*

Okeke glanced at Boyd. He was doing his best to look calm and professional. Impartial.

*Are you really on my side, guv?* she wondered. There was no way to be certain at this point, was there? If he'd had another delivery in a cardboard box, would he have told her? He was playing the stony-faced, task-focused cop for Hatcher, and the I've-secretly-got-Jay's-back role for her. Could she trust him?

'All right,' said Hatcher. 'I don't think any of us have the time or the energy for this nonsense. Get your phones out, Okeke.'

'You're not looking through my phones without a warrant,' she replied.

'If you're being straight with us, Okeke... then why don't you just show us right now? Unlock them and let us have a look,' Hatcher demanded.

Boyd nodded. 'She's right.' He looked directly at her. 'Sam, I *know* you've got nothing you want to hide.'

'We can get a warrant,' said Hatcher. 'Very easily and very quickly. Trust me.'

Okeke sat back in her seat and glanced up at the dead camera in the corner of the room. 'I see that's been switched off. So I think we should cut all the bullshit... don't you, ma'am?'

'Oh? And what bullshit is that?' Hatcher asked.

Okeke laughed dryly. 'That these Russians have got their fingers wrapped tightly round your neck.'

Hatcher blanched.

Okeke glanced at Boyd. 'And yours too, guv.'

Her Madge scoffed. 'Really? And that's what you think is it?'

'I know Boyd got a warning package, ma'am. From the Salikovs. And I'm guessing you got one too.'

Hatcher looked shaken. 'What? That's utterly ridiculous!' She turned to Boyd and skewered him with a look of outrage.

'Okeke knows,' he said with a sigh. 'I told her. She knows everything I know.'

'This is...' Hatcher glared at him, then back at Okeke. 'This is...'

'Maybe she's right, ma'am,' Boyd said. 'Maybe we need to start talking plainly.' He pulled out his work Samsung and his personal iPhone. 'On the table and turned off. All of us,' he said. 'Because, like it or not, we're all three in this bloody mess now.'

KARL SET his beer down on the table and dropped a couple of packets of smoky-bacon-flavoured crisps between them. 'I spent most of this morning assigning tasks to my development teams so I can take a few days off,' he said. 'But I've also been consolidating last night's research.'

'Sounds ominous,' muttered Jay.

'Well, it is actually, bro.' Karl pursed his lips.

Jay grinned nervously. 'C'mon, bro – don't leave me hanging.'

Karl sighed. 'Sorry, man... Look, Rovshan Salikov was best friends with the KGB, back in the day.'

'What day?' Jay asked.

'Cold War times. You know, before we were born... back in the eighties.'

'I was born by then. *You weren't*, little bro.' Jay leant forward and opened one of the crisp packets.

'Right, well, small detail. Anyway, this guy was besties with the KGB, based in Georgia and he was a middleman for their dirty-ops slush fund. So then along comes the nineties, Gorbachev with his glasnost, Yeltsin... the fall of the Berlin Wall. The fall of the Soviet Union. All that good stuff. So, amid all the chaos, this guy Salikov was given the job of hiding some of that KGB money and also a shit ton of money from the Communist Party's coffers.'

'Hiding it where?' Jay tossed some crisps into his mouth.

Karl shrugged. 'Who knows? Switzerland? Panama? Shell companies? Under his floorboards? The point is, he knows where it's all stashed and that's kind of how he became rich. The rest of his money has come from whatever dirty businesses he's sunk his fingers into over the last few decades.'

'So he's a rich bastard,' said Jay. 'Which I knew already.'

'No, see, it's more complicated than that,' Karl explained. 'Yes, he's the boss of a criminal organisation, but he was also the trusted bagman for a lot of money that wasn't his.'

'It was the KGB's – you told me that already. See, I'm listening,' Jay said, giving his brother a pensive nod and a smile.

Karl didn't return the smile. He looked deeply concerned. 'Well, they're called the FSB now... and it would seem that they want all their money back. Like, yesterday.'

Jay licked the bacon flavouring off his fingers. 'So... what does that mean? Has he fallen out with them? Are they enemies now?'

'Well, if he's not prepared to give it back, then probably. The point is, bro... the shit pile you put one of your big clodhopping boots in may be bigger than you realised. Salikov's getting on. His eldest son died recently... and I'm just saying FSB connections... Salikov's primary heir is dead, so then you go and threaten the spare?' Karl looked at Jay, who'd frozen with a finger still in his mouth. 'The FSB are the same gnarly bastards who did the whole Novichok thing in Salisbury.' He nudged Jay. 'So, uh... maybe you don't want to be licking your fingers, eh?'

Jay slowly lowered his hand and looked at it.

'I'm kidding!' Karl laughed.

'Ah, right,' replied Jay, unamused. 'Hilarious.'

~

'ALL RIGHT,' said Boyd. 'The phones are off. Again. What's said in here stays in here, all right, ma'am?'

Hatcher nodded.

'So? Who's talking first?' he asked.

'I will,' said Hatcher. 'Salikov's lawyer has been in contact with me. They're expecting me to put every resource I have into locating Mr Turner. I say "expecting"... I mean *demanding*.' She turned to Okeke. 'They're not going to accept *I'm doing my best* from me, do you understand?'

'And if the police find him?' Okeke asked.

Hatcher shook her head. 'We bring him in, charge him and put him on remand.'

'Effectively handing him to the Salikovs, then,' Okeke said. 'If he's shoved into a prison on remand, they'll find a way to get to him.'

'Boyd?' said Hatcher, giving him a pointed look.

'We'll make sure he's kept safe, inside,' said Boyd. 'Just tell us where he is, Sam.'

She shook her head. 'I don't know.'

'I thought we were all speaking plainly and honestly,' said Hatcher.

'Well, in that case I wouldn't tell you if I did know,' Okeke replied curtly. 'Sorry, but if we're being honest here... I wouldn't tell either of you anything at this point – and I don't know how you could possibly expect me to.'

'Okay,' said Boyd. 'I can understand that.'

'I could have you arrested,' said Hatcher. 'For aiding a criminal fugitive.'

Okeke raised her brows and looked at the phones on the table. 'And I would still tell you I know nothing. I'm not handing over my *innocent* boyfriend to them. Is that clear?'

'You do understand, Okeke...' Hatcher said. 'If they don't get a result from pressuring me, or Boyd, they'll come for you.'

Okeke sighed. 'I actually don't know where he is, ma'am. He took off. He has no phone. In fact, Sully's lot have it now, right?'

Boyd nodded. 'And they've hacked it.'

'Right. So at this point in time you probably know more about his activities over the last few days than I do.'

'I DON'T GET why Hammond had to kill Louie, though. I mean, neither of us really heard enough to get him into trouble,' Jay said.

'Well, it's not down to what you know, is it?' Karl said. 'It's what Hammond *thinks* you know that's the problem.'

Jay shrugged. 'All I heard was some shit about "getting the job done" and "staying calm" and "if you stop, he'll get better". Something about "a cup of blue tea".'

'To Hammond that would sound enough to make you a problem, bro,' said Karl. 'People have been taken out for knowing much less. Thing is, Jay, you told me that while Hammond was tied up that you told him you "knew everything", right?'

Jay nodded. 'I was just trying to put the shit up him.'

'Well, there you go – that is what's dumped you in the shit, bro. You drew a fucking cross-hair on your forehead, by saying that.'

'Jesus, Karl...' Jay said. 'You're meant to be making me feel better, not scaring the crap out of –'

'I'm just keeping it real.'

Jay looked at the open bag of crisps and suddenly had no more appetite for them. Nor the beer in his hand. 'So basically what you're saying is that I'm screwed?'

'Well, I wouldn't be thinking of going back to Hastings if I were you. Seriously, bro... I'm not even sure if it's a good idea to stay in the country.'

Jay suspected that if the police were after him too, then asking Okeke to send over his passport so that he could book an EasyJet flight to Costa del Wherever was a non-starter.

'I could nick a boat perhaps? Sail across the Channel and ditch it somewhere off Calais?' Jay improvised.

Karl laughed. 'Then what?'

Jay scowled. 'I'd work something out.'

'UNDERSTAND THIS,' said Hatcher. 'If I don't give them what they want, they won't hesitate to make their displeasure known.'

'And what they want is Jay,' Okeke said.

'Perhaps there's a deal to be struck?' suggested Boyd.

Hatcher shook her head. 'I call them back and say I have a counterproposal...?' She shook her head again. 'No. I'm sorry, but I'm not going there.'

'You have a strong bargaining position,' said Okeke. 'You're the Chief Super! They need you onside if they have any further plans in Hastings.'

'For God's sake!' Hatcher snapped. 'Do you honestly think

I'm in their camp for backhanders?! Some filthy bloody money? Do you?!' Her hands were balled into tight, bulging, white fists.

*Jesus*, thought Boyd, speaking plainly appeared to be getting them nowhere. 'Okay,' he said, 'maybe trying for a deal is pushing our luck.'

They lapsed into silence. There was little more to be said.

'I just can't help you, Okeke,' said Hatcher eventually. 'I'm really sorry.' She glanced at Boyd, clearly expecting him to say the same.

*And I have to.*

'Sam,' he began, 'I've got no choice here. I'm going to have to find him with or without your help. I've got to bring him in.'

'He saved your life when we met Nix,' Okeke said coolly. 'You owe him.'

'I'm afraid we're done here.' Hatcher raised a hand. 'I don't want to hear any more.'

'I know,' Boyd answered Okeke. 'But, Sam, this is –'

'I said we're done!' barked Hatcher. She reached for her smartphone and stood up. 'I don't want to hear another word about Nix, all right?'

Okeke shot a glance at her. 'Ah, so you do know what happened then?'

Hatcher glared at her. 'Once this is over, there's no way I can have either of you under my command. You do understand that? When this has been settled, you should both think about putting in for a transfer. And do not think about crossing me. You have nothing on me, whereas I have a very long list where the two of you are concerned.'

She went to the door and rested her hand on the handle. 'I want as little to do with this bloody nightmare as possible. I'm not *bent*, Okeke. I've never taken any kind of backhander in my entire career... but I'm also not stupid. This isn't a hill I'm prepared to die on.'

BOYD WATCHED Okeke from the CID's main-floor window as she headed across the tarmac towards her Datsun, a plume of cigarette smoke lingering in her wake.

She looked defeated as she pulled the key fob out of her shoulder bag and blipped her car. He hoped she'd look up and see him watching her. And then what? A smile? A wave? A thumbs-up?

Nothing he could gesture through the plate glass was going to make up for the fact that – in front of Her Madge – he'd told her there was nothing he could do for Jay. There hadn't been a private moment to whisper anything else to her; Hatcher had gestured for her to leave the station... and she had, without glancing his way even once.

She was obviously leaving the station with the very clear impression that this time round they were on different sides. That his job was to locate Jay and, in all but name, hand him over to be executed by the Salikovs. And that he was prepared to do it.

It was that or him.

Or Emma.

Boyd watched her car pull out onto Bohemia Road and turn left then downhill towards the seafront. He headed back to his desk feeling like the world's biggest piece of shit.

# 34

DC Warren and DI Shannon were waiting for Boyd beside his desk, both with printouts in their hands, waggling them to get his attention like eager kids in a classroom.

'All right,' he said, sighing as he sat down. 'Who's first?'

'Me,' said Warren. He placed his sheet down on the table, a grainy printout from a CCTV camera that showed a white van at a petrol station.

'We heard back from O'Neal. He's just been interviewing Greg Howler. He did a vehicle swap with Jason Turner yesterday morning,' he said quickly. 'This is Howler's van.'

Boyd had asked Warren to do an ANPR check on *Jay's* big van, but, for once, the lad had shown initiative and skipped straight to Howler's van. On any other case that would have been great.

'And here's a picture of him paying in the station.' Boyd looked at the grainy image of Jay. He was wearing a baseball cap and towered over the counter like a wrongly scaled miniature in a diorama.

'Where is this?' he asked.

'It's the petrol station on the A27, just beyond Lewes,' Warren told him.

'Good job, Warren,' he said mildly. 'And Turner's van?'

'On the way to the station. CSI will go through it for anything that might help.'

'Right.' Boyd gave Warren a nod and waved him off before looking up at DI Shannon. 'And what have you got for me?'

'His half-brother's new name. He changed it by deed poll from Craymore to Craig.'

'Karl Craig?'

The DI nodded, then grinned. 'Sounds like a shitty blues singer, eh?'

Boyd really wasn't in the mood. 'So what do we have on Mr Craig?'

'He's been a bit of a slippery customer, to be honest... Hasn't got any socials that we can find. It's a legal name, obviously, but he's been sure to use it very sparingly. Under the name Craymore, he's had form in the past, boss. He took part in some G8 protests, Extinction Rebellion. Anti-vaxxer stuff. He's even been rumoured in the past to have links with that Anonymous hackers bunch, but –'

'That's all very interesting, Shannon, but may I cut to the chase?' Boyd interrupted.

'Sir?'

'Do you have an address for him?'

'Unit Seventeen, Hamble House, Eastern Terrace Mews, Brighton,' Shannon said.

Boyd nodded. Brighton it was, then.

'Well, there we go, sir. Turner's probably gone over to hide at his brother's place.'

Crap. Jay, the stupid idiot, was going to get himself caught in record time. Boyd gave DI Shannon an appreciative nod. 'Good work.'

*This feels like shit. Utter shit.* He was damned if he was going to hand over the address to Hatcher yet, though.

'Okay, then...' He sighed. 'I suppose we'd better go and pay Mr Craig a visit.'

'Right.' Shannon hesitated. 'Are you coming along, guv?' The DI was clearly used to his regular guv – Flack – remaining station-based.

'Yup.' Boyd nodded. 'I need to get some fresh air.'

Maybe there was some way he could hamper, delay or even sabotage the visit; perhaps give Jay a chance to make another run for it. The Keystone Cops came to mind – a careless blunder or two might just give Jay a head start. He looked around for the perfect candidate and saw him across the floor at his desk tucking into a Greggs pastry. Hastings CID's very own super cop.

'Let's bring DI Abbott along too.'

'Right.' Shannon looked uncertain.

'Have a pool car ready to go in ten minutes, all right?'

Boyd watched Shannon weave his way through the desks, like a ball bearing through a marble run, and tap Abbott on the shoulder.

Then Boyd got up and reached for his jacket, which was draped over the back of his seat.

On the floor at the rear of the chair was a folded piece of paper. It must have fallen out of one of his pockets. He bent down and scooped it up. It was a torn corner from a Post-it note.

He unfolded it and found a nine-digit number. A phone number.

He recognised the rounded handwriting. It was Okeke's.

# 35

'Are you safe here?' Karl shrugged. 'Shit, I dunno. I guess maybe for a couple of days. That is unless you told anyone else you were coming to stay with me.'

'Just Sam,' Jay replied.

'Okay. But no one else knows?'

Jay shook his head.

Karl walked across the open floor to the kitchen in the corner. He opened a cupboard. 'I mean, this place isn't rented under my name anyway. So that'll buy us a little more time. You want something for lunch? I got some pad thai pots.'

Jay shook his head. He wasn't hungry.

'The company owns the old brewery. They let me rent it for a few hundred quid.' Karl poured out a bowl of granola for himself.

'Oh. I thought this was *your* place,' Jay said.

Karl grinned. 'It is. I own the company. And the company owns this. It's a handy way to sidestep the usual taxes, bro.' He grinned. 'I probably pay less tax than you do.'

Jay frowned. 'But you're bloody minted!'

'It's unfair, I know. But the loopholes are there. You'd have to be a dumbass not to exploit them. What's good for Zuckerberg is good for me.'

Jay nodded. 'Right. Clever.'

'My snail mail, not that I have much of that, if any, goes straight to work. I prefer it that way.' He poured in some soya milk, then glanced at Jay. 'The bigger your footprint, the more vulnerable you are. It pays to have small feet, bruv'.'

Karl joined Jay in the lounge area and sat cross-legged on the beanbag, breakfast bowl in hand.

'Who are you vulnerable to?' Jay asked.

'The System,' Karl said. 'The police state, MI5, the squinty little government gremlins who monitor the troublemakers and build their little dossiers. The more data points they've got on you, the more leverage they have. That's why I don't do Facebook or TikTok... or whatever.'

'Ah.' Jay nodded knowingly. 'Well, I mean, I just use it for, you know, the dumb stuff. The games...'

'The pop quizzes? The "Name Your Fave Movie", 'Which Star Wars Character Are You?" stuff, those things, uh?' said Karl.

Jay nodded. 'It can get pretty boring working on the door.'

Karl laughed.

'What's so funny?'

'See? That's the crap we develop at Unit Seventeen. The dumb games, the quizzes, "What's Your Porn Star Name?" crap. We churn it out, upload it and then all the beautiful data comes pouring back in.'

'What kind of data?'

'Well, look, take "What's Your Porn Star Name?" for starters... Your first pet's name and your mother's maiden name – put them together and bingo. What's your name?'

'Rex Cobbley,' Jay replied. He smiled. The name actually kind of worked.

'There you go, two pieces of data I just wangled out of you.

Classic security questions. With that and your address, I'd be able to hack into your online bank account pretty fast.'

'Please don't,' Jay grimaced.

Karl chuckled. 'It's probably not worth my while. Anyway, you play one of those games and your info is coming straight to me, along with every other bit of information you've leaked about yourself. Your favourite films, superheroes, ice cream, your post code, the website you go to next, whether you buy something... and, if you do, what it is. Your political persuasion –'

'I don't have one.'

'No? Oh, you do, even if you don't know it, bro... and the things you like or share... the things you linger indecisively over – all that good stuff comes in a big old river of information to people like me.'

'What do you do with it?' Jay asked, looking slightly horrified.

Karl shrugged. 'Sell it by the truckload to the highest bidder. I'm telling you, Jay, if I pulled your IP number up, there'd be enough info linked to it for me to totally freak you out. It'd be like going on a blind date with some creepy stranger who's been stalking you their whole life.'

'Shit.'

'Best-case scenario?' Karl continued. 'You're constantly hit by banner ads that seem to be spookily on point. Right?'

Jay nodded.

'And the worst case ... bad people *gaslight* the fuck out of you. Think of your Facebook feed as your window looking out to the world outside. If I controlled what you saw in that window, I could tell you it's raining when it's actually sunny. I could hook you up with lots of other people who I've also fooled into believing it's raining... then you could all chat together about how much it seems to fucking rain all the time!'

Karl shook his head. 'That, my dear naive brother, is how we end up with the Trumps of the world.'

Jay gazed out of the window onto the mews down below. The world he was presently occupying was totally different from anything he could even have begun to imagine just yesterday.

'Anyway...' Karl said. 'Bro... back on topic. We've got to think about getting you away.'

Jay turned to look at him. 'Where to?'

'On a plane and out of the country, mate. It's safest for now. Take a little holiday.'

'How am I going to do that?' Jay asked. 'Jesus. Why is this happening to me? I don't want to leave the fucking country, bro. I just want to go home. I don't even have my passport...'

Karl raised a finger. 'Leave that to me.'

# 36

oyd found a desk phone away from all the others and dialled the number.

Okeke answered immediately. 'Guv?'

'Yes. Sam... I –'

'First, tell me you're not on your regular phone.'

'No,' he replied softly, 'because I'm not a complete idiot. Sam, look, I just want to say –'

'I get it,' she cut in. 'Well... I hope I do. That was for Hatcher's benefit, right?'

'Yes,' he replied quietly. 'She's watching me like a hawk.'

'And can I trust *you*?' she asked.

'If you're asking me whether the Salikovs have paid me a personal visit yet, then the answer's no. As far as they're aware, I'm onside, following orders and doing my best.'

He heard her sigh with relief.

'Sam, I'm going to do what I can to hamstring this operation. To give Jay a chance, but if I do anything too obvious, I'll become part of their problem. You do understand what I mean by that?'

She hesitated.

'Sam?'

'Obviously,' she said finally. 'So I'll ask again: have they threatened you yet? You know... directly?'

'No,' he said firmly.

She paused again. 'I want to trust you. Look, Boyd... if they've dropped another severed ear at your house, or even just mentioned Emma's name... this is exactly the conversation you'd be having with me, right? Trying to win my trust, trying to reassure me that you've got Jay's back. Because, let's be honest, it would come down to a choice between my Jay or your Emma, right?'

'I'm telling you they haven't... Not yet anyway.'

He heard her breath rustling down the line.

'Look, this call has to be brief, Sam. We're on the move.'

'What do you mean?' she asked.

'We've got his brother's address in Brighton and I'm going over with some lads to interview him this afternoon.'

He heard her breath catch. Then: 'Luckily, Jay's not there.'

'Well, whether his is or he isn't... we'll be there in just over an hour.' He looked around the office to make sure no one was watching him. 'Sam, I get you can't trust me, for obvious reasons. But what I can do to help you, I will, okay?'

She paused.

'I hear you.' She paused again. 'Thanks, guv.'

DI Shannon drove and Boyd took the front passenger seat. In the back, DI Abbott grumbled and wheezed on one side, while O'Neal kept them entertained with woefully unlikely tales of his Tinder exploits on the other.

Boyd had decided to bring O'Neal along with him so that

he could report back to Her Madge that he was doing his job thoroughly.

'So, O'Neal, how're things over on Flack's team?' asked Boyd.

The young lad leant forward. 'Good, yeah. We did a raid on a cuckooed flat last week. It was pretty bloody mental. We nicked three foot soldiers and a big stash of spice.'

'And they had several modified shooters stashed in the house,' added DI Shannon. 'Nasty little shites had taken over the home of a disabled woman.'

'She was wheelchair-bound,' said O'Neal. 'They'd just parked her in the back room with a telly turned up loud and some water. Felt bloody good throwing those scrotes into the back of the van.'

'So it's a bit more of an active role, eh?' said Boyd.

'Well, you know... not gonna lie.' O'Neal grinned.

'It's a bit like whack-a-mole, though,' said Shannon. 'You shut one place down and pull a few low-level scum off the street, then the very next day another one pops up the next street over.'

O'Neal laughed. 'It's the gift that keeps on giving.'

Boyd looked across at Shannon. 'The drugs business... keeps us all gainfully employed, right, Shannon? Busting down doors? Nicking minnows?'

Shannon nodded but kept his eyes on the road. 'So what's the plan when we get there, guv?'

'You and me, we'll interview Karl Craig. O'Neal, Abbott... while Craig's busy with us, you two take a look around his place. See if there's anything amiss.'

'Amiss?' echoed Abbott, who was halfway down a bag of cheesy Wotsits. 'Like what?'

'Like Jason Turner being there, for starters. Or any sign that someone else has been bunking over. You know... two cups on the side instead of one? Sleeping bag?'

'Ah, okay. Gotcha, boss,' Abbott said, tipping the rest of the packet into his mouth and showering his jacket with orange dust.

*Christ. He really is a deadweight.*

## 37

---

J ay went out onto the metal fire-escape steps at the front of the old brewery, rolled himself a cig and lit up.

He looked down at an old cobblestoned forecourt that he imagined had once been host to horse-drawn carts and then belching old trucks laden with barrels of hops. Sometimes he wondered whether he was an old soul stranded in the wrong century. There were too many gadgets and gizmos nowadays, too many memes and fads to keep up with. He figured he'd been one of the last people in Britain to learn that those green and yellow squares popping up on his Facebook page with monotonous regularity were results from a word-game fad that had come and gone.

He took a pull on his cigarette and let out a rolling ball of smoke.

And now, just because he'd been incensed at the injustice of some posh tosspot literally getting away with murder, he was somehow the marked man of not only a mafia family but perhaps also the Russian secret service.

'What the actual fuck?' he muttered to himself.

Karl was right. He was going to *have* to stay away from Hastings, which had been his home town for the last fifteen years. To be fair, it had been his only home town. Before Hastings, he'd been moved from a foster home in one town to another. Jay knew he'd been a nightmare child; he'd been bad-tempered and big, an unhelpful combination when it came to appealing to prospective dewy-eyed adopters. Karl, on the other hand – three years younger and far more wily – had cottoned on pretty quickly that a few well-deployed manners and a cute smile went a long way.

Now, Jay's evacuation plan was going to have to be simple and low key; he'd get a lift with a trucker through the Chunnel and show-off his brand-new fake passport in Calais. Then he'd wing it from there. He had his burner phone to keep in touch with Okeke, and Karl said he'd set up a pre-paid debit card for Jay that he could use abroad, virtually untraceably. The card and the passport would be enough for him to re-establish himself somewhere else. Greece or Crete had been Karl's suggestion. Money would go further in those places and it was still largely a cash economy.

Plus, it was fucking nice over there.

'*Seriously, bro... you could get work in a bar. Or you could recycle old furniture to your heart's content for ex-pats wanting to do that whole* Mamma Mia-*chic thing.*'

It sounded good, to be honest: sun, sea, cheap beer. And maybe he could entice Sam to come out and join him once he was settled.

His burner phone buzzed in his pocket. *Speak of the devil.*

'Hey, babycakes,' he answered.

'Jay,' she said quickly. 'I just got a call from Boyd. He's on his way over with some of his team to interview Karl.'

'*What?*' Jay shook his head, dumbfounded. 'How the hell did he figure –'

'Detecting. It's his job, love,' she said gently.

'Shit! But... if he's on our side, why's he –'

'Listen, Jay, he *is* on our side. That's why he gave me the heads-up. You've got to get out of there, though. And quickly.'

Jay took a long pull on his roll-up.

'Like, right now, okay?'

'It's okay, Sam. The only *listed* address Karl has is his workplace. They'll head there first. I've got a little time.'

'Well, then don't waste it!' she said.

'Wait! Sam... what about you? Are you okay?'

'What? Yes, I'm fine,' she assured him. 'But, babe, you need to –'

'Sam,' Jay cut in. 'I've been talking with Karl about the Salikovs –'

'You did *WHAT*?!?'

He held the phone away from his ear. 'Relax. It's okay, it's okay,' he said. 'He's not going to shop me to them, is he? But listen – I think I might be in bigger shit than we realised.'

He explained to Sam what Karl had told him about Rovshan's special relationship with the Russian secret service. 'I really have kicked the wrong molehill, haven't I, babes?'

She sighed. 'You can say that again.'

He told her that Karl was getting someone on the dark web to knock up a fake passport and that he was going to lie low abroad for a while.

'Okay, that's good,' she told him. 'It's good that you're thinking ahead.'

'I was thinking Greece,' Jay said. 'It's cheap. And warm. I'll head off as soon as Karl's got me that fake passport. You could join me.'

'Yeah, hun – look, we can discuss this later, okay?' He heard her breathing heavily.

'Are you running?' he asked.

'No, I'm packing some things. Just in case,' she said. 'Babes, just get your arse out of Karl's place and I'll speak to you later, okay?'

'Okay.'

'Okay,' she said again. 'You got enough money?'

He smiled. 'Yes, mum.'

'Right. Then bugger off.'

'Love you, babycakes.'

'Love you too,' she said, and hung up.

# 38

---

**B**oyd led his team up the metal steps to the first floor of the old brewery, their heavy feet clanking as they climbed to the top. 'So, Rachel, your PA, said –'

'Assistant developer,' Karl quickly corrected. 'FYI, she's one of the best coders I've got.'

'Ah.' Boyd nodded, rightly chastened. 'She said the company owns this place, not you?'

'Uh-huh. And lets it to me for a nominal fee,' Karl said.

'It's a nice place, Mr Craig,' said Boyd, pausing at the top. 'Very *Dragon's Den*.'

'Karl is fine,' he replied as he beckoned them over to the lounge area of his open-plan living space. 'So what's my idiot big brother gone and done now?'

Boyd sat down on a leather sofa beside a tall window that looked over cobblestoned mews with a row of boutique shops opening onto it. 'He assaulted someone,' he replied.

'At gunpoint,' O'Neal added.

Boyd glared at him. 'Allegedly,' he said. 'It was clearly a misguided attempt at some sort of vigilante justice. He thought he'd picked out the right man for a murder that occurred last week.'

'Oh.' Karl nodded. 'Was it the wrong bloke?'

It pained Boyd to nod, but he managed it. 'It was a case of adding two and two together and coming up with five. Jason's done a runner, obviously, and I'm just here to ask whether or not he's been in touch with you.'

Karl looked around at them all. 'Four plain-clothes detectives. It's a bit overkill for a case of mistaken identity, isn't it?'

'We have to take this seriously because of the gun that was reported,' said O'Neal.

'And as Jason's only blood relative,' Boyd continued, 'you're top of our list to talk to.'

'So you thought he might come and seek me out?' Karl said.

Boyd nodded and looked around at the dark and industrial-looking space. 'It's a good place to lie low, a place like this.'

'That's why I like it.' Karl smiled. 'Tucked away, off the street but still in the middle of Brighton. You wouldn't know this place was here, eh?'

Boyd pulled out his notebook. 'Right, well, I've got a few questions, then we'll be on our way.'

Karl nodded.

'Do you mind if my colleagues have a look around while we talk?' Boyd asked.

'Looking for Jay, huh?' He laughed. 'He's way too big a chump to fit underneath my bed.'

Boyd smiled. 'I know. But all the same...'

'Help yourselves,' Karl said.

Boyd nodded at O'Neal and Abbott, who got up and left the room. 'Now then,' he said, 'we've been through Jay's phone and, to be fair, it doesn't seem like you and Jay interact that much.'

'Not really,' Karl said truthfully. 'We don't have a lot in common. We're related, but that's about it.'

'You share the same background, though. You were both fostered, and both spent time in care homes?'

DI Shannon studied him. 'And you say you're actually *brothers*?'

Karl shot him a look. 'Yes, amazingly... despite the different skin colour, we do share the same blood.'

'Turner's quite a lot different,' said Shannon defensively. 'It's not just skin colour.'

'He had a very different experience from me,' Karl said. 'I got a long-term foster home from twelve onwards. Jay, on the other hand, did a lot of bouncing around until he eventually stopped being the state's responsibility.'

'You stayed in contact, though?' said Boyd.

'At first,' replied Karl. 'But then that petered out. However, I reached out to Jay about seven years ago.'

'Through Facebook?' Boyd asked.

'No way,' Karl shot back. 'I wouldn't touch that site with a bargepole. Through LinkedIn.'

'Right.' Boyd noted that down. 'And what's the deal these days? Do you get together at all for birthdays and Christmases? That sort of thing?

'Not so much... We share an occasional pint. Like I say, we don't have that much in common. But family's family, right?' Karl replied.

'When was the last time you spoke to him?' Boyd asked.

Karl gazed up at the rafters. 'I can't remember. A few months maybe? It was before Christmas at any rate.'

Boyd noted that down too. 'And nothing since?'

'No, not a thing.'

DI Abbott emerged from one of the doors off the main area. He shook his head at Boyd.

'Do you have much contact with your old foster family?' asked Boyd.

'Christmas cards and birthday cards.' Karl smiled. 'I always visit for Mother's Day, though. You know, a box of Hotel Chocolat and a bunch of flowers. My foster mum was good to me.'

'Has Jay ever met your foster parents?' Boyd asked.

Karl shook his head. 'No. It's not really his family, is it? I wouldn't want that, anyway; it would be like me rubbing his face in it. I had a much easier childhood than he did.'

O'Neal emerged through a doorway. 'Nothing in the bedroom, guv!' he called out.

Boyd reached into his jacket and pulled out one of his business cards. He handed it to Karl. 'Jay may well get in touch. Do him a favour and give me a call if he does,' he said.

'How's that doing him a favour?' Karl asked.

'He's wanted for aggravated assault,' Boyd said. 'Better we catch him before he adds any other offences to the list, don't you think?'

'Assault.' Karl shook his head. 'That's not Jay. No way. He's not a violent bloke.'

'There were mitigating circumstances,' Boyd said. 'It was an old mate of his who was murdered. It hit him hard. If he gives himself up, a magistrate would probably look sympathetically at his case. But not if he gets into more trouble while he's on the run.' Boyd paused. 'Mr Craig, do call me, please. I know Jay a little. He's a good bloke. I'd hate to see him get into even bigger trouble.'

'If he calls,' Karl said with a nod, 'I'll let you know.'

Boyd got up from the leather sofa. 'Thanks for your help,' he said.

'Anything I can do.' Karl led them back towards the stairs, stopping beside his kitchenette island. 'I really don't see him having a gun, though. Please... detective, if you do corner him and he decides to run like an idiot... don't set SWAT after him, or whatever they're called. Coppers seem to be quite trigger-happy these days.'

Boyd smiled. 'This isn't America yet.'

O'Neal pulled out a packet of cigarettes from his back pocket and began to fumble inside the box for one.

'Uh, not in here, please, mate,' said Karl.

Boyd twisted around and scowled at O'Neal for his unprofessionalism.

'It's a bad habit, dude,' said Karl, placing Boyd's business card on a metal tray and tapping it. 'I'll give you a ring if I hear from him, okay?'

Boyd's eyes were glued to the tray, where a packet of Rizzlers sat. He shot a glance at Abbott and Shannon, wondering if they'd clocked them. Neither seemed to have noticed.

'Thanks,' Boyd said, and swiftly herded the other three detectives towards the metal stairs that led down to the brewery's cluttered and dusty ground floor.

## 39

'I said get your ruddy feet DOWN!'

Roland didn't like the way the three men had made themselves at home in his penthouse apartment. He'd had them all remove their shoes and boots in the hallway (because the lounge had a thick cream carpet) to which they had grudgingly agreed, but all three seemed to be flaunting their irritation by putting their bare – grubby – feet up onto whatever piece of furniture was closest.

'Ronaldo' uncrossed his feet and swung them off the coffee table and back onto the floor. He grumbled something in Georgian. Gregor barked back at him like a kennels' old-timer putting a new dog in its place.

'What did he just say?' asked Roland.

Gregor wafted a hand. 'Is nothing. Relax.'

'Tony Soprano' had his bare feet up on one of the white suede armchairs and he'd been absently picking at the dry skin between his toes as he thumbed through channels on the wall-mounted TV. He rolled his eyes, uncrossed his legs and lowered his feet to the carpet as well.

Roland couldn't imagine why his father had retained

these uncouth apes, imported from his motherland, when he could have hired some properly trained, indeed house-trained, professionals. Men, ironically, like those two doormen at CuffLinks: polite, well-dressed, physically fit, English-speaking muscleheads. Ex-servicemen – that's who Roland would hire.

He wandered over to the French doors and out onto the balcony. The sky was beginning to darken' the day had slipped by and so far he'd heard sweet FA from that slapped bitch of a Chief Super.

*Jesus. Nanny McPhee meets Morticia fucking Addams.* She vaguely reminded him of his house matron at Dunstan College: prim and proper but shaggable in a have-her-scrubbed- and-sent-to-my-tent kind of way.

Karovic had cautioned patience earlier today when Roland had called him for an update: 'They will find him, Mr Hammond. Just give the police some time.' Well, it was time he'd rather not spend with these Neanderthals cluttering his living space. And time was something he really couldn't afford to waste. The longer Turner remained at large and alive, the greater the risk that he was going to share what he knew with someone who could piece it all together.

'Screw you, Karovic,' he muttered. He pulled out his phone, scrolled down and found the number for the wretched woman.

Chief Superintendent Margaret Hatcher answered after the second ring. 'Who is this?' she asked.

'It's Roland Hammond,' he replied impatiently.

He heard her gasp. 'Uh... now, this is *not* what was agreed. We speak *only* via your lawyer, Mr Karovic. I can't afford to have a call directly from your family. Certainly not on this pho–'

'Be quiet,' Roland spat. 'What's happening? What's the progress? I need an update.'

'I... look, I really can't have this conversation with you. Not now and not on this phone,' Hatcher tried again.

Roland ignored her. 'Where's Turner? Do you have any fucking idea yet?'

'We're doing our best.' He could hear a slight tremor in her voice. Good. He rather liked that. Fear made folks up their game a little. 'We think he may have gone to ground... in...'

'Yes?'

'Brighton. Somewhere in Brighton.'

Roland felt a spike of adrenaline lift his hopes slightly. 'So how do you know he's in Brighton?'

'Through the vehicle he's currently using,' Hatcher replied.

'What? Number-plate recognition?' Roland asked.

'Yes. His vehicle was logged by CCTV at a service station on a road heading into Brighton,' she replied. 'But look – that's all that I have for you. And we should end this conversation now.'

'Fuck it!' Roland hissed. 'I will tell you when we're ruddy well done!'

He heard her gasp again. She obviously wasn't used to being spoken to like this, the silly cow.

'Look, Mr Hammond... I have put all my available resources on this. I assure you we will pick him up again in the next few –'

'What, hours? Days? This is not good enough.' Roland liked how his voice was sounding down the phone right now: a little deeper, a hard edge, a touch of menace. 'The arrangement has changed,' he told her.

'What? What do you mean the arrangement's *changed*?' she replied.

'All you have to do now is simply *locate him*. We'll do the rest.'

'I... no, Mr Karovic told me that we're to locate him, charge him and put him on remand. Then... after that...I'm done.'

'Ah, well, you see... the old boy's obviously given you the wrong impression. We just need you to find him and give us his location. That's it. And then you're done.'

Hatcher paused. Roland could hear the ambient noises of the police station in the background. 'I believe it would be more discreet and better for all of us if he's simply arrested and —'

'As soon as you identify where he is, my dear, you're going to pick up your phone and call this number. By the time your plods turn up to arrest him —' Roland smiled – 'there'll be no sign of him. Not a scrap. He'll have vanished. Escaped the Sussex Police all over again. Do you see? Very tidy. Very discreet.'

'That's not... not possible. There'll be operational logs, radio reports to and from the SIO. I can't simply terminate an unresolved manhunt.'

'That's your problem to sort out, not mine, you stupid bitch!'

He ended the call and grinned. How many times had he fantasized about saying that over and over to Matron as he took her roughly from behind. The momentary endorphin rush slowly evaporated and he realised that just maybe he'd ended the call prematurely.

*Oh, deary me. I think this woman needs a visit.*

# 40

Boyd watched DI Abbott and DI Shannon walk across the petrol station forecourt and enter the shop. Shannon had just filled up the pool car. Abbott, of course, needed the bloody toilet. O'Neal had been surprisingly quiet on the drive back from Brighton.

'You all right, O'Neal?' Boyd asked, making eye contact with him via the wing mirror as O'Neal, behind him, looked up from his phone.

'Uh. Yeah. No. Fine, sir'

'I've not seen much of you recently...' Boyd said, smiling. 'Since you went over to the dark side.'

O'Neal grinned back at him in the mirror. 'There's a bit more action going on in Flack's team, sir.'

'So it seems.'

'Hey, I heard Warren made the Knight arrest,' O'Neal said. 'Nice one.'

'Yup. After nearly being bayonetted to death.' Boyd winked. 'See? There's action on the main floor too, you know.'

O'Neal nodded and turned his attention back to his phone.

Boyd could sense the unease. This wasn't just down to O'Neal being on another team.

'What did you make of Karl Craig?' he asked.

He saw an anxious expression flit across the lad's face.

'O'Neal?'

He looked up and met Boyd's eyes in the wing mirror again. 'He's got a cool place, right?'

*I've got to know.*

'O'Neal, did you see it?'

'See *what*, sir?'

'Did you see it?' Boyd repeated. 'When he put my card down?'

O'Neal hesitated before finally nodding. 'Yes. He's not a smoker, sir.'

'Right,' he replied. 'So why did he have cigarette papers?'

'My thought too, sir.' O'Neal lowered his phone. 'Why didn't you ask Craig about them, sir? I was surprised you didn't pick him up on that.'

Boyd turned in his seat to look at him. 'Her Madge has got you watching me, hasn't she?' he said.

'What?! No! Of course not!'

The DC was a crap liar. 'Don't be an arse,' said Boyd. 'She asked you to report in on me, right?'

'Sir... I... she...'

'O'Neal, I said don't be an arse. Spit it out. She's asked you to spy on me. Correct?'

'She said she's lost confidence in you,' he blurted. 'She said she was concerned you might be dragging your feet on this case.'

'Did she say why?' Boyd asked.

'Jay,' O'Neal replied. He shrugged. 'You're friends with Jay and Okeke. So... obviously...'

There was an awkward silence.

'Jay's been staying there, hasn't he?' said O'Neal finally.

'You're giving him a chance, aren't you? You should have followed up on those Rizzlers, sir.'

Boyd could have come up with some BS answer, but he knew O'Neal already had sussed him out. 'You think I'm cutting Jay some slack?' he said.

O'Neal broke eye contact and looked out of the window. DI Shannon was on his way back across the forecourt towards the car.

'O'Neal?' Boyd said urgently.

'Hatcher said I had to let her know the moment I spotted anything dodgy.' He sounded genuinely remorseful. 'She said... you might be *compromised*.'

'Christ.' Boyd closed his eyes and let out humourless huff. 'Seriously?'

'She said you might be involved with Jay... in blackmailing someone.'

'Oh, for fuck's sake! And you believed that, did you?'

Shannon paused just outside the car to stuff a can of Red Bull into the pocket of his anorak and to shove the petrol station's till receipt into his wallet. Boyd saw DI Abbott emerging from the store, hoisting the belt of his sagging trousers up over his belly and clutching a sandwich.

'Well, have you?' Boyd asked.

'What?'

'Snitched to Her Madge on me?'

O'Neal nodded slowly, looking down. 'I'm really sorry, sir.'

# 41

Hatcher pulled into her driveway and swung round so that her Nissan Juke was facing out, ready for work tomorrow.

As she turned, her headlights picked out the reflection of a dark-grey SUV parked snugly up against her leylandii bushes, a thickset man in dark-blue joggers and a puffer jacket standing beside it.

'Shit!' she yelped, her foot stamping down on the brake pedal. The car lurched and stalled.

The man stepped over to her driver-side door and, before she could think to engage the central locking, he'd pulled the door open.

'No! Please...!' she recoiled.

He put a finger to his moustache and two pink lips emerged from beneath it. 'Shhhhh...'

He pointed towards her front door. She turned in her seat and noticed for the first time that her front door was wide open.

'You... in,' he said softly. 'Talk. Inside.'

*Oh God.* She recognised the Slavic accent and realised that her worst nightmare had finally turned up. She'd been dreading a moment like this, ever since they'd first made contact with her two years ago.

Zophia Salikov had looked to be in her early twenties – about the same age or thereabouts as her son, Julian. But instead of being all blue hair and pink Doc Martens, she'd worn a corporate suit and her blonde hair had been scraped back into a tidy bun.

The unexpected encounter with the young woman had been brief and to the point and had taken just a few minutes. Just long enough for Salikov to explain who she was, what was going to be happening on Hatcher's turf and that her cooperation, namely a blind eye, would be required. That brief conversation had taken place one sunny Sunday morning in the parking area of quaint little farmers' shop and nursery just outside Beckley. The brazenness of it – with customers only a few yards away putting plants and bags of potting compost into the boots of their cars – had shocked Hatcher. Zophia Salikov had informed her that her father only ever asked once, then she'd casually shown her a photo of somebody whom Mr Salikov had had to ask a second time.

It was an image that would come back and visit her every night thereafter. If that poor somebody had survived – and Margaret Hatcher hadn't been able to work out whether the victim had been male or female – it would have been a life without sight, sound, taste or smell.

'In!' said the man again, jerking his finger towards her porch. She got out of the car and headed slowly towards the front door. Another man was waiting there for her, younger, skinny, with long dark hair pulled back into a man bun. He smiled, showing gold fillings, and waved at her to proceed inside.

*Oh God. Is this it? Is this how it ends... in my own home?*

'I'm in here!' a voice called out from her lounge. She stepped into the room and saw that Roland Hammond had made himself comfortable in one of her armchairs.

Beside him, standing to attention with hands behind his back, was a wiry old man with a silver crew cut and pock-marked cheeks.

'Take a seat,' said Hammond. 'Please.'

She sat down on the sofa. 'What's going on?' She took a deep breath to steady her voice. 'Where's Mr Karovic?'

Hammond grinned. 'We're currently operating under different rules. Dad's not so well these days,' he said, wrinkling his nose, 'so I'm minding the shop.'

'Look. I told you on the phone –'

'I know. That you're doing your very best,' he cut in. 'But I'm afraid that's not working for me.'

She glanced at the man standing beside Hammond, both his hands remained resolutely, worryingly, tucked out of sight behind.

'Now, I've been exceedingly patient. It's been a few days and I really would have expected that one of the best resourced, best trained police forces in the world would have managed to track down an amateur like Mr Turner by now.'

'I told you over the phone... we... we've made progress,' she said.

'*He's somewhere in Brighton,*' Hammond responded, mimicking her voice.

'We... we're pretty sure he has been staying in Brighton.'

'*Has been,*' Hammond echoed. He shook his head and tutted. 'Has been. See? That's what I'm talking about. You're always a step behind. You need to be ahead of him. Antici-pating him.' Hammond lurched in the armchair, his voice suddenly rising. 'For fuck's sake, he's not James Bond, – he's just a *stupid fucking bouncer!*'

'We can only work with the leads we have,' she replied. The attack in her voice sounded good. It made her feel a little bolder. 'He was in Brighton yesterday morning. He may have moved on. We're working to find out where he is right now. We will find him.'

She watched Hammond as he pushed a strand of wavy blond hair back off his forehead and ran a tongue across his top lip. He stared down at her flat shoes, then let his gaze wander to her ankles, up her tights to the hem of her dark skirt, then up to her shirt and tie. He chuckled. 'You know, I really do like a mature woman in uniform.'

His eyes met hers and she fought hard not to look away.

*It's intimidation... That's all this is. This little prick is giving you a scare. Stay calm.*

He picked up a brass letter-opener sitting on the side table and casually inspected it. 'I know I don't sound very Georgian,' he said, smiling. 'It's not an easy language to learn, to be honest. But that doesn't stop me from being one.'

Hatcher remained stony-faced.

'Yes,' he continued, 'don't make the mistake of thinking that Salikov blood *isn't* flowing through my veins.' He waggled the tip of the blade in her direction. 'In our family we have a tradition, all to do with eyes, ears and tongues. Hear no evil. See no evil. Speak no evil. Do you see?'

She nodded. She knew all too well.

'Now, I'm sorely tempted to help myself to one of your sharper kitchen knives and demonstrate that for you, but Father assures me that you're a handy asset so...' His gaze wondered to the framed photographs on her teak display cabinet. 'Is that your son?' he asked conversationally.

She remained perfectly still.

'Julian,' said Hammond. 'That's right, isn't it? He's Julian Hatcher and he's at Brighton University, I believe?'

Her heart froze.

Hammond lifted a ragged opened brown envelope with a cellophane window from the side table and pulled out a folded piece of paper. 'And this is a rent renewal form for... What's his address again? Ahhh... there it is.'

'Please!' she blurted.

He laughed and looked up at Gregor. 'And there's our leverage.'

'Please,' she begged again. 'He's just a boy! He's got nothing to do with th–'

'He has everything to do with this... if I say he does,' he replied, looking back at the photograph. 'Because I'm in charge. He's a rather good-looking lad, isn't he? At the moment, that is.'

Hatcher felt the blood drain from her face.

'I'm leaving this room in the next few minutes with either Turner's location or this letter,' Hammond said.

'Oh God, no...' she pleaded. Then before she could stop herself: 'Boyd...'

Hammond frowned. 'That's the inspector who interviewed me, right?'

'Yes,' she said. 'DCI Boyd.' She noticed a flicker of a reaction on the wiry old man's face.

The old man leant over and whispered something to Hammond.

His brows raised in surprise. 'Oh? Really?' He turned back to Hatcher. 'Gregor tells me we've already reached out to Boyd before. So... what's he to me? Like I said, I want an address. Now.'

'I think...' she began. She knew there'd be a price to be paid for this down the line. 'I think... I *suspect*... that Boyd knows where Turner is. He may even be in contact with him. They're friends.'

Hammond smiled. 'Well, that *is* interesting. Very interest-ing. He is helping him, is he?'

'Y-yes. I... I believe so,' she said.

Hammond's face widened to a troll-like grin. 'So we have a naughty dog. See how good we are together, Margaret! Well now... I see no reason to waste any more of each other's time... Where am I going to find DCI Boyd?'

# 42

Boyd drummed his fingers on the dashboard impatiently as DI Shannon nudged the car through the traffic. The stop–start pulsing of red brake lights was starting to give him a headache.

'See, this is why I don't ever drive to Brighton,' muttered DI Shannon. 'It's literally quicker to drive back to London along the M25 and back down the A21 than it is to drive the thirty bloody miles between us!'

'It's five past five,' said DI Abbott. 'Rush hour, ain't it?'

'Oh, well done, sunshine,' said Shannon. 'You just earned your "State the Bleedin' Obvious" *Blue Peter* badge.'

'At this rate it'll be gone six thirty before we get back to the station,' muttered Abbott. 'And there'll be sod-all overtime. Sutherland's as tight as a camel's arse.'

'You'd just spend it in Greggs, Abbott,' said Shannon. 'He's doing you a favour.'

'Oh, piss off,' Abbott muttered. 'Cockwomble.'

Boyd tried to tune out their wittering noise. His mind was on the quiet young DC in the back. O'Neal had already reported back that his SIO appeared to be dragging his feet;

Boyd wondered how long it would be before Hatcher passed that information back up the chain to the Salikovs themselves. Or would she simply switch him out of the operation for Flack? Or even DI Shannon?

His work phone buzzed in his pocket. He pulled it out to see it was the Chief Superintendent herself. *Speak of the devil.* He turned to the others. 'Hold it down, fellas. It's Her Madge calling.'

The car was instantly silent.

'Evening, ma'am. We're on our way back from Bright–'

'Boyd...' She was breathing heavily, as though she'd just been for a run.

'Ma'am?'

'Boyd...' She wheezed again. 'The... the Salikovs...'

He switched hands and ear so the phone wouldn't bleed her voice straight to Shannon sitting in the seat beside him.

'Yes? What about them?'

He thought he heard her choke back a sob.

'Ma'am... are you okay?'

'*They're coming for you...*'

Boyd looked round at the others; all eyes were on him.

'Pull over,' he ordered Shannon.

The DI signalled left and put the hazard lights on. He pulled out of the sluggish stream of traffic and onto the hard shoulder.

Boyd unclipped his belt and quickly climbed out of the car, slamming the door shut behind him. 'What's happened?'

'There's no... fucking time,' she said. 'They came here, to my home. They've just left and they're on the way to yours...' She took a deep breath. 'Boyd... I'm sorry.'

Then the call ended.

He kept the phone to his ear as he looked at his three colleagues sitting inside the car, curious eyes still on him, trying to read what the hell was going on. He kept his face neutral.

*Emma.*

He called her number. It rang several times, then went to voicemail. 'Emma, it's Dad. If you're in the house, get out of it *now*! Then call me straight back.' He ended the call and texted her the same message. She had to be at work or on the way there. Either was good.

He called Okeke's burner phone. She answered instantly. 'Guv? Have... you spoken with Karl yet?'

'They're coming for me,' he blurted out.

'What?!'

'I've just spoke to Hatcher. The Salikovs went out to her place. It sounds like they've done a number on her. And now they're on the way over to my house!'

'Fuck!'

Beckley, where Hatcher lived, was a half-hour drive to Hastings. Forty-five if they got snarled up with the nearly-home-now traffic on the A21. 'Okeke, I can't get hold of Emma. Either she's at work, or on the way to work or...'

He didn't want to vocalise the last 'or'. He really didn't.

'I'm on it,' she replied. 'I'll go find her and pick her up. Then what, guv?'

He had no bloody idea. He hadn't got anything even remotely resembling a plan – just blind panic.

'Look, find Emma... please! Find her, then call me as soon as you've got her. I'll work out the next steps.'

'On it.' She ended the call.

OKEKE DIALLED THE CLUB. Jay's boss answered. 'CuffLinks?'

'Luigi... it's Jay's other half, Sam.'

'Ahhh! The lovely Samantha! Yessss,' he oozed disarmingly.

'Listen! When is my big man coming back to work? We're missing him!'

'No, listen. Luigi... is Emma Boyd behind the bar?'

He tutted. 'No. She said she might come in early to help with stocking up, but she's not turned up yet. It's no problem. I can –'

'Shit.'

'Hey? What's up?' Luigi asked.

'Look, when she does turn up, get her to call me... immediately. It's urgent, okay?'

'What's happened, Samantha?'

'Just tell her to call me, okay?'

'Yes, okay.'

She hung up and tried Emma's number; after several rings the line was bumped to voicemail. Boyd would have undoubtedly left her a message. There was no point doing the same bloody thing. Instead she thumbed a quick text, then looked at the time on her phone. It was twenty past five. If the Russians had just left Beckley, then Okeke could beat them to Boyd's house. She might even spot Emma walking down the hill into the old town.

She grabbed her coat and shoulder bag and flew out of the front door.

# 43

'I know, I know,' said Emma softly. 'And, you know, it *was* pretty shit of me.'

'Very shit, I think you could say,' replied Daniel. She could hear him absently strumming his electric guitar while they spoke.

'I mean, fuck... you dropped me like a shit second season.'

She smiled. 'Nice.' Even though Daniel was baring his soul and effectively telling her there was little chance of a second chance because she'd broken his bloody heart... he was still finding some wriggle room for some *bants*.

She took that as a good sign.

'I just... I was an idiot,' she continued. 'He kind of, I don't know, he seemed a lot more mature...'

'Thanks,' Daniel replied. 'None taken.'

'Look...' She checked her watch; she was going to be late. She'd texted him for a chat and he'd called literally as soon as she'd stepped out of the shower. Her hair was hanging down her bath robe in wet, tangled ribbons and Ozzie was side-eyeing her from the floor as if to remind her she really needed to get a move on.

'Look,' she said again, 'I get that you want us to be friends only, Dan. And I'll take that. It's more than I deserve it but maybe...?'

She heard the soft zzzzing of a strummed chord. 'I... shit... I dunno, Emma.'

'Please,' she whispered. 'I miss you, Dan.'

She heard him clack his tongue. 'I missed you too. That's the prob–'

The front doorbell rang and Ozzie let loose a barrage of deafening barks.

'I gotta go, Dan. There's someone at the door. Can we talk in about ten minutes? I'll be walking down to work... and –'

'Sure. Okay.'

She opened the door to her bedroom and let Ozzie cascade down the stairs barking loudly all the way.

'All right,' she said. 'Ten minutes.' She ended the call and followed Ozzie down the stairs. It was too early to be Dad standing with an apologetic 'duh' face and no door keys to let himself in, so it was most likely the Amazon guy with her order of vegan chocolate.

Ozzie was right up at the inner door on his hind legs, barking at the frosted glass. She was about to drop her phone into the bathrobe's pocket when she saw there were two texts she'd missed.

One from Dad. And another one from Sam Okeke. She skipped her dad's – it was almost certainly something about working late – and opened Okeke's message instead.

GET OUT OF HOUSE ASAP!

'What?' Emma paused at the bottom of the stairs. Three dots were dancing at the bottom of her screen... Another message from Sam was writing another one:

I'm in my car. Come to pick you up!

It had to be Sam at the door then. Emma hurried down the hall, pulled open the inner door and flicked on the foyer light.

Ozzie barged past her onto the coarse-haired mat and then proceeded to bark at the figure standing just outside in the dark.

She was about to reach for the handle when a third message pinged onto the screen from Sam.

BAD PEOPLE coming fOr You gEt OUT!!!

Emma froze. The figure outside wasn't wearing a high-vis jacket, so not Amazon, and was far too tall to be Sam. She reached for Ozzie's collar and took a step back from the front door with him still barking ferociously at whoever was waiting patiently outside for her to answer.

She was just taking another step back when something hit the front door hard from outside and it rattled inwards, the old stained glass shattering as it did so.

Standing before her was a tall, skinny man with black hair scraped into a man bun and a grin that glinted with gold fillings. In one hand he was holding a gun with a long, extended barrel on the end of it.

Ozzie was barking ferociously now and lurched forward suddenly, freeing himself from Emma's tight grip. The skinny man raised his gun…

OKEKE TURNED inland along the Bourne, heading up the gentle slope to Old London Road, looking for the right-hand turning onto Ashburnham Road. She'd been frantically scanning both sides of the street, wondering whether Emma preferred the promenade side or the shop side, but so far there was no sign of her walking to work.

As her Datsun pulled up the steepening hill, the entrance to the old town's High Street ahead and All Saints Hall on her right, she had hoped that she might catch Emma striding downhill, but there was still no sign of her.

'Okay,' Okeke muttered. 'Still at home, then.' She peddled the clutch to shift her Datsun into a lower, more responsive gear. 'Come on, come on, you lazy old bitch! Come on!' The engine went from a throaty rattle to a whine as it sped forward, and finally the turning for Ashburnham appeared.

Okeke swung the car right, causing a bus heading downhill to brake suddenly and flash its headlights angrily at her.

GREGOR KNOCKED the young man's arm upwards and the gun puffed a muted gunshot into the hall's ceiling. He pulled a coat from one of the hooks to his left and flung it over the dog charging towards them.

It had the effect he was after. The dog paused to shake it off, giving him enough time to flip it over onto its back and jam a wellington boot into its snapping jaw.

'Get the girl!' he shouted in Georgian at the young man as he scrambled to find something to tie around the animal's drooling muzzle.

Roland watched the frantic scramble from just outside the front door, over Soprano's beefy shoulders. He was actually rather impressed with the speed, agility and no-nonsense brutality of these chaps. He'd been somewhat underwhelmed with the three uncouth louts when he'd first met them. They looked like three inhabitants from Borat's Kazakh village: scruffy, undisciplined and all reeking of stale cigarettes and beef jerky. But they had the dog and the girl subdued within seconds with the only sound being the dog's bloody barking.

All of a sudden, it was quiet. Gregor had the panting dog trussed up, Ronaldo had the girl in his arms, one hand over her mouth and the barrel of the gun's silencer rammed up under her chin.

Soprano hurried into the house and vaulted up the stairs

with his handgun at the ready. A few moments later, he hurried back down and shook his head. 'No person.'

OKEKE WAS HALFWAY up Ashburnham Road when she noticed a dark grey SUV parked in the road right outside Boyd's house. She kept on going uphill, keeping her speed slow but constant as she drove past. The front door was wide open and the lights were on. Through the window, she thought she caught a glimpse of a thickset man with a beard stepping into the lounge to look around before disappearing back into the hallway.

She pulled over twenty yards further up the road and twisted in her seat to look out through the rear window. Several figures emerged from Boyd's house, heading down the short path to the pavement. She thought she recognised the wavy blonde hair of Hammond among them. Behind him was a tall, skinny man with his arms wrapped around a figure with a towel over her head... It had to be Emma.

'Oh, shit, shit, shit,' she whispered.

The headlights of the SUV suddenly glared to life, blinding her. She ducked down low in case any of them noticed her watching them from so stupidly close by. She heard the vehicle's engine rumble and saw the beams of the headlights swing across the low canopy of her car as it sped past her and off up the road.

She sat up and furiously tapped the vehicle's quickly receding registration number into her phone. The SUV turned at the next left and swung out of view, leaving Ashburnham Road seemingly eventless and quiet, save for the distant squawk of seagulls circling in the dark sky above.

'Oh God...' she whispered. 'Oh God, they've got her.'

# 44

Soprano drove, with Roland in the front passenger seat, while Ronaldo lay across the middle seat with the girl squirming beneath him. Gregor was in the rearmost seat, wrestling with the dog.

'There is tape! In bag!' shouted Gregor. He gestured a finger towards the passenger-side footwell. Roland reached down and found the bag. He unzipped it and blindly rummaged inside. His fingers brushed across the tacky side of a broad wheel of plumber's tape. He pulled it out and handed it back to Ronaldo, who quickly wound it several times around the girl's wrists, bit with his teeth to sever the tape and tossed it to Gregor.

A few minutes further along the road was a turn-off for an empty car park. Gregor shouted something from the back and Soprano took the turning and drove towards a remote corner of the car park, away from the Homebase store's well-lit front entrance.

'Why are we bloody stopping?' snapped Roland.

'We need plan! What is plan?' Gregor replied, look of incredulity on his face.

Roland realised the old man was right. He'd hoped for

Boyd, but he'd got whoever this young woman was instead. And a grumpy, seemingly wild dog. He needed to re-jig things. Instead of extracting an address out of the detective in the comfort of his own home, he was going to have to broker some arrangement with him. The girl – presumably Boyd's daughter – was sure to get him what he needed.

One location, for one girl, unharmed. Tonight.

'Right, yes. Park there,' he said, pointing at the spot that Soprano was already steering the vehicle towards. 'Yes! That's it! That's good!'

Soprano pulled into the corner furthest from the store and shadowed from the nearest amber street light by the low boughs of a yew tree, and he turned the engine off.

There was silence for a few moments. Time for him to gather his thoughts, marshal a new plan. 'Okay,' he began. 'All right... let me think.'

He looked down at the girl trapped beneath Ronaldo. The silencer of his gun was resting heavily on her cheek: a reminder – as if she needed it – that before she could suck in enough breath to let out a scream, half her head would be smeared across the upholstery. She was in a white bathrobe and, he guessed, little else.

Roland pulled the towel from her head and lifted a finger to his lips to ensure she understood that they were going to have a conversation that would be very quiet, and very calm. Then he spoke softly: 'Hello there, lovely ... what's your name?'

Her wide eyes locked onto him and for a fleeting moment she looked vaguely familiar.

'E-Emma...' she whispered.

'Emma?' He smiled. 'Okay, Emma. My name is Roland. That was your home we just entered, I take it?'

She nodded.

'So your daddy's the detective called Boyd?'

Emma hesitated for a moment before conceding another nod.

Roland reached down and gently pulled her bathrobe down to cover her exposed bare legs. 'It's probably best not to tease these horny hairy monkeys...' he said, still smiling. 'They've got work to do yet.'

He looked up at Gregor, who was busy wrapping tape around the dog's muzzle. 'Why have we got a dog, Gregor?'

The old man bit into the tape and tore the wheel free. 'Is extra leverage.' He shrugged. 'We do dog as warning first. Then we do girl.'

Roland nodded. 'Yes. That's good. That's clever.'

BOYD HAD the pool car to himself. He'd left the other three out in the cold and stranded somewhere along the A27. Tough shit. They could call a patrol car or an Uber. He'd switched on the siren and lights and was now speeding along the hard shoulder past the slow-moving traffic heading towards Lewes and, beyond that, Hastings.

'Shit, shit, shit!' he hissed to himself as if that was going to expedite his journey in some way. Okeke had to get there first. She was just ten minutes away. In fact, she must have collected Emma by now.

He fumbled for his phone, which was resting on his left thigh, and managed to knock it down into the handbrake's recess.

'OH, FOR FUCK'S SAKE!!!' he screamed as he fumbled for it.

Then the damned thing's screen lit up as it started buzzing. He glanced down and saw a sliver of Okeke's face – a picture from the barbecue last summer of her and Jay with bottles of beer in their hands.

He managed to extract the phone from the well and answer the call without swerving into the stationary traffic or onto the verge. 'You got her?'

'I'm... so, so sorry...' Okeke said.

There were more words – she was still talking – but those were the ones he heard and parsed. He slowed the car to a crawl, pulled over and switched off the siren.

*So, so sorry...*

He mentally shook himself. 'Say all that again,' he replied. He heard Okeke's breath hitch. In the year and a bit that he'd known her, this was the first time he'd heard an edge of raw emotion in her voice. And it terrified him.

'Sam?!'

'They've got her, Boyd. They've got her,' she said.

'She's alive?'

'Yes. I... I saw them bundling her into an SUV...'

*An SUV. Of course an SUV. Bastards.*

'And they took off. I went inside your house. There was a bullet hole in the ceiling, your dog's gone as –'

'Jesus Christ. Was there any blood? Tell me there was no –'

'There was no blood. None at all. I promise. I think the bullet hole must have been a warning shot. There's no sign inside of any blood or restraint or... or... Looks like they just kicked your door in and snatched Emma. That's it.'

*That's it?* He wanted to bellow into the private bubble of the car, because that wasn't it, was it? Emma was alive for now, but this was the start of something that could well end up with her returning in pieces.

*Keep your shit together, Bill.* It was Julia. *Our daughter needs you. You screw this up and I'll haunt you for the rest of your life.*

'They obviously want to do a deal,' said Okeke. 'That's what this is about. They clearly want to do a swap. They're not going to kill her. They're –'

'I know,' he cut in, just to shut her up for a second. 'I know, all right.'

He needed to think. The goons had just been to Hatcher's place and God knows what they'd done to her. She'd sounded very shaken, but alive... so maybe – maybe – this was going to be their modus operandi – to scare the living shit out of everyone, but they didn't intend to leave a pile of bodies in their wake. This wasn't about Emma or him, after all. This was about Jay.

'Okeke, where are you?' he asked.

'I'm parked up near your house,' she replied.

'We need to get our heads together. We need to figure out a plan, okay?'

'Yeah.' Okeke's voice was rock steady again. He heard her light up a cigarette. 'Right,' she said, all business-like again. 'Not your place or mine.'

'So where?'

The phone speaker rustled as she slowly exhaled. 'I've got an idea.'

# 45

'Oh, you shitting little arsehole!' Warren snarled. 'You total bellend!'

RipperZ99 was hopping up and down in a squatted posture over Warren's prone body, teabagging him endlessly. Warren could hear the kid cackling insanely over the voice comms. He sounded as though he was about seven.

'Oh, just go away,' Warren snapped into his microphone as he tossed the Xbox controller onto the sofa. Getting sniped yet again by the same, probably spotty, little American kid was bad enough, but the unsportsmanlike dancing over his body was bloody infuriating.

'Yo pussy! Yo pussy! Yo pussy!' the kid was yee-hawing over the game's comms.

*Oh, to be able to reach through the screen and slap his little face.*

Warren decided he'd had enough ritual humiliation for one night and logged out of the *Call of Duty* death match. He pulled off his headset and let it drop onto the sofa beside the controller. There was nothing worse than feeling like a doddering old man in your early twenties, but honestly... there was no chance of keeping up with the trigger-reaction time of some prat a third his age.

He decided to salve his wounded pride with a microwave dinner. His mum had left him a week's worth of pre-made dinners in repurposed plastic takeaway tubs. All his favourite hits: spag bol, corned beef hash, chilli con carne – complete with the appropriate accompaniments of pasta, mash and rice. Like little aeroplane meals in a tub: no thinking or planning required – straight into Chef Mike for five minutes and voila!

He got up off the sofa and was halfway to the kitchen when he heard someone hammering on the front door. He course-corrected and went to answer it. He pulled the door open, expecting either a DPD driver or Cecille from next door enquiring about her wandering tabby cat.

Boyd and Okeke shoved past him and into his hallway, and a rather surprised Warren closed the front door quickly behind them.

'Guv? Okeke? What's...' Warren spluttered.

'Warren,' said Boyd. 'Can we come in?'

He looked from them to the closed front door. 'Um... sure. What's going on?' He had a sneaking suspicion his mum might have asked them to check up on him.

Boyd strode into the front room and headed to the sofa.

'Stop!' Warren cried, quickly reaching around his boss to retrieve his controller and headset.

Boyd checked to make sure there was nothing else he could squash and sat down heavily. 'We need to stop overnight,' he said briskly. 'Is that okay?'

'What? Like, you mean a sleepover?'

The faintest flicker of smile came and went. 'Yes, a sleep-over, Warren.'

Okeke sat down next to Boyd. 'We telling him all or not, guv?'

Boyd nodded. 'Might as well.'

'Warren,' she began, 'the Russians have kidnapped Emma and they're after Jay.'

'Sorry... what?' said Warren, totally bemused.

'The Georgian mafia...' Boyd corrected.

Warren felt as though he'd turned three pages over at the same time. 'Russians? Georgians? Mafia? What the f–'

ROLAND HAD KICKED his three Georgian minions out of the SUV. He could see them through the tinted glass, smoking and talking quietly. Inside it was just himself and the girl with her wrists taped behind her back and her dog who was panting and snorting on the back seat.

'Well, Emma...' he said. 'I'm awfully sorry about my goon squad. They can be a tad heavy-handed.' He looked at the V of her robe's neckline. 'Tsk... they should have brought some clothes along for you. Sorry about that too.' He reached out and fingered the hem of her robe. He hesitated for a moment; there was something indescribably delicious about this situation. He could... if he chose to, jerk her robe wide open and she couldn't do a thing to stop him. He had the power and the privacy to do what the hell he wanted.

*But this is work*, he told himself. *Very important work.*

Part of getting ready for his new role – taking over from Father – involved making grown-up decisions about work and play. There was a time and there was a place. He tugged the two sides of her robe together so that there was less skin on show to distract him.

'Now, I need to have a chat with your dad, Emma. Don't worry – it's just a little chat about some business.'

'Please... please don't hurt –' Emma whispered.

He put a finger to his lips to shush her, then smiled. 'Relax.

No one's getting hurt tonight. Not while I'm in charge. I just need you to give your old dad a quick call. All right?'

Roland pulled his phone out from his pocket, swiped it to unlock it and brought up the telephone keypad. 'There – be a lamb and just tap his number in for me, would you?'

'I... I can't... my hands...' she said.

'Oh, of course, your hands!' He laughed softly and rolled his eyes. 'Silly me. Tell me the number, then.' He winked. 'Off you go, Emma...'

BOYD'S PHONE suddenly started buzzing. He glanced at it; *Unknown Caller* flashed up on the screen. He let it buzz three times before sucking in a deep breath and answering.

'Yes?'

'Is this Detective Boyd?'

'Yes.' He recognised the younger man's voice from their interview. 'Hammond?'

'Well guessed.' Hammond chuckled. 'Now look – I've got a bit of news for you. I've –'

'I know,' Boyd cut in. 'You've got my daughter.'

A pause. 'Well, that's... a little disappointing. I was hoping to surprise you.'

'I can guess what this is about,' Boyd continued. 'But first I need to hear Emma's voice.'

'Yes. Of course, DCI Boyd. I wouldn't expect anything less.'

Boyd could hear rustling, then Emma's laboured breathing. 'Dad...'

'Jesus. Are you hurt, Ems? Where are you?' he asked.

'N-no...' she stuttered. 'I... I'm f-fucking terrified, Dad! We're in Hastings! I'm –'

The phone rustled as before and it was back with Hammond. He was chuckling again. 'She's a pickle, isn't she?'

'All right,' said Boyd. 'So tell me what you want.'

'You know what I want, Boyd. I want Jason Turner, obviously. And I happen to know that you know exactly where he is.'

'I'm still trying to find him,' Boyd said.

Hammond tutted. 'We're going to get this sorted tonight, Boyd. One way or another. So let's not waste time playing silly games. Where is he?'

Boyd glanced at Okeke and Warren. They would have heard everything leaking from the phone's speaker. He was sorely tempted to say where Jay was, but that was his only leverage. If he told Hammond, then getting Emma back in one piece would rely entirely on the bastard's good faith.

'I know several places he's likely to be,' Boyd said.

'Brighton, I believe,' said Hammond.

'He's not where we thought he was. I need time. I'll need to get in touch with him and find out where he's planning to hide out this evening.'

Hammond sighed. 'Very well. You do that. But listen carefully: you'd better find out fast or –'

'If you touch her, Hammond... if you *fucking touch her*, I'll come for you.' Boyd was shouting now. 'Do you understand? I'll make it my life's work to hunt you down. Catch you on your own, I'll take my time with you, you piece of shit... and then I'll kill you!'

'Oh, very impressive, detective,' cooed Hammond. 'You almost gave me goosebumps. Now, you go and call Turner – there's a good dog. It's nearly six, Boyd. We'll talk again at half past and I want that location... or you'll hear us slice off a little piece of your daughter. How does that sound?'

# 46

'Jay, you big plank – you left your bloody Rizzlers in plain sight.' They were dangling from Karl's fingers as he opened one of the big oak doors for him.

Jay winced. 'Bollocks... That was dumb.'

'Yes, it fucking well was.'

'Was it Boyd?'

Karl nodded. 'Yeah, one DCI Boyd and three other knuckle-draggers.'

Jay stepped inside and Karl closed the brewery's main door with a booming thud. 'Boyd's no knuckle-dragger,' he said. 'He's smart.'

'Well, he didn't mention the Rizzlers, so maybe not so smart,' Karl said, handing them over. 'Where did you go?'

'Wetherspoons,' replied Jay.

Karl shrugged. 'Classy. There's more atmosphere down here,' he said, indicating the basement and the dust-covered innards of the brewery.

'What did Boyd say?' Jay asked.

'He asked about our history. Childhood stuff. Were we close? Did we see each other much? That kind of thing.'

'And you said?'

'All the time. We're like besties,' Karl said, grinning.

Jay dropped a brow. 'Right. Hilarious.'

'I told him we don't see each other much. Once or twice a year.' Which wasn't far off the truth. 'Are you sure this Boyd guy is actually on your side? I mean... he didn't give me any vibes that he was.'

'He is,' replied Jay. 'He's solid.'

'Bruv, seriously,' Karl said. 'He's a cop and he's got a job to do.'

'We're friends,' Jay said stubbornly. 'He'd have been going through the motions.'

'Yeah, well, Brutus and Caesar were friends. And that didn't work out so well, did it?' Karl pointed out.

'I trust him.'

Karl shrugged again. 'Fair enough. It's your scalp, not mine.'

'How long ago did they leave?' asked Jay.

Karl tapped a code into a number pad by the main door, and an unseen bolt *clunked* into place. 'About three hours ago. Come on, Jay... The dust down here plays havoc with my allergies.'

They climbed the metal stairs back up to Karl's apartment. 'I'm going to order in some Chinese,' said Karl. 'Any requests?'

'Ribs,' said Jay.

Karl smiled. 'Of course, ribs.' He was about to dial when Jay's burner phone buzzed in his back pocket. He pulled it out quickly.

'Sam?'

'Hey, baby,' she replied. 'How are you coping?'

'Okay, so far,' Jay replied. 'I think. What about you?'

'There've been, uh... developments,' she replied briskly. 'Boyd's here with me. I'm going to put you on speaker phone. Hold on...'

Jay studied the tiny buttons on his cheap Nokia and saw that it, too, had a speakerphone button. He did the same.

'Hello, you there, Jay?' Boyd's voice suddenly echoed around the cavernous room.

'Hey, guv!' Jay replied.

'Where are you?' Boyd asked.

'Back at Karl's place.'

Karl shot him a *WTF are you doing?* look.

'Say hi, Karl,' said Jay.

'Jesus...' Karl muttered. 'Hello... again, Detective Boyd.'

'Karl,' Boyd replied. 'Now, Jay, listen. The Salikovs have grabbed Emma.'

'Oh shit,' Jay said.

'They're talking about a deal – you for Emma,' Boyd continued. 'But I don't trust them. Not for one second. I need you to keep yourself safe, Jay. That way we've got leverage for Emma. Do you understand?'

'Shit' was Jay's response. He bit his lip. 'Jesus, this is all my fault, guv. I'm... so –'

'There's no time for this,' Boyd said. 'They're calling me back in less than half an hour. They want your location.'

And now Jay could hear the emotion in Boyd's voice. 'Okay,' he replied. 'Okay. What do you want me to do, guv?' He could see where this was heading. It was a very simple equation. His life for Emma. And he'd caused this. The least he could do was make it right.

'Surely they can be stalled,' cut in Karl. 'I mean... look, if Jay's the prize and your daughter is the only way they can get him... we've got bargaining space, right?'

'What we have is twenty-five minutes,' Okeke replied.

'So we need a plan,' said Boyd. 'And fast.'

'I counted just four of them,' said Okeke slowly. 'And one of them was just that prat Hammond...'

There was silence on both ends of the call as they all digested this.

'These Russian dudes, I presume, have guns?' said Karl eventually. 'I mean, I'm no expert, but we can't win against guns.'

'With the element of surprise on our side,' said Jay, 'maybe we've got a chance...'

# 47

'Why... why is it so important?' asked Emma hesitantly.

Roland looked up from his phone. 'What?'

'Why do you *have* to kill Jay? He... he's a good guy,' she said.

The three goons had disappeared. More precisely, Soprano was somewhere outside having a cigarette. Gregor and Ronaldo had spied a KFC across the car park and had gone to get a family bucket.

'It's business,' Roland replied. 'Now do please shut up. I'm thinking.'

The dog whimpered from the back seat. 'Could you at least cut the tape around his muzzle,' asked Emma. 'He's struggling to breathe.'

Roland turned to look at her. 'And what? Let him bite me?'

'He won't,' she replied. 'He thinks you're a friend now.'

'That I very much doubt.'

However, Roland was a big believer in the cyclic nature of karma; a good deed now could well play a part in resolving this shitty mess later. He got out of the car, and Soprano whipped round.

'Relax,' said Roland. 'As you were.'

He fished inside his jacket and pulled out a flick knife. The very same one he'd used on that bouncer a few days ago. He opened the boot of the SUV and looked down at the trussed-up dog; it was making startled whale eyes at him.

'Easy mutt,' he said softly. He bent down, carefully ran the sharp blade along the silver-coloured tape and peeled it back. The dog's mouth opened immediately, and he thought the bastard was about to take a chunk out of his face; instead he got a grateful lick.

Mother had had a Jack Russell when he was younger. They were snappy little rat-faced yobbos that growled at him every time he returned home from boarding school and snarled every time he'd approach her for a polite hug.

He much preferred bigger dogs. They seemed less bad-tempered. 'Sorry about all this, old chap,' he said gently, ruffling the spaniel's long ears. 'It'll be over soon enough.'

With that, he closed the boot and got back into the warm vehicle.

'Thank you,' said Emma.

'I like dogs,' he replied curtly. 'Some, anyway.' He looked at his Rolex. Another twenty minutes and he was going to call that copper back.

'Bait?' repeated Okeke. She looked at Boyd.

'Yes,' replied Jay. 'I can be bait. For a trap. I'm up for it.'

Boyd rubbed his bristled chin absently. A trap sounded like the start of something possible, but they had to be open-eyed about this. They were up against three or four armed men. One of them, admittedly, was nothing more than a playboy wimp with a weak bladder... but guns had a habit of levelling things up for the weakest of arseholes.

'Karl, that brewery downstairs from you,' said Boyd, 'it's cluttered, full of blind spots. If we could lure them there, is it possible we could find a pinch point and jump them?'

*Christ, if Charlotte could hear me now.*

'It is,' said Karl. 'It's basically a giant metal labyrinth. It's full of pipes, vats, pumps... There are plenty of things to smack your head on and trip you up. It's perfect.'

'All right, then,' said Boyd. 'So that's our spot and Jay's our bait.' He looked at Okeke. She took a deep breath and nodded.

'We'll have the element of surprise...' he said, 'and it's Karl's home ground, but apart from that, what have we got?'

'I have a crossbow,' said Karl.

'Can you use it?' Boyd asked.

'Oh, yeah,' he replied. 'Short range it's as good as any gun.'

'That, I presume, means you're in?'

'For my big bro? Of course I'm in,' Karl replied.

'I'm in too, sir.' Boyd looked across the small lounge at Warren, who nodded. 'I'm serious, sir.'

'Warren,' Boyd cautioned, 'this isn't your problem.'

'I'm in. I'm not letting anyone else push me around tonight,' Warren said firmly. Seeing the confused expression on Boyd's face, he added, 'Don't ask.' Then, 'I've got a katana upstairs in my bedroom.'

'What the bloody hell's a –'

'It's a Samurai sword,' Jay answered.

'I've got a taser, guv,' said Okeke. 'And some PAVA spray.'

Boyd nodded slowly. 'Of course you have.' He ran a finger along his lips. 'So it looks like we're doing this.'

He was acutely aware that he was the one most invested in this plan. Jay could've run, Okeke too. And Warren? The lad was an innocent bystander.

'Thank you,' he muttered. Then cleared his throat. 'I mean it. Thanks. All of you.'

Emma, hands now bound in front of her, accepted a chicken drumstick from Roland. She wasn't hungry in the slightest, plus she didn't eat meat, but from the depths of her memory came a nugget of pop psychology: that this small gesture now might lead to a life-saving moment of hesitation from her abductor later.

'Thanks...' she said, taking a bite out of it.

Outside the SUV, the three Georgians tore hungrily into the bucket of deep-fried chicken. Roland, however, pulled a face at the greasy chicken, opting to stick with the fries.

Ozzie had wriggled onto his bound feet and a pair of nostrils were flaring over the headrest. 'Give him a fry,' Emma said. 'You'll have a friend for life.'

Roland nodded. 'Here you go, boy.' He pulled one from his carton and watched it vanish instantly as he dangled it over the back seat.

*Connect with him. Talk.*

'You... you're not what I expected,' she said. 'You know, as a Russian mafia boss?'

'Half... and not even Russian,' he replied. 'Half Georgian. There's a difference.'

'Do you speak any... whatever the others speak?' she asked.

'Georgian.' He shook his head. 'I tried. But I was raised in the UK.' He shrugged. 'What's the point, though? Anybody with common sense and enough roubles to bribe their way in comes to Londongrad.' He grinned. 'They love it here. They've all been working on their English for years.'

'Is that what this is all about... just money?' Emma asked.

He shook his head and laughed. 'Just money? There's no such thing as *just money*. You might as well call oxygen "just oxygen".' He glanced at his men outside. 'Money is what makes those peasants do *exactly* as I say. If you had more than money than me, I'd be the one with gaffer tape around my wrists.'

'Roland... is that your first name?'

He nodded. 'Roland Sebastian Octavian Hammond. You know, once upon a time the Hammonds were established *old money*. English old money, that is.'

'But not now?'

He looked at her. 'That's why my mother married a Georgian twenty years her senior.' He pulled a face. 'She got herself a billionaire, and Rovshan got himself a trophy wife and a golden visa. A mutually beneficial arrangement. It worked out well.' He laughed humourlessly. 'And then they had me. The spare heir.' He looked down at his watch again. 'All right – it's nearly showtime...'

'Roland?'

He looked up at her. 'What?'

'Please... tell me...' She took a deep breath. 'Am I going to survive tonight?'

Roland turned back to his phone.

'There's got to be a way that nobody gets killed tonight, right? It's got to be –'

'Enough!' he snapped. 'Be quiet and eat your chicken.'

# 48

'We lure them into the brewery, lock them in and call 999: *Gunshots heard inside this address. Hurry. Send armed police.* That sort of thing,' suggested Karl.

'That's if they *all* go in,' replied Boyd. Karl's suggestion didn't account for one or more of them being parked up somewhere nearby with Emma in the boot. 'If they hear blues-and-twos coming, the driver will be off.'

'With Emma,' Okeke added. 'That doesn't work, Karl.'

Boyd checked his watch. It was 6.29 p.m. 'Okay, we're going to have to park this. Hammond will be calling me any second.'

'Good luck, guv,' said Jay.

'Thanks. I'll call you back as soon as we're done.' Boyd ended the call and looked down at his phone's screen, waiting for it to light up again.

'*Clement. Lamb. Vigour,*' said Okeke. 'Do you want me to write the location down?'

Boyd nodded. His mind was racing. They'd picked a What3-words address in the very middle of the building, rather than at the entrance. He was in two minds about it. If Hammond suspected a trap, then a location that required them to go into the old brewery screamed ambush. He'd just have to hope that Hammond was as stupid as he looked.

'It's going to be okay, sir,' said Warren. 'We've got this.'

The phone suddenly lit up in his hand – *Unknown Caller*.

'Right then,' he muttered, and tapped the screen to answer. 'Boyd.'

'Have you made contact with Turner?' asked Hammond.

'Yes.'

'Right. And did he tell you where he is?'

'He told me where he'll be staying later tonight. Yes,' Boyd answered.

'Well, I want to know where he is *right now*, not where he'll be *later*!'

Boyd wasn't certain where Hammond was calling from. Emma had blurted 'Hastings'. He hoped they still were and hadn't got a head start on the way to Brighton. Either way he had to build in time to allow them to get to Karl's place first.

'I don't know where he is as we speak,' he said. 'He's scared, obviously. It sounded like he was in a public space. A pub or a bar maybe.'

'So how long is he staying there?' Hammond asked.

'Until closing time, I expect,' Boyd said.

'And then – good grief, this really is like pulling teeth. Where will he be later, Boyd?'

'He has a place to bunk down. That's where his stuff is.' Boyd took the scrap of paper from Okeke. 'It's a What3words location. Do you use that?'

'Yes. Of course, I'm not an idiot.'

Boyd read out the words and Hammond repeated them back to him.

'That's it.'

'One moment.' Hammond put him on hold. A moment

later he was back on. 'That looks like a business premises to me.'

'Yes, that's what I thought too.' *Distract him.* 'May I speak to Emma again?'

'Your daughter's fine. Is Turner with anyone else or is he alone?'

'Alone. He doesn't know who to trust. He doesn't know anyone in Brighton. I want to speak to Emma now.'

'You'll get to speak to her again once I have Turner. I'll call you again when we've found him.' The call ended abruptly. Boyd lowered the phone. He realised his hand was shaking.

'Guv?'

He looked up at Okeke and Warren. 'I think he's going for it.'

'Did he give a specific time?' asked Okeke.

He shook his head. 'It's unlikely they're anywhere near Brighton yet. Doesn't make sense for them to set off without knowing which direction to head. When they arrive, I expect they'll stake out the building and wait for Jay to turn up, hoping to get him before he goes inside. We need to make a move.' He stood up. 'We have to get there ahead of them.'

Okeke and Warren got up quickly.

'Warren, you're with me. You drive.' He realised his hands were too shaky to take the wheel himself. 'Okeke, we'll meet you there.'

'On it.' She grabbed her bag and headed for the front door.

'Sam!' he called out after her.

She stopped.

'I'll call you when we arrive. Let you know if the coast's clear.'

She nodded, pulled the door open and was gone.

Boyd turned to Warren. 'You'd better get your ninja sword.'

JAY CARRIED the old wooden mannequin down the metal stairs, its wooden peg-feet clanging loudly on each step in the darkness as he descended to the brewery's abandoned work floor. It was heavier than it looked.

'Are you okay down there, Jay?' Karl asked.

'I need a light here or I'm going to go arse over tit,' Jay complained.

'Wait for me at the bottom. I've got a torch,' Karl said.

The clanging finally stopped as he touched down on concrete. The plan – which was a pretty big word for what they had come up with – seemed wildly optimistic. They were setting up a 'squat' among the innards of the defunct brewery, which basically meant putting this stiff, cumbersome and utterly unconvincing Victorian window dummy into a sleeping bag and making it look as though it was huddled around a glowing camping light.

Karl joined him at the bottom of the stairs, a sleeping bag under one arm and a full carrier bag in the other.

'What have you got there?' Jay asked.

'Some more props,' Karl informed him. 'A thermos, radio, tins of food. Some beer. Gotta make it real, right?'

'I like your thinking.'

'There's a couple of large empty drums in the middle of the floor. I guess fermenting vats. We could set up in one of them.' Karl panned the torch towards the dust-choked labyrinth of pipes and valves in front of them.

'This looks good.' Jay nodded. 'Perfect.'

The space resembled a tangled jungle made from scrapyard junk. Not only was the ground floor crammed with the bowel-like clutter of pipes and valves, but it had also become a depository for all the office furniture and bric-a-brac that presumably had occupied the floor above once upon a time. There were wooden chairs and old desks, filing cabinets and stools all stacked untidily in what little floor space was left.

'Follow me,' said Karl. He stepped forward, picking his way past some wooden bar stools – they had nice, thick oak legs and padded leather seats – ripe for upcycling, Jay noted. 'Mind the trip hazards,' Karl pointed out.

Jay glanced at the brick floor. There were potholes where loose bricks had been dislodged, creating block-shaped, ankle-breaking dips in the ground. He hefted the heavy mannequin onto one shoulder and had just begun to follow Karl when he felt his Nokia buzz in his pocket. 'Hold on a sec, bro.'

He set the mannequin down, fished out the phone and answered the call. 'Have they called yet?' he asked.

'Yes,' replied Boyd. 'Warren and I are on our way over. Sam's bringing up the rear.'

'Is Sam okay?' Jay asked, concerned.

'She's tooling up,' Boyd said. 'Listen, Jay... I told them you sounded like you were in a pub and were planning to stay as late as you could. So that's hopefully going to buy us a few hours to get ourselves in place and ready.'

'Are you sure?' Jay asked.

'No, I'm *hoping*,' said Boyd. 'I think they've only just left Hastings. They wouldn't have known which way to head until I told them. Plus, I think I heard seagulls their end.'

'There're seagulls here too, you know, guv?' Jay pointed out.

'Right, fair point. Jay, listen. Set up the bait and get yourself hidden as quickly as possible. I'll text you when we're close.'

'We're gonna set up a camp inside a huge beer vat,' said Jay. 'Make it look like I've been hiding out in there.'

'That's good,' Boyd said.

'You've seen what it's like downstairs?' Jay asked.

'Briefly. A bloody mess.'

Jay chuckled. 'It's ambush heaven, guv. They won't know what hit them.'

'Hopefully. That's the plan.'

'You ever see that film *Predator*, guv? You know the one with the invisible a–'

'Jay?'

'Yeah?'

'Crack on, eh?'

'Right.'

'I'll contact again when we're close. All right?'

'Roger that.' Jay ended the call and tucked the phone back into his pocket. Karl was looking at him.

'He said we've got to get this done super quickly,' said Jay. 'We could have visitors at any time.'

'Shit,' Karl said. 'Okay then... Let's do this.'

# 49

Roland was relieved to be on the move again. Sitting around waiting was like meekly asking Fate to pick a direction and decide the future. Waiting was for farm animals in slaughter pens. Not for him.

He had the girl's mouth taped up. He was onto her. She was chatting to distract him. Chatting to try to forge a bond with him. Well, that little plan of hers had been swiftly foiled with a rag in her mouth and some gaffer tape over her flapping lips.

He'd taped the dog back up too. If it suffocated, so be it. Once they'd put a cap in Turner's head, they could do this girl and her dog, firebomb the place with petrol and make like ghosts into the night.

A few hours from now he'd be back in his penthouse flat, washing the smell of petrol and blood off his hands, and those vulgar apes could grunt back to whatever basement cage Rovshan kept them in.

And he could relax once more.

The really annoying thing was that he shouldn't have been bothered with any of this. None of it. If Mummy, the silly bitch, hadn't had one of her gin-fuelled panic attacks and caught him

ALEX SCARROW

off guard ringing him like that, he wouldn't have been overheard by Tweedledum and Tweedledumbass outside the club.
His endeavour would have been well on its way to a quiet and
very satisfactory conclusion.

The old man would be lingering at death's door by now,
confused and weak. Mummy would be dutifully weeping her
crocodile tears on one side of his bed and he would be on the
other, reassuring the insane old bastard that the Salikov business would be safe in his hands. And mere inches away from
him, on his father's bedside table, dissolved and undetectable
in his herbal tea, would be the cause of his rapidly deterio-
rating condition.

Roland's FSB contact at the embassy had told him they
called the slow-acting nerve agent Blue-T. Blue because of the
gradual but increasing hypoxia it caused over several weeks.
The prisoners they'd tested it out on had died with discoloured
gums – the normal healthy pink had been reduced by the
absence of oxygen in the blood to an almost blue-grey hue.

The 'T' part of the name hadn't been explained. *Maybe T for
toxin?* he wondered.

The agent had provided him with a bottle of liquid with an
eyedropper lid and instructions that just one drop a day would
do the job, untraceably, within a month. Any more than that
would accelerate the hypoxia and attract suspicion. The initial
symptoms would be fatigue, fuzzy-headedness, an inability to
concentrate. Given that Rovshan had been working long hours
over the last year to smoothly migrate his fortune to London,
those symptoms would be seen as work exhaustion.

Nothing that some bed rest and a nice cup of tea couldn't
fix.

His mistake had been assuming that Mummy Dearest
would actually fucking cope. All she had to do was add one
drop of the bloody stuff to Father's tea every morning and, since
he was paranoid right now that *they* might be after him, he

retained no domestic staff. There were no butlers, Michelin-star chefs or suspicious housekeepers to peer over her shoulder. It was simple. Or should have been.

Roland checked the maps app on his phone. They were roughly halfway there, approaching a town called Lewes. But the traffic was slow-going. It was nearly seven in the evening and the little people were still grinding their way home in their little cars.

In broken, appalling, Russian he told Gregor that, once they arrived, the other two were to go in, find Turner and deal with him. They should take an ear and then torch the place. He and Gregor would stay in the vehicle.

Gregor nodded and then elaborated the plan in Georgian to Ronaldo and Soprano.

'OKAY, so I think it looks totally staged,' said Karl. 'I mean, it looks like what it is: a mannequin wearing a hoodie, propped up on a fricking chair.'

Jay nodded. The camp chair was a bad idea. It looked like a poorly crafted diorama in a rundown museum. 'Yeah, it's a bit much. Right, back to plan A, then: I'll just lie him down in the sleeping bag.' He lifted the bulky thing off the chair and laid it down on the floor of the vat.

The vat had an access hatch at the bottom, there presumably to allow someone inside to clean it out between batches of whatever hooch they'd once brewed here. Jay squatted down and peered out at the dark labyrinth outside.

They only needed it to appear convincing enough for one of the Russians to crawl in to get a closer look. Jay would be waiting inside, out of view – and whoever had drawn the short straw and looked inside was going to get a plank to the head.

Meanwhile, Karl would be tucked away in a dark nook

further within the tangle of pipes and abandoned furniture with a clear sniper's view of the vat's crawl-space entrance. The moment Jay whacked the first one, he'd take out the next with his crossbow. With two men down, the odds of success would be way better.

Jay propped a balled-up jumper under the mannequin's head and pulled the sleeping bag over the oversized Pinocchio figure. He switched on the camping lamp and the radio, dialling it to Heart FM and dipping the volume so that it was little more than the leaking tsk-tsk-tsk of a pair of large, ill-fitting headphones.

'All right,' said Karl. 'We'd better hide.'

~

'THAT'S THE ENTRANCE,' said Boyd.

Warren turned off St George's Road, then drove through a narrow archway and down a gently sloping ramp into the cobblestone mews.

'Just here will do,' he said.

Warren parked up and turned off the engine.

'What now, sir?' he asked.

'Sit tight,' Boyd replied. 'I'm going to do a recce. Keep your eyes peeled for an SUV.'

He got out of the car, gently closed the door and poked his head round the corner to check out the enclosed area. It was 7.41 p.m. The row of boutiques opposite the old brewery were closed, but several lights from inside them spilled across the damp cobblestones. A light aerosol drizzle was producing a bloom of amber around the single street light and a gentle soothing hiss. He could hear the muted sound of music coming from a cabaret bar on the corner of St George's Road and Paston Place and the occasional swish of passing tyres on wet tarmac.

He couldn't see any other parked vehicles in the mews, nor, more to the point, any suspicious, lurking figures. It looked as if they'd beaten the Salikovs there. He pulled back out of view and sent a quick text to Jay's phone.

Boyd here – outside Karl's. Where are you?

A moment later the reply buzzed back.

Inside. Trap set. Hiding. Locked and Loaded.

Boyd couldn't help a fleeting smile. Jay's naively cavalier banter felt like a reassuring force field; fate or fortune tended to take care of the recklessly optimistic. It was the wary, worried or vexed who tended to wind up splattered. Just ask Wile E. Coyote.

We're waiting on Sam. Going to check her ETA. Sec...

Jay's reply came back swiftly.

Copy that, guv.

Boyd dialled her phone. She answered after the fourth ring.

'Guv?'

'Yup,' he replied softly. 'Me and Warren are parked outside Karl's place. It looks like we've got here first.'

'Thank God,' she replied.

'Where are you?'

'Fifteen minutes out. I'm just entering Brighton now. How's Jay doing?'

Boyd managed another smile. 'He's ready. Look, park up on St George's Road *outside* the mews. Come on foot to join us. Let's have a car outside the area that we can get to if we can't get to mine.'

'Makes sense.'

'I'm going to speak to Jay, to see what their set-up is, and I'll call you back.'

'Okay.'

He ended the call and dialled Jay. It took a while for him to answer.

'Guv? I thought we're on silent running. Texts only?' he said.

'Just don't shout,' Boyd replied. 'How have you rigged things in there?'

Jay explained. It sounded clever. Very clever.

'Nice one,' said Boyd. 'We're going to find a place nearby to hide the car.'

'There's, like, a narrow rat-run beside the building,' Jay told him.

Boyd squinted into the orange gloom. He could see a narrow alleyway running down the right-hand side of the old brewery. 'I'm looking at it,' he confirmed. 'We might tuck ourselves down there. That'll give us eyes on the entrance.'

'Aren't you coming in?' Jay asked.

'No. We'll be the early warning,' Boyd said. 'If all four men get out of the car and enter the brewery, Okeke can grab Emma, and me and Warren will sneak into the brewery behind them as backup.'

'What if they split into pairs?' Jay wondered.

Boyd suspected Hammond was likely to do that – send in the heavies while he sat tight in his SUV. 'Then I'll figure something out. You just focus on jumping whoever sticks their ugly mugs into your trap.'

'No probs, guv. Me and Karl have got this.'

'Okay.' Boyd smiled. 'Thanks again, Jay.'

'It's just like old times, eh, guv? This time last year or thereabouts? Team Boyd versus the bad dudes!'

Boyd shook his head. 'Right, yup, we should plan to do this every year.'

He heard Jay chuckle.

'Stay sharp, big man.'

'Will do, guv.'

Boyd ended the call and returned to the car. 'Warren, take the car to the end of that alley. We need to get it off the mews,' he said. The entrance was cluttered with wheelie bins and a stack of wooden pallets. Good. He could put those back after Warren had driven through, to try to disguise the entrance. It would also be a handy place to observe the old brewery from.

Boyd got out. 'I'll clear a way through. Take the car down as far as you can go. See if there's an exit at the far end as well. This might be our run-like-hell escape.'

'Yes, sir.'

He closed the door gently, jogged over towards the bins and began to clear an opening for the car. A moment later Warren eased it through the gap and rolled slowly into the cluttered alley. He paused beside Boyd and lowered the window.

'You want some help?' he asked.

'No, you stay with the car,' Boyd replied. 'If this situation goes tits up, I want you already behind a wheel and good to go.'

'Right.' Warren leant over the back seat and picked up his samurai sword. 'Do you want this?'

Boyd looked at it sceptically. 'Is it – no offence, Warren – a proper sword?'

'You mean, is it sharp?' Warren nodded. 'Very. You can actually cut paper with it.'

Boyd winced. He imagined he'd end up doing more damage to himself than anyone else. All the same, at the moment he was armed with nothing more than his fists.

'All right, I'll take it. Thanks,' he said.

# 50

They entered Brighton on the Moulsecoomb road, heading south towards the seafront.

Gregor twisted in the front seat. 'We nearly here.'

Roland nodded. They had several hours to go before the pubs served last orders and began turfing out their customers. He was in two minds as to whether or not to head straight for the What3words location Boyd had given him, to try his luck. Maybe Turner was already tucked up for the night? It probably made more sense to sit tight and wait for the rest of Brighton to settle down and go to sleep, especially if he was going to burn Turner's hidey-hole to the ground.

He glanced at the jerrycan of petrol in the footwell. He was right: firebombing the place after they'd capped Turner was the right move. It would destroy any forensics left behind and delay, if not prevent, the body's identification. Fires tended to hide a multitude of sins and left in their wake a useful and prolonged smokescreen.

'Tell him to find somewhere nearby that we can park,' said Roland. 'We'll sit tight for a bit.'

JAY WAS GETTING bloody cold inside the damp metal vat and was beginning to cramp up. He wondered if this hastily thrown-together plan was going to wind up getting them all killed. He'd spent an hour so far crouched on the wet floor beside 'Steve' – his wooden sleeping wooden companion – which had proved more than enough time for second thoughts to kick in. The four of them – five, if Sam's colleague, DC Warren had come along – had chosen to square up to four Russian mobsters. If this had been a film, they'd have been pretty good odds...

*Because, let's face it, bad guys in movies can't hit shit with their guns.*

But this wasn't a film, he reminded himself. It was real-world. Which meant that bad-guy bullets tended to follow the laws of physics rather than the on-screen requirement for a convenient and happy ending.

There was another alternative here. He could give himself up. Once he heard that oak door creak open, he could emerge from his hiding place and let them know he was there and ready to exchange himself for Emma.

She was a good kid. Far too young to be involved in something like this. Certainly far too young to end up in a ditch with a bullet in her head. And all this was his fault anyway. If he'd taken Sam's advice and left this to the police...

Or maybe he could just charge at them – do a Jason Statham, karate-kick the crap out of them all and save the day.

*Jesus-effing-Christ. You're not Jason Statham! You're a part-time furniture restorer and door-monkey for a strip club.*

So maybe not. He'd get a yard towards them and then drop dead like a slab of beef on the ground. His have-a-go hero moment would be over before it had begun. The guv was probably right. He should sit tight and stay quiet. Karl was right too

– they had the element of surprise, and this was the perfect place to pull that off.

Christ, though. All this... *all this*, because he and Louie had decided to sneak a quick spliff away from the entrance to CuffLinks...

~

*Louie took a long pull on the joint, leant back against the brick wall and handed him the glowing doobie.*

*'Cheers,' said Jay. 'Hello, you big beauty.' He grinned as he welcomed the crinkled roll-up.*

*'Shit,' muttered Louie. 'Tonight's really dragging out, isn't it?'*

*Jay nodded. He'd much rather have been back in his workshop, some chilled music on the iPhone, a cup of tea and digestive biscuit on the side, and applying the finishing touches of lacquer to Mrs Patton's La Rochelle.*

*One day, one bloody day, he was going to make his passion pay more than pocket money. Hastings was a treasure trove of antiques locked away in attics and basements, corners of care homes and dusty mezzanine floors. Forgotten lovelies that could be restored with little effort and upsold to gullible DFLs with fat wallets.*

*His silent reverie was interrupted by Louie gently nudging him. He was grinning. 'Hello,' he whispered, 'Someone's throwing their teddies out...'*

*Jay cocked his head.*

*'No, listen! No... stop. STOP! Just listen!!'*

*Some bloke was having a hissy fit on his phone. Louie nodded at the entrance to their smoking alley. Someone, maybe the phone guy, had paused just out of view, the breath from their mouth drifting across the entrance like clouds from a steam train.*

*'You need to keep doing it!' The voice sounded young. A voice that had either broken late or was eternally doomed to remain marooned*

in a higher-than-normal register. 'If you stop, he'll get better. Don't you get it?'

Jay turned to Louie and mouthed 'fuck'. Louie did the same.

'Oh, you think?' continued the man. 'He's not an idiot.'

There was another long pause, during which the man finally stepped into view. Jay and Louie instinctively pulled further back into the darkness.

'No, it's <u>not</u>. Not if you know what to look out for. And he will — trust me. It's blue tea...'

Jay realised he was holding his breath in case a cloud of his own breath drifted from the darkness into the light cast from the lamp across the street.

'Just keep your shit together, all right?' The young man stepped slowly past the alleyway entrance. 'Right... well, just calm the fuck down.'

Louie suddenly sneezed. Loudly. 'Shit,' he mumbled.

The man on the phone was now completely silent. Louie gave Jay a nudge to say, 'I got this,' and quickly emerged from the alleyway, disappearing round the corner and out of view.

'Hey, mate...' he heard Louie say in a lowered voice, 'you might want to watch what you say out loud in future, eh?'

There was a long pause. Then: 'What the hell did you just hear?'

'Nothing that I want to know about, old son,' Louie responded with a friendly laugh. 'But... I won't be drinking any tea you make, any time soon.'

There was another, very, long pause.

'So? Are you coming in or what?' asked Louie.

'Yes,' the man replied slowly. 'Yes... I am.'

JAY CHECKED HIS WATCH. It was 8.37 p.m. He'd been crouched in the vat for over two hours now and was wondering how much charge was left in the camping lamp's battery. The lamp was important; it was there to draw them in like moths, to allow them to see that their prey was sparked out on the floor in his sleeping bag and safe to approach.

He decided to check in with Karl.

**You still there, bro?**

The ellipses bounced several times as he tapped a reply.

> **Y. But getting v cold now.**
> **Should have brought**
> **my own thermos.**

JAY'S MEMORY of that overheard conversation was still playing in his mind. The 'tea' comment was a detail he'd completely forgotten about.

**Have you heard of something**
**called 'blue tea'?**

> **Blue tea? Nope.**

**I think it might a kind of**
**Russian thing?**

Karl's reply took a few moments coming back.

> **It's blue-T, you muppet. The**
> **T stands for trimethyl**
> **mercury.**

**What's that?**

**VERY dangerous stuff.
Why you asking?**

**It's what this bloke mentioned
on the phone. I think he's
using it to poison someone.**

There was another long delay, during which Karl's jiggling ellipses came and went several times. Finally he came back with a reply...

**Shit. It's a toxin the Russian
spooks use. The Salisbury
poisoning guys.**

**Right. I knew that.**

**Sure you did. *eyeroll***

Jay let the screen on his phone go dark and then he whispered to himself.

'Bloody hell.'

# 51

Okeke parked her car on double yellow lines several dozen yards beyond the entrance to the mews. St George's Road was reassuringly busy. The cabaret club on the corner throbbed with noise from within and the scattering of boutique wine bars and restaurants along the road all seemed to be doing a brisk business. She grabbed her duffel bag from the back seat and slung it over her shoulder, then thumbed a quick text to both Boyd and Jay that she was parked up and coming on foot.

'Right,' she muttered under her breath. She ran a quick diagnostic on her mental state.

*Anxious? Yes.*

*Shitting it? Yes.*

*Ready? Ready as I'll ever be.*

'Here we go,' she said softly.

She walked as casually as she could back up the street towards the entrance to the mews, just in case the Salikovs were watching. The entrance was signposted with a list of the various little businesses that operated out of the units clustered within: a nail salon, a tattooist, a sandwich place and a few others – none that were likely to be open for business now. She paused by the entrance, lighting a cigarette to give her a reason to linger, and she scanned the faces she could see through the various windows. No one seemed to be looking at her or reaching for a phone.

Reassured, she ducked out of the drizzle and into the archway, down a short gentle slope of rain-slick cobblestones and into the dark enclosed space beyond.

BOYD HEARD THE FOOTSTEPS FIRST, then saw a shadow slanting up the brick wall like some old Hitchcock film. Okeke merged into view and she paused as she stepped into the gloomy cul-de-sac.

One solitary, fizzing street light bathed the cloistered area in a sinister, sulphurous orange that glistened off every slick surface.

He whistled to her softly. Her head turned his way and he waved her over.

'Any sign of them?' she asked.

'None yet,' he replied.

She dug into her duffel bag. 'Taser?'

'You have it. I've got Warren's ninja sword.'

'Then at least take the PAVA spray,' she insisted. 'Sword versus gun? I know where I'd put my money.'

He took it from her gratefully and stashed it in his coat pocket.

'Where's Warren?' she asked.

Boyd thumbed over his shoulder at the alleyway behind him. 'Down the far end with the car,' he replied. 'We're lucky. It's not a dead end, so if this all goes wrong, we've got that way out too.' He looked at her. 'How're you doing?'

'I'm ready,' she replied. She looked out at the mews,

towered over by the brewery on their side and opposite the grubby rear of a row of business-below, bedsits-above town houses.

'What's the plan?' she asked.

'We watch them come in and enter the building.' He pointed to his right. 'I'm guessing Hammond will lead from the rear and stay in the car.'

'So we'll have two, maybe three of them to deal with,' Okeke added.

He nodded.

'What about Emma?'

'If I can see an opportunity, I'll take it. Otherwise... we'll deal with the heavies first.'

'Deal with... as in *kill*?' she asked and gave him a shrug. 'I guess there's no such thing as being a little bit pregnant?'

Boyd chuckled softly. 'Well, we're here, right?' He waggled Warren's katana. 'It's us or them.'

'Christ...' She blew out a cloud. 'I can't believe we're actually doing this.'

'The last time round, if I recall correctly,' he said, 'we turned up with just a baseball bat and some pepper spray. We're marginally better off this time.'

Okeke looked down at the yellow-handled taser in her fist. 'I feel a little underdressed,' she said.

'Did you do a spark test on that?' he asked her.

She rolled her eyes, removed the protective cap and half-pressed the trigger. A blue spark arced from one spike to the other. 'It's good.'

'I just hope to God they've brought Emma along,' he said. 'And that she's all right.'

Okeke put a hand on his. 'Guv... they want Jay. He's why they're here. Their only leverage is Emma.' She squeezed. 'She'll be fine.'

Boyd nodded. She was right. 'Jesus Christ, Okeke... what kind of shit-stick plan have we just tossed together?'

She laughed. 'It's the best shit-stick plan we've got.'

# 52

Roland looked again at his watch. It was gone quarter past eleven. Their SUV was one of the last few vehicles dotted around the Marine Parade parking area. From here he had a clear view up Paston Place. The patrons emerging from the Bristol Bar, overlooking the seafront and the parking area, had thinned out.

An hour ago, it had still been buzzing with mid-week activity. Now, things were going quiet. Turner, if he'd been nursing a pint of beer out there somewhere, and if he had any wits about him, had presumably been among the throng.

His men were getting twitchy, looking repeatedly at their watches too.

'All right,' he said to Gregor. 'Let's get this done.'

Soprano turned on the engine, pulled out of the parking spot and swung across the empty seafront road and into the street that Roland had been gazing down. As they drove slowly up Paston Place, Roland scanned the faces of people emerging from the wine bars and restaurants. Turner would be easy to spot. He was tall, broad, and his head was shaved to the wood.

Soprano drove up the gently sloping street and turned right

onto St George's Road. He slowed the car to a halt. They had stopped beside a building that looked like a Turkish desert fortress, with white-washed walls and a crenelated top. On the wall facing them was a sign – Bombay Bar – and beside that in absolutely fabulous lettering... *Proud Cabaret.*

*Christ*, mused Roland. *We've been lured into the bloody gay ground zero for Brighton and Hove.*

'What is it?' he asked. 'Why have we stopped here?'

Gregor pointed at an opening off the street a dozen yards beyond the nightclub's main entrance. 'Location is down there.'

*Dammit.* Virtually right next door to this club. He wondered if that was deliberate. For the first time he wondered if this was some kind of set-up. No. More likely that Turner felt safer hiding out close to a busy venue, he reasoned.

Except it didn't look that busy tonight.

'Well, what are you waiting for?' he replied. 'Let's ruddy well get this done.'

Soprano rolled forward along St George's Road, turning right into a tight archway that led down a short ramp into what appeared to be a small cobblestone courtyard. He immediately switched the SUV's headlights off and stopped, blocking the way in or out.

They waited in silence for a moment, listening to the *tac-tac-tac* of drizzle on the windscreen as their eyes adjusted to the amber gloom cast from a single desultory street light.

'Turner is there...' said Gregor, pointing towards what appeared to be some sort of old warehouse. Its brick walls had been painted white, a *long* time ago, and what little paint remained clung to them in ragged pale patches like an unpleasant skin condition.

Ronaldo said something and Gregor replied.

'What did he say?' asked Roland.

'The dog. What to do with dog?'

He glanced behind to see the top of the spaniel's head, two

glinting eyes and puckering nostrils. The vehicle obviously still reeked of KFC.

'Shoot?' offered Gregor. He shrugged. 'Not needed.'

The girl jerked in the seat beside him and pleaded something behind the gaffer tape, her eyes wide and glistening.

'We're not shooting the dog,' snapped Roland. He felt irrationally angered by that suggestion. 'We're not fucking savages over here, all right?'

Gregor shrugged again. 'You boss.'

Roland turned to Ronaldo. 'Walk him out onto the street. Tie him up somewhere.'

Gregor translated and the young man shook his head, but nevertheless climbed out of the SUV and opened the boot. He cut the tape that was bound the dog's paws, secured a tether of rope around his neck and jerked him out of the vehicle and down onto the ground.

'Hurry up,' snapped Roland.

He watched them walk up the gentle slope, through the archway and out of view.

'He'll be fine,' he said to Emma. 'Someone will find him in the morning.'

Ronaldo returned a couple of minutes later on his own and climbed back into the rear seat.

*Okay then...* Roland took a deep breath. *Showtime.*

JAY'S PHONE LIT UP. He had a text from Boyd.

They're here. Just parked up. Waiting.

He quickly tapped out an acknowledgement, then forwarded Boyd's message to Karl.

'Shit just got real,' he muttered under his breath. He took another look around the interior of the metal vat at their 'camp-out' scene. From where he was crouched inside, just beside the maintenance hatch, it still looked horrendously fake: Steve lying on his side under a sleeping bag, with a beanie pulled down over the round wooden head – it was a joke. The table leg Jay was clutching like a baseball bat suddenly felt as impotent as a wound-up wet tea towel.

*Come on, Jay. Stay cool.* The voice started out as Sam's, but then seemed to morph into Jason Statham's. *You got this, mate. You got the jump on these Russian pussies.*

Right. He did. The small transistor radio on the floor, warbling softly on what remained of its battery power, changed tunes to an eighties classic: 'Everybody Wants to Rule the World'.

He adjusted his grip on the leg and took a deep breath. 'Game on, pussies.'

*Attaboy*, voiced Jason Statham.

~

BOYD WATCHED the man return to the SUV without Ozzie. His first thought was that the bastard had just killed his dog. But then why walk him out into the street to do that?

*They've dumped him.*

For some reason that gave him a glimmer of hope. Maybe there was a sliver of humanity inside that vehicle. Someone – perhaps Hammond, maybe one of his thugs – was unwilling to slaughter an innocent animal.

The SUV was blocking the ramp out of the mews. Their only other escape route, then, was back down the alleyway where Warren was waiting.

He glanced at Okeke. She nodded, presumably noting the exact same thing.

So, this part of the plan was going to have to be fluid. It would be down to chance and opportunity. If Ozzie had been in that car, then Emma presumably was too. That was good. But, *somehow*, he was going to have to sneak up on the SUV, surprise and take out whoever was sitting in there with her, grab her and run for it.

Just then the doors of the SUV opened, and he counted three figures emerging from it. He looked again at Okeke and raised four fingers.

She nodded. *Yes... there were four of them.*

He watched them stretch, then reach into their jackets and pull out what appeared to be long-barrelled handguns.

Silencers. Of course, they had silencers.

*And I'm sitting here holding a samurai sword. Bloody marvellous.*

One of them, a stocky man, was carrying a jerrycan in one hand. Petrol. So they were going with the same MO as Nix, then. Whack the target, set the place on fire and slink away into the night.

The three men spread out slowly, cautiously studying the mews and the dark doorways to the small business premises opposite. Finally they focused their attention on the large double oak doors of the brewery. They approached it slowly, and Boyd and Okeke instinctively drew back deeper into the shadows of the alleyway as they drew closer.

One of the figures paused to look down into the alley. Silhouetted against the glow of the street light, his poise looked vaguely familiar to Boyd.

*We've met before.*

It wasn't Hammond. Then with a shudder he remembered – it was the wiry old bastard with bad teeth who'd nearly put a bullet in his face back at that trailer park a year ago.

# 53

Gregor was suspicious by nature. He was suspicious of the old brick building in front of him with its large oak doors. He was suspicious that the location they'd been given was this cloister-like enclosure with dim lighting and only one apparent point of egress. If he was planning an ambush, he'd pick a place just like this. He'd fought Afghans and Chechens in his time, and their tactics had been identical – lure the enemy into a pinch point, then fire from all sides.

But this was England. He doubted that their prey, a frightened nightclub doorman who was on the run from the police, was likely to have recruited a band of battle-hardened urban fighters to help him.

He glanced back at the SUV. Rovshan Salikov's heir – that cowardly, idiot man-baby – was hiding in the vehicle, 'bravely' guarding the girl. Gregor had no time for him and was giving serious thought to migrating his services to one of the other rich Russian families in Central London. Rovshan was an old man – and a sick man these days. When he died, there was no way Gregor wanted that idiot man-baby as his new boss.

Stupid bosses had a way of getting their minders killed.

Hector, his brother-in-law, set the jerrycan down and reached out with one of his big hairy hands for the old rusty hoop of one of the door handles.

'Wait,' said Gregor.

He snapped on a torch and inspected the entrance thoroughly, looking for sensors or tripwires, or any other simple device that their man might have erected to warn him that someone was entering the building. He could see nothing. He aimed the torch into the thin gap between the doors and looked for any sign of something set up on the inside. Again, nothing.

He turned to Hector. 'You and me will go inside,' he said in little more than a whisper. 'One headshot. A quick kill. Nothing more. We take a photo to show the job is done, then we burn this place.'

Hector looked at him. 'No ear?'

'Not this time.' Gregor looked over at his young nephew. 'Alek, you stay out here. You watch the car. You see anyone else enter, you text me. No shouting. Understood?'

Alek nodded.

Gregor gently leant against one of the big oak doors, testing it for any suspicious resistance. But it swung in gently with the softest of creaks.

KARL HAD BEEN FILLING his time on his phone, tapping increasingly worrying terms into the search engine on Tor, the dark-web browser, and getting equally unsettling results. The FSB, formerly the KGB, seemed to have more in common with a ruthless drug cartel than they did the intelligence-gathering organ of a global superpower.

They were, in all but name, an OCG with fingers in every criminal activity he could think of. So then it begged the question: what the hell was going on between them and the Salikovs? A turf war? A vendetta? A disagreement on the spoils? Why the hell would they want Rovshan Salikov poisoned?

And why the hell was his only surviving child doing it?

'What on earth have you stuck your foot into, bruv?' he muttered quietly.

He was half tempted to quietly extricate himself from his hiding place amid the tangle of discarded furniture and make a discreet exit while he still could, but then he heard it... the creak of a door slowly swinging inwards. He switched his phone off and tucked it away.

He caught a glimpse of light through the bowels of the brewery, reflecting off the wet brick floor, glinting off damp pipes and rusting storage hoppers. Then with a soft *snick* the light vanished.

*Shit. They're here.*

IN THE COMPLETE DARKNESS, Gregor's eyes gradually adjusted. His once-around with the torch had given him the lay of the land. It looked like some kind of defunct brewery: a nightmare to move around without torch light, but it would be better to sneak up on their prey in the dark rather than advertise their approach.

A minute passed and at last his eyes were acclimatised enough to make use of what little amber light was stealing in through the tiny, grime-encrusted windows. He could make out dim outlines and shapes. The basic geometry of the place. That was enough to forge a cautious start.

Hector nudged his arm and whispered, 'Gregor, look'.

He turned towards Hector's voice and spotted the muted glow of cool bluish light emerging from somewhere in the middle of the cluttered floor. It could have been the light cast from a smartphone screen. In fact, it probably was.

A smile made his teeth glint in the gloom.

*Fool. We have you.*

He led the way, slowly and silently advancing towards the faint light, pausing every few seconds to study the floor for trip hazards. Better him take point than clumsy Hector, who had all the agility and spatial awareness of a wounded elephant.

As he got closer, Gregor paused again. He could hear music playing softly. It echoed as if it was playing at the bottom of a deep well. It was an English pop tune that he vaguely recognised.

*The idiot*, he mused. His last quarry – that little weasel Gerald Nix – had been scared enough to hide himself properly. This guy was almost begging to be found.

He stepped carefully around a stack of wooden pallets and finally got a clear and direct view of where the soft glow was coming from: it looked like a water tank. There was a small oval hatchway near the ground, like the entrance to an igloo, and the pale light was spilling out from within.

Gregor glanced back at Hector and indicated with two fingers that he had eyes on the target. The fool was making their job too easy, quite literally: he was a fish that had hopped into a barrel, ready to be shot. Gregor continued forward, bearing right, until he had a clearer view of the inside of the container through the maintenance hatch.

The man was lying on his side in a sleeping bag on the floor, his back to the entrance – another dumb error. Beyond his sleeping form was a lamp – the source of the cool-blue-tinted light. He had a woollen cap pulled down over his head, to keep him warm.

Despite him looking fast asleep, it would be a mistake to assume he was. The music from the radio was broadcasting his presence and drowning any chance of his hearing the soft scrape or rustle of anyone approaching.

*Very well, little fishy.* They didn't need any information from the man; they just needed him to be dead. And a photo to prove it. Gregor cocked his head. *Perhaps we will have an ear. Then* Hector could scatter the petrol all around.

Gregor raised his gun and lined up the target down the extended barrel. He had a clear line of sight to the back of Turner's head.

He pulled the trigger and a muted *phut* spilled out from the silencer.

The body jerked slightly on impact. But that was all. He smiled.

*Quick. Clean. Done.*

~

JAY RECOILED. The mannequin's head had just twitched, like someone shaking an annoying fly off their face or sneezing silently. It took him a couple of seconds and the sight of several splinters of wood scattered across the floor of the drum to realise that Steve had just taken a shot to the head.

*Shit, shit, shit.*

He rose from his haunches until he was standing over the hatch and raised the table leg up over his head, ready to bring it down hard on the first thing that dared poke through. His whole body was trembling with fear and exhilaration.

*Come on, mate. Would Jason Statham be trembling?*

He heard a rasping voice whisper just outside the vat, followed by a man groaning with effort, then he saw the stark, bright beam from a torch flood in through the maintenance hatch.

A voice whispered softly as the beam angled around; a cloud of breath swirled in the light. Then, at last, Jay heard another tired groan and the rustle of clothing against the lip of the hatch. The torch entered first, held by a gloved hand, followed by an outstretched arm.

Jay fought the urge to swing down too early.

He needed to swing down on a head, not a hand.

There was another scraping sound against the side and a grunt of irritation, then finally a head of thick, closely clipped grey hair emerged into the vat, followed by a narrow pair of shoulders.

The man seemed to catch sight of something in his peripheral vision and looked up at Jay... Their eyes met for a brief instant.

Then Jay swung the table leg down hard.

# 54

The table leg came down with the precision of a guillotine, but the old man managed to raise an arm and deflect the blow with his elbow. His torch went flying across the vat as he collapsed forward into the container.

Jay raised the table leg to swing it down again, this time hopefully on the top of the scrawny bastard's head. But the old man moved with surprising speed, bringing his legs in behind him and rolling away to one side. Jay had to take a step forward to reach him.

The arm that had held the torch and taken the blow might well be broken but the other one was fine, and he noticed the old man fumbling inside his jacket for something. Jay caught sight of a gun, the extended barrel of a silencer making it too cumbersome to whip out quickly.

He swung down again on the hand holding the gun and knocked the weapon out of the wiry little git's fingers. It skittered across the floor of the vat and out of reach for either of them. Jay decided to go after it, stepping awkwardly over the mannequin in a bid to get to it first. But the old man caught his ankle and brought him down. A moment later he was on top of

Jay: lightweight but surprisingly strong. One hand went straight for his eyes, and Jay managed to close his eyelids a fraction before he felt sharp fingernails digging into them.

'Fuck off!' Jay yelled, shaking his head from side to side, trying to dislodge the man's probing razor-sharp fingers. He flailed blindly with his big fists, aiming punches at where he guessed the man's face was, but kept missing or landing ineffective glancing blows.

*I need to see, I need to see...!* The bastard could be pulling out a knife for all he knew. Jay pulled his head up and forward and managed to catch a couple of the probing fingers in his mouth. He bit down hard.

He heard the man scream as his mouth filled with blood and his teeth scissored down on yielding gristle and bone.

~

KARL HEARD the thwack and grunt of Jay launching his attack inside the vat. He could make out a second, thickset, man crouching down low just outside the hatchway, peering into see what the fuck was going on.

*Now, mate! If you're doing this... it has to be now!*

He lined up the sight of the crossbow on the side of the man's head and pulled the trigger. The bolt thudded home, but into his shoulder. The beefy man let out a howl of shock and staggered back from the open hatch.

Karl frantically pulled on the stirrup to recock the crossbow and fumbled for another bolt. With both of his hands shaking violently, he made a pig's ear out of setting the bolt the right way round on the barrel track, giving the startled Russian time to pull out a torch and aim it squarely at him.

He was dimly aware that he probably looked like an idiotic deer caught in the headlights of a speeding car. He didn't have time to check whether the bolt was set properly. Karl fired again. This time the shot went completely wide of the mark and clanged off something somewhere out in the darkness. Barely a second later, the wooden desk he'd been hiding behind lurched as a ragged hole appeared amid a shower of splinters.

Karl scrambled backwards out from his hiding place, but the crossbow's left arm got caught on the leg of an upended bar stool. He wriggled it frantically to free it, just as another ragged hole burst through the table right next to his head.

'Fuck, fuck, fuck!' he hissed as he struggled to free the crossbow from the clutter around him.

A third hole exploded through the desk, this time lower... He felt something punch his thigh. He screamed with the shock of it.

He finally managed to free the crossbow and stagger out of the sniper's nest of furniture. He needed to find another hiding place and quickly, so he could reload the crossbow and see how bad his leg was. He'd learned enough from films to know that if there was any spurting, he needed get pressure on it fast.

THEY HEARD the scream echo from within the building, and so did the third man waiting just outside the doorway. Boyd saw him step warily inside.

'Shit, they're going to need our help.' He got up and immediately felt Okeke's hand on his wrist. 'What're you doing?'

'It's Jay in there,' she hissed. 'Your focus is Emma.'

She was right, of course. 'Swap,' she said, holding the taser out for him. With her other hand, she grabbed the handle of Warren's katana and pulled it out of its sheath with a coarse rasp. She held her hand out for the PAVA spray.

'Sam...' he said, handing it over.

'You get Emma,' she replied, and she was gone, sprinting towards the brewery's open door.

Boyd looked back at the SUV. The dark windows were giving nothing away. If Hammond had heard the scream, he hadn't reacted yet.

Boyd emerged from the alleyway and hugged the pools of shadow as he sprinted across to the far side of the mews where the closed business units were. He waited for a moment in a doorway to see if his dash across the cobblestones had been spotted. But, still, there was no response: no car doors swinging open, no headlights. Nothing. Hammond wasn't paying close enough attention.

He began to creep forward, staying close to the doorways and shop windows, using the wheelie bins, pallets, empty delivery boxes as cover between his duck-and-run advances. He was now just a dozen yards from the side of the SUV and there was still no response from inside.

From where he was crouched, Boyd only had sight of the front bumper and hood of the vehicle. If he made a dash for it, one of several bad things was likely to happen: a door would open and a shot would come his way; the SUV would growl to life and reverse back out of the mews, taking his daughter with it; or, worst of all, he'd here the muted crack of a gunshot and his daughter's lifeless body would come tumbling out.

He ducked down low and dialled Warren's number.

The lad answered immediately. 'Boss?'

'It's all kicking off here. Warren... can you get the car out at the far end?'

'Yes. It's clear.'

'Bring it round. Block the archway to this place!'

'I'll... try, but...'

'Do it!' Boyd ended the call, unsure what his next move should be. Should he sprint for the vehicle or wait for Warren to block its escape?

OKEKE STEPPED in through the open door. She could hear objects clattering and falling in the darkness and the grunting and straining of two men locked in a close struggle somewhere nearby.

One of them was almost certainly her Jay.

She tried to map the layout inside from the faint outlines she could make out, and swiftly began to pick her way forward, heading towards the sound of the struggle – towards the flickering beam of torchlight that was sending confused, Escher-like shadows leaping across the brewery's low ceiling.

She held the can of PAVA spray out in front of her, finger on the nozzle, desperately regretting that she'd given the taser to Boyd. The sword she had in the other hand, the blade raised, but resting on her shoulder, ready to swing down if needed.

*Oh, fuck, it'll be needed.* She had just better be sure she didn't decapitate Jay or Karl by mistake.

She took several more cautious steps into the bowels of the ground floor, stopping suddenly as she bumped noisily against a metal drum that grated loudly along the brick floor. She stopped dead in her tracks and ducked down.

A torch snapped on just beyond the drum and swung wildly around. She heard a young man's voice calling out. 'Gregor? Hector?'

Footsteps approached and a moment later the young man who'd been waiting outside the door came into view, stepping past her, crouched in the rapidly diminishing shadow cast by his torch. He had his gun and torch aimed in parallel, checking the corners and nooks around him, just like in the films.

Then he began to turn her way.

She got up, leapt towards him and, as the dazzling torch beam illuminated her, she sprayed the PAVA where she hoped his face would be. The young man instantly let out a yelp of surprise and pain. The torch dropped from his grasp and clattered to the ground, but not the gun. Light strobed as he fired off four shots in rapid succession, aiming blindly, manically.

The torch was spinning on the ground like a sped-up lighthouse beam, picking out her, then him, then her, then... She got a glimpse of his face contorted with agony, eyes clamped shut, both hands holding the gun, the long barrel swinging wildly.

She brought the sword down instinctively, the blade biting deep into one of his wrists. The gun flickered again; this time she thought she felt the puff of displaced air whistle past her ear and she heard the clang of the bullet finding metalwork.

Without thinking, she jerked the blade free of his arm, pulled back and swung it horizontally. It made a whooshing sound. A sound that she knew was going to stay with her if she managed to survive tonight. Then it made contact, the momentum carrying it well into whatever part of him she'd managed to catch with her wild swing.

The gun clattered to the floor beside the torch.

It was immediately followed by her assailant, his legs buckling as he dropped to the ground, tugging the sword out of her hand and down with him.

As the spinning torch slowed down like a Wheel of Fortune, its beam settled on the man. He was on his knees, both hands holding onto the sword as if it was a lifeline. The blade was embedded in his left side, six inches below his armpit. His mouth was opening and closing; his eyes were rounded and glazed with shock.

He slowly wilted, like a time-lapse video of a snowman melting, and collapsed onto his side.

Okeke looked down at him and realised that he was young, barely in his twenties.

'Karl!! For fuck's sake... Gimme a hand!!!'

Jay's voice jerked Okeke out of her shock. She bent down,

scooped up the gun and torch and hurried towards the sound of the fight.

Jay had finally managed to leverage his bulk and strength to get on top of the older man and now had both his big hands around his throat. He was still unable to see what he was doing; his right eye was filled with blood streaming from a deep gash above his brow, the other eye was filled with grit, dust and tears. The scrawny little Russian goblin had managed to fumble blindly with his good hand, found the table leg and cracked Jay on the side of the head with it. The sharp end of a nail or screw sticking out of the wood had gashed his skin, but luckily not embedded itself into his skull.

So Jay was now effectively fighting blind, trying to blink through the crap in both his eyes to get a glimpse of what the old bastard was going to try next, while he did his utmost to throttle him.

Rather than wait to find out, Jay suddenly realised that knocking him senseless might be quicker. He lifted the man's head up by the neck and cracked it back down onto the ground. The man instantly stopped squirming. Just to be on the safe side, Jay did it a second time, then waited with his hands still around the man's neck for a few moments longer to see whether or not that had done the trick.

The man remained still. Jay took a chance and let go with one hand so that he could wipe the streaming blood out of his right eye.

The man seemed to be out cold.

He got up and looked around the floor of the vat. There, beside Steve's shattered wooden head, was the gun. He stepped over the sleeping bag and picked it up.

He briefly held the gun on the old man, wondering yet

again what Jason Statham would advise.

*Put a cap in him, old son. He'd do the same to you.*

If this had been another film, the decision would have been made for him. The old man would have suddenly reached for some hidden weapon and Jay would have had no choice. But instead he remained still. Concussed. Out for the count. Maybe already dead.

He heard movement outside the hatchway and swung the torch and gun towards it as a face peered in. 'Is that you, Sam?' he whispered hopefully.

'Oh, thank God,' she rasped. Then: 'The gun, sweetie... Lower. The. Gun.'

BOYD WAS JUST BEGINNING to wonder whether Warren had got lost when he heard the screech of tyres and an over-revved engine coming from St George's Road. The archway suddenly filled with the glare of headlights as Warren parked their car askew across the entrance.

And that *finally* triggered a response. The rear door of the SUV swung open beside Boyd and he heard a foot go down hard on the cobbles.

'Hey! Move your ruddy car!' Hammond screamed.

Boyd scooted quickly from behind the bin and crouched, hiding behind the open passenger-side door.

'Hey! I said MOVE IT!' Hammond shouted again.

Boyd peered over the rim of the door and saw that Hammond was approaching Warren's parked car, one hand gesticulating at him to move, the other holding a gun behind his back.

Another couple of steps up the slope and Hammond would be close enough to pop a shot at Warren through the wind-screen. He slipped the safety catch off the taser and raised his arm so that the red dot was aimed squarely at Hammond's back, right between the shoulders. It had been ten years since he'd had any training with one of these things, but the drilled-in procedure was to shout out a warning – 'officer with taser' – before pulling the trigger.

He pulled the trigger.

The cartridge lid blew off and the attached dart shot across and lodged into Hammond's back. He yelped in pain, but what he didn't do was immediately hit the deck and convulse. It had malfunctioned. Instead, Hammond spun round and raised his gun at Boyd's head.

'You cheeky fucking bastard,' Hammond actually screeched, and pulled the trigger. The glass of the open door shattered. Boyd decided not to trust the door's metal panelling to block the next shot and dived – well, more sprawled – over the SUV's still-warm hood to the far side.

Now on the driver's side he crouched, waiting to see if Hammond would come around the rear of the vehicle to finish him off. He tried to peer through the car's shaded windows, hoping to catch a glimpse of his daughter inside. Her face could have been mere inches away from him, but all he could see was his own frantic reflection.

'Just stay put, Boyd...' whispered Hammond. 'I only want to talk. Make a deal.'

There was a momentary pause. He could hear Hammond's ragged breathing. Hammond could undoubtedly hear his too.

'Your minders have been taken out,' Boyd said, hoping they had. 'So let's draw a line here. Just give me Emma, and you and me are done.'

'I need Turner dead, Boyd. You know that.'

'It's all over, mate. I know everything he knows. You're going to need to kill me too.'

There was no answer.

'You're in trouble, Roland. Aren't you? That's what this is

about, right? What is it? Some side deal? Some arrangement that's got you in a fix?'

He could hear Hammond breathing heavily.

'Look, backup's already on its way,' Boyd said. 'If you want to sort something out, we need to crack on with it...'

He heard the car door open and felt the SUV wobble as Hammond jumped in and got into the driver's seat.

'WAIT!' Boyd shouted.

The SUV roared to life and, with tyres screaming, it lurched backwards out of the mews, smashing into the side of Warren's parked car and pushing it effortlessly aside into the street.

Boyd hurried after them, just in time to see the SUV's red tail lights disappearing round a corner.

'FUCK!'

JAY AIMED the torch down at the body. 'That's the third one,' whispered Okeke. 'One was waiting outside, two went in.'

A crossbow bolt was lodged in one of the man's shoulders and another squarely embedded in the middle of his chest. He was dead.

'And you're sure it was just the three?'

She nodded. 'Plus, whoever stayed in the SUV.'

Jay looked left and right. 'Karl?' He raised his voice. 'Karl?! Where are you?'

They heard something scraping the ground. Okeke panned her torch around and called out, 'Karl! You okay?!'

'I'm pretty sure I need an ambulance here.' Karl's voice echoed out of the darkness. Her torch rested on him – he was slouched over a metal barrel with the crossbow lying at his feet and blood pooling on the brick floor around one trainer.

He flexed his foot. 'I can feel my leg still... That's a good sign, right?'

## 55

'He's going to live,' said Okeke. 'He has a broken femur, but luckily the bullet didn't hit any arteries as it passed through.'

Jay glanced at his brother, who was stretched out on his leather sofa. He was groaning softly, despite being loaded up with painkillers. Ozzie, who Warren had picked up, was sitting tidily beside the sofa, head cocking one way then the other with each moan.

'But he's going to need the hospital, right? Sam?' Jay said.

She nodded. 'Yes, of course. Stitches, a cast. Antibiotics. And an explanation, by the way, for what is quite clearly a bullet wound.' She picked up one of the mugs of black coffee on the kitchenette counter and took a slug.

'Guv?' She looked at Boyd. 'What now?'

Boyd cursed and lowered his phone. 'Hammond's not ringing.'

'Guv? We need to get a AFW out there. I mean, right now.'

He shook his head. 'If we do, we'll end up with a bloody siege.' He shook his head again. 'The bastard's totally lost it. He's...'

'At least put in an ANPR alert so we can track his whereabouts.'

'NO!' snapped Boyd. 'I don't...' He ran his fingers through his beard. 'Hammond's panicking. He's got a gun and he's got...' He couldn't say it; he picked his phone up and looked at it again.

They heard Warren's footsteps clunking up the stairs. 'Boss! I've parked the car out of sight, and I just checked –'

Okeke waved him over. 'The boss is busy... What is it?'

'I checked on the hitmen. They're dead. Stone-cold dead.' He bit his bottom lip. 'Jesus. Okeke... you actually used my sword! I mean, it's literally lodged in his –'

'I don't want to hear,' she cut him off. 'Really. I'm trying not to think about –'

'The other one's...' Warren muttered, and shook his head. 'It's a massacre down there.'

'Dammit!' Boyd slammed his phone down. 'Ring me, you bastard!'

'He won't yet,' said Okeke softly. 'He's probably on his way back to Hastings. He's –'

'Okay, just... shhh,' said Boyd. 'Let me think... Let me think.'

*Hammond's panicking. He's got Emma, a gun and he's probably driving like a maniac.*

The last thing Boyd wanted to add on top of that was a frantic high-speed car chase across several counties with Hammond likely to wrap his SUV around a tree, killing his daughter in the process. He just hoped that Emma was keeping cool, keeping her head down, and was strapped in.

*God, please let her be strapped in.*

'Guv,' Okeke prompted. 'We do need to think about our next move.'

He shook his head. 'I need to speak to him, Okeke! I need to talk him down!'

'Well, he'll want to speak to you too,' she said calmly. 'So let him get his shit together first. Let him find a pit-stop and call.' She grabbed his hand. 'He has Emma for a reason. She's his bargaining chip. Let's focus on how we work with that. On what we say when he does call. Okay?'

She was right. He looked up and nodded at her. 'Yes. Okay.'

Okeke let out a deep sigh. 'Fuck me, I need a cigarette.' She fumbled inside her jacket for a lighter.

'Out on the fire escape,' wheezed Karl. 'If you don't mind.'

'Just one thing?' cut in Jay. 'What do we do with those three bodies?'

'Two,' said Warren.

They all looked his way.

'Two bodies,' he said. 'Downstairs. One with a sword stuck in him, one with arrows.'

'Shit!' rasped Jay. 'I thought my guy was, you know... dead.'

'Didn't you check?' asked Okeke.

He looked at her. 'No. Did you check yours?'

She clasped her eyes shut for a moment. 'Baby, I really didn't need to.'

'It's okay, though. I've got his gun,' said Jay, eager to make amends. 'I'll go and check downstairs is clear.'

Boyd shook his head. 'No, we stay together. He's no doubt fled. Like Hammond.'

'What if he's gone to call in reinforcements?' asked Warren. 'Shouldn't we get away from here?'

Warren was right. If Hammond could rustle up three heavies, he could probably rustle up three more. 'We should be somewhere else. Anywhere else.' Boyd looked at them. 'All right, let's get Karl downstairs. Warren, get the car.'

## 56

What. The. Actual. Fuck?

Roland banged the steering wheel with his fist several times. Those stupid, half-shaved imbeciles had blundered into an ambush. He'd assumed – naively, it seemed – that if there was one thing they could do right, it was to take care of themselves in a scrap.

*All right. Well, fuck 'em. They're down. What now?*

He glanced in the rear-view mirror at the girl in the back. Her wide eyes locked on his, waiting to know her fate. 'Your dad just messed everything up,' he said with a sigh. 'I really was going to let you go, Emma. But that can't happen now, can it?'

He heard her mumble something from behind the tape.

'I'm going to have to make sure he gets a little piece of you, Emma, so that he realises he can't mess around with me again.'

She whimpered.

'It's really not my fault. You can't blame me.' He turned in his seat to look back at her. 'I'm in a bit of a jam here. I'm not a meanie, but... he's got to know I'm serious. You understand.'

*And he says he knows how much of a fix I'm in.*

That ape Turner only had half the picture, though – he was

pretty certain he was incapable of putting two and two together.

*But has Boyd worked it out?* Roland could imagine it wouldn't be too much of a stretch for him to piece together what was going on. A change of management. Out with the old, in with the new.

He could call his FSB contact. He had a number if not a name. They were on the same page as him; they wanted the same outcome – Rovshan dead. They'd get back what was theirs, and Roland, as promised, would get a share of it.

He pulled his phone out and dialled the number. It took a while for someone to answer.

'Who is this?'

He recognised the thick accent. The man sounded half asleep.

'Roland Hammond.'

'Why are you calling at this time?' He sounded angry. A pause. 'Is it done?'

'Not yet. There's been a... well, look, there's been a bit of a hiccup.'

There was silence on the other end of the phone.

'He may get to find out what's been going on,' Roland blurted.

'How?' The man sounded awake now.

'I... I was, shit, it wasn't even my fault,' Roland bleated.

'If he knows... then it is *your* problem.'

'If he knows, I'm fucking dead!' Roland said.

'Your problem,' the man repeated calmly.

'And you don't get your fucking money back? So if you don't help me, it's your problem too!'

'There are always other ways. Do not call me again.' The call ended.

Roland stared at his phone. 'Shit.' He redialled the number.

This time there was no answer, and after a dozen rings he realised no voicemail either.

'SHIIIIIIT!!!' he howled, tossing the phone into his lap. He gazed out of the windscreen at darkness. He was parked in a layby off a coastal road. Beyond the thin line of saplings in plastic chutes and the nettles lay nothing but shingle and waves. He had no bloody idea where he was. Sussex. Somewhere. He'd just driven until he'd found somewhere remote enough to stop and get his shit together.

*Think. Roland. Calm the fuck down and think.*

He took several deep breaths. 'Okay... okay...'

So, even though this was their ruddy idea in the first place, the Russians were leaving him to it.

*Think. THINK! Options. Options.* He let out another long breath. All right... The copper said he was open to a deal. He had definitely said that. Maybe that was the way forward. He needed to find out how much Boyd knew, because clearly *he knows something*, and make a deal. Maybe he could have his daughter returned in one piece if he agreed to back off and shut up.

Or he could call Mother and tell her to finish the old man off right now, if she could put her glass of gin down for long enough. He was weak, probably sedated, but certainly asleep. He could tell the silly cow to reach over and put a pillow over his fucking wrinkled face. Two minutes, maybe three, and she'd be done. Crisis over. And in the morning she could call Mr Karovic... and cry her crocodile tears for his benefit. *He was so exhausted... so frail... so...*

'All right,' he mumbled. 'Okay.'

## 57

Boyd's phone rang just as Warren was about to drive them out of the mews.

'Hold it!' He looked down at his phone. 'He's calling. I'm going to put it on speakerphone.' He nodded, then lifted a finger to his lips for them all to keep silent and answered: 'Boyd.'

'That was bloody stupid, Boyd!' Hammond began. 'We had a deal! Your daughter could be with you right now if you hadn't fucked it all up!'

*Keep this calm. Talk him down.*

'Do you really want me to send your daughter back in pieces?' Hammond screeched. 'Because you're going the right way about it!'

'I'm sorry,' Boyd said. 'I'll take more care this time round. Can I speak to her?'

'Fuck off.'

'Hammond, I need to know she's okay, otherwise... there's no way we can arrange anything. Let me hear that she's all right, then we can have a second go at fixing this.'

Boyd waited and finally he heard the phone rustling and the sound of tape being pulled off skin.

'Dad?!' she called.

Ozzie barked at the sound of her voice. Boyd reached out and grabbed his muzzle.

'Hey ho – you found your dog, then? Good,' Hammond said.

'Put Emma back on!' Boyd demanded.

'No. She's alive. You heard her. That'll do for now. Let's talk.'

Boyd sighed. 'All right.'

'Trust me, Boyd... I don't want any more shit tonight. No more tricks.'

'No tricks,' Boyd agreed.

Several seconds passed, then...

'Right, cards on the table, Boyd. You said you knew what this is all about. Before we sort anything out, I want to hear it. I want to hear what you fucking well know.'

Boyd looked at the others, a finger to his lips again to remind them not to make a noise.

Okeke nodded. *Tell him.*

He nodded assent. The more they knew, the greater their leverage. Hammond needed to hear this, even if some of it was based on guesswork.

'The Russian secret service wants your father dead,' said Boyd. 'And that's what Turner and Collins overheard you planning – his murder.'

Hammond was silent.

'I don't know whether this is about revenge, money or what. And frankly I don't give a shit. But I know that if this feeds back to your father, you're dead. Right?'

'That's... an interesting theory,' Hammond replied finally.

'And accurate,' Boyd said.

He heard Hammond laugh – an edgy flutter of breath that sounded almost frantic. 'He's double-crossed some dangerous people. If you're thinking you can play games with them... Boyd, you have no idea who you're messing around with.'

'The FSB,' Boyd said.

There was another long pause.

'Right... and so... you fuck with me and you're fucking with them too. But luckily for you I'm still prepared to make a deal with you.'

Boyd shook his head. 'I'm not an idiot, Hammond. I don't want to spend the rest of my life watching what I eat, or wondering whether my front-door handle is smothered with Novichok.'

Hammond chuckled. 'Right, Boyd. Exactly right. Because those sons of bitches don't ever forget.'

'And I really don't give a shit what happens to your father,' Boyd continued. 'I just want this over. I want Emma. So... Does that put us on the same page? Is there an arrangement we can come to?'

'That's all well and good, Boyd. But Turner knows about this too.'

'Turner's dead,' Boyd replied.

Jay opened his mouth, and Boyd flung his finger out to shut him up. 'Your men got to him first. They didn't manage to saw his ear off or firebomb the building, but they got him.'

'And I suppose you got them?'

Boyd nodded. 'Yes.'

'Well... then that's better,' said Hammond. 'So it's just us... who know about –'

'Yes,' Boyd replied.

Hammond laughed. 'Well, we seem to have each other over a bit of a barrel, don't we?'

'My side of the deal's easy,' said Boyd. 'Turner's body will be found. Your minders too. I'll wrap the case up and not tell your father what I know, and you'll...'

'I'll take Emma back to your house.'

'Tonight?'

'Yes, of course, tonight,' said Hammond. 'So what's your next step?'

'I'll come back to Hastings. Check she's there and that she's okay. Tomorrow I'll follow up on my investigation in Brighton and I'll happen to find Turner's body. And the others.'

'And I'm supposed to trust that you won't grass me up to my father?'

Boyd let out a sigh, with what he hoped sounded like genuine disinterest. 'Like I said... one less Russian mobster in London? I really couldn't give a toss.'

He heard Hammond sigh, with what sounded like relief. 'All right, then.'

'All right,' Boyd mirrored. 'Then we're done.'

The call ended abruptly.

'Well?' he asked the others.

'He's bullshitting,' said Jay. 'He's going to hang on to her until he's confirmed what you told him. She's his only chip.'

Boyd nodded; he suspected the same.

'He's playing for time,' said Warren. 'He'll be back with more men. What are you going to do, sir? Should we tell Sutherland and Hatcher now? They'll know what to do.'

'No.' Boyd looked down at his phone. He had what he wanted. 'Change of plan.'

# 58

By the creeping grey light of dawn, Roland parked the battered SUV outside Rovshan's grand town house. Battered was too dramatic a term for the vehicle – it had a dented rear bumper and the red plastic around one of the brake lights was broken. The other car had probably fared worse.

He turned round in his seat and looked at Emma, bound, gagged and lying prone across the back seat. 'I'm going to walk you inside, and you're going to keep perfectly quiet, do you understand?'

She nodded.

He opened the driver-side door and stepped out into a peculiarly still and peaceful morning. Eaton Square's trees were alive with the chirping of birds, and coming from another street nearby he heard a beep as someone unlocked their car.

It was 5 a.m. Unlike New York, it seemed that London *did* manage to find an hour or two on the clock to grab forty winks. The workmen who were currently in the process of stripping out the basement and ground floors of the house presumably wouldn't turn up until at least eight or nine. So, apart from the security chap who kept an eye on the building overnight, he would have the place to himself for a few hours.

Good. Time to compose himself. Time to grab a coffee and change his clothes. And to think how best to explain to his father about the mess that was last night. *You hire cretins, Father. Village idiots! We really should think about employing better security personnel.*

Then he'd take the short walk across to the hotel to see the old man.

*Can I take a couple more men back down to Hastings to fix the mess that the cretins left? It'll be straightforward with decent men. No mess. No fuss. We'll deal with that copper first. A small house fire and it'll all be sorted.*

Rovshan had been a pushover last time. He'd been so tired and lethargic from the blue-T Mummy had been slipping him that he'd seemed almost keen for Roland to just get on with the job. It wouldn't be long now.

Roland opened the rear door, quickly looked around to make sure there were no early delivery men in the square, and hauled Emma out of the vehicle and onto her bare feet.

'Not a fucking sound!' he hissed in her ear.

He gently closed the door and led her up the stairs to the front portico. The main door had a keypad and Mummy had convinced the old man that, security issues withstanding, it made sense for her son at least to have the code if he was going to use it as a London base for the time being.

Roland tapped the six-digit number into the keypad and the front door gently *snicked*. He pushed it open and dragged Emma inside.

The hallway was a mess: paint-flecked sheets covered the marble tiles; the walls that had once been rich dark mahogany were now stripped back to bare bricks. Stepladders remained where they'd been erected, and large plastic tubs of paint and lining plaster littered the floor.

*It's a fucking travesty.* If Rovshan didn't die in the next fort-night, the entirety of this beautiful Regency-period home was going to end up being blinged to death.

Roland led Emma across the floor, past the grand stairs, towards the door at the back that led to the utility rooms, the laundry room and the old staff kitchen.

'I could do with a coffee,' he said as pushed the door open and led her in. 'You can make yourself useful.' He pulled a knife out of a drawer and cut the tape around her wrists. Then peeled the tape from her mouth. 'Kettle's there; cups are there,' he said, pointing them out.

'I... I'm not making you a bloody coffee!' were the first words out of her dry mouth.

He waggled the knife in front of her face. 'You'll do as you're told, you silly bitch.'

'Why am I here?' she replied, refusing to move. 'What're you going to do with me?'

'You're going to be my guest for a little while.'

Roland heard muted footsteps behind him, turned and was met with the sight of Miko Karovic crossing the sheet-covered hallway floor.

'Roland,' he called out softly. 'There you are.'

'What the...? What're you doing here?' Roland glanced at his Rolex. 'At this time?'

A second man emerged from behind Miko. Roland recog-nised him – he was Father's personal chauffeur from back home in Georgia. Another pock-marked and scarred face, another village idiot who presumably went way back with his father.

'Davit,' said Karovic, 'stay with the girl.'

'Miko? What's going on?' Roland asked.

The old lawyer glared at him for the briefest moment, before turning on a courtroom smile. 'Let's go up to the music room to speak with your father,' he said.

'He's here?! Now? What's he doing up *at this time*?'

That cool, cadaverous smile again. 'He has some early business to attend to before the workmen arrive.'

Roland stood aside as Davit stepped into the kitchen and approached Emma.

'Come along,' said Karovic. 'Better not to keep your father waiting.'

～

KAROVIC PULLED the doors open and gestured at Roland to step into the room. In the bay window facing the French doors was his mother, sitting in the exact same seat as she'd been the last time he'd visited. Only she wasn't holding a gin and tonic, nor was she her normal groomed and made-up self.

Beside her in a wing-backed leather chair, turned away from the doors and facing the tall bay window, was Rovshan. Roland recognised his old hands resting on the arms, lumpy with prominent varicose veins and protruding knuckle bones.

Roland took a couple of slow steps, conscious of Karovic pulling the doors shut as he retreated.

'Aren't you coming in too?' Roland asked.

Karovic shook his head. 'Not this time.'

As the doors closed, Roland thought he caught sight of a genuine smile sliding across the bastard's snaky face.

*Something's happened.* He felt his insides turn to liquid. 'What's going on?' he demanded. 'Why are you up so early, Father?'

'I'm up *late*,' Rovshan replied softly. He leant slowly forward the creak of the seat reverberating loudly in the empty room. His pale, lined face appeared round the edge of the chair's winged back. 'How did your business in Hastings go, son?'

Roland felt a small sliver of relief.

*He's going to read me the riot act for the balls-up.* Fine. He could handle that. He had it straight in his head now. It had been Gregor's fault. It had been Gregor's idea to go blundering in without checking the place out first.

'Not as well as hoped, Father,' he began. 'Those idiots you sent down with me really screwed things up.'

He noticed his mother shaking her head, vigorously yet almost imperceptibly.

*What's she trying to...?*

'They screwed up, eh?' Rovshan tutted. He let out a long rasping sigh. 'Come here, son. I... I'm too tired to raise my voice.'

Roland walked across the room and joined them overlooking Eaton Square. He could see his father in his entirety now. He was dressed today in a suit and waistcoat, with one of his burgundy silk ties hanging loose around his collar. In one hand he held a cigarette with a long and drooping ash head. In the other his phone.

'Mistakes...' Rovshan began. 'I blame no one, so long as they correct them.'

Roland felt the tension in his body release a notch. This was going to be a dressing down, then. A lecture on leadership, a rap across the knuckles for his carelessness. A teachable moment for the time when he would one day be running the family firm.

'Betrayal, however...' Rovshan swiped at the phone's screen and jabbed it with one of his gnarly fingers.

*'He's double-crossed some dangerous people. If you're thinking you can play games with them... Boyd, you have no idea who you're messing around with.'*

'The FSB.'

A long pause. *'Right... and so...you fuck with me, then you're fucking with them too.'*

Rovshan Salikov tapped the screen to pause the playback, then he dipped his hand into the left hip pocket of his waistcoat. He pulled out a small brown bottle with an eyedropper lid.

'KGB tea,' he said, placing it gently on the side table.

'Oh, God.' His mother's barely restrained composure collapsed at the sight of it. She let out a small yelp of fear and began to sob into her hands.

Roland felt his gut roll over inside his belly, a somersault that almost made him retch.

'Miko!' Rovshan called out.

The doors clicked open. Roland spun round to see the old lawyer standing in the doorway, and beside him was a scruffy and dishevelled-looking man, a foot taller.

'Mr Boyd,' said Rovshan softly, 'you can now get your daughter and leave.'

# TWO WEEKS LATER

# 59

Okeke reached out and rubbed Jay's back as the big man's shoulders heaved with grief. She watched him catch his tears in a scrappy handkerchief. She caught Boyd looking sympathetically over at them. She wiped away the tear that had escaped down her cheek and scowled back at him.

The coffin had disappeared behind the drapes and the rollers ceased their squeaking as 'Come Up and See Me' faded away to silence.

'And let us now say our final goodbyes to Louie David Collins, a gentle soul taken far too early from this world to be with Our Lord in the next...'

~

Boyd left Jay and Okeke to console Louie's family and emerged from the crematorium into daylight. Scudding clouds crossed the blue sky as pools of light and shade bathed the crematorium's garden with subtle and shifting tones.

The car park was full, as had been the seats inside. It was

good to see that Louie had had a decent turn-out. There was nothing so bleak as attending a funeral in an official role and discovering you'd just doubled the numbers. He'd been to a few like that.

He spotted a solitary figure, a woman, standing beside a car. He didn't recognise her at first, dressed in her civvies.

It was Hatcher.

He nodded politely and ambled over to her.

'Morning, Ma'am. I wasn't expecting to see you here,' he said.

'Sutherland told me you were attending on behalf of the force,' she replied. 'Can we walk and talk?'

He glanced at his watch. He needed to be somewhere else by midday. 'I've got a bit of time.' He looked around; they had the garden to themselves.

Hatcher led the way along a gravel path, between two patches of daffodils that had chanced an early arrival.

'How are you doing?' asked Boyd.

She nodded. 'Okay. I'm thinking of extending my sick leave. I've even considered the prospect of early retirement.'

'What?' Boyd asked, surprised.

'I... All this has forced me to re-evaluate my work–life balance,' she explained.

Boyd smiled. 'As in: *they don't pay me enough to put up with this kind of crap?*'

She nodded. 'Policing is policing until you get to force-command level, then it turns political.' She looked at him. 'First Gerald Nix, then Sutton, and now with Salikov – I keep getting leaned on.'

'Leaned on?'

'Leant on, then.'

'No, I wasn't challenging your English,' he said, chuckling lightly.

'I had a visit from a couple of gentlemen a few years ago.

Not long after I met Zophia Salikov for the first time,' she continued. 'They didn't say as much but they were obviously MI6.'

'Jesus.'

She took a deep breath. 'Last year, I was made to bury everything that went on with Nix and had to take your shit for it. And now this whole Salikov incident is to be buried too.' She stopped and turned to him. 'Well, I've had enough. It's time you knew: Rovshan Salikov has a deal with MI6.'

'What kind of a deal?' Boyd asked, astonished.

'Immunity. His dirty money gets whitewashed. He's left alone, plus he gets MI6 protection.'

Boyd shook his head. 'So which government minister did he bribe to get all that?'

'It's down to what he knows,' she replied. 'Essentially where the KGB stashed their blood money back when things went pear-shaped for the Soviet Union. They had connections with a number of criminal families. Rovshan Salikov was one of their go-to men. One of their "trustees".'

'And he's rolling over for MI6?'

Hatcher nodded. 'Something like that. He'll help them locate and recover it, and in exchange they'll keep him safe, comfortable and living the good life.'

'So, his son, Hammond... I'm guessing –'

'Was approached by the FSB to silence his dad.' She shrugged. 'With a promise that he'd be their new tame, *controllable* trustee.'

'And what's happened to him?' Boyd asked.

She shook her head. 'I don't know. And I don't want to know.'

'MI6 presumably have him?'

Hatcher shrugged. 'I get the distinct impression that he's no longer around.' She glanced at him. 'Do you happen to know anything about that side of things?'

He hesitated for a moment too long.

'Well, I'll take it that you do,' she continued. 'I heard on the grapevine that there was a "turf war" between some unsavoury types in Brighton round about the time we were looking for Mr Turner.'

He nodded. 'I heard about that too.'

'A couple of dead East Europeans. Georgians? One shot by a crossbow. One, apparently, attacked by a samurai warrior.'

'Really? Blimey,' Boyd said.

They resumed walking through the garden. Boyd could now see the first of Louie's family and friends emerging from the building.

'So where does this leave us, ma'am? You were quite clear before that you weren't prepared to have me or Okeke under your command any longer.'

'For obvious reasons,' she replied. 'It makes command somewhat awkward if your junior officers think they have something on you. And what about you, Boyd? I'm somewhat uncomfortable having a DCI under my command who's prepared to go off-procedure when it suits him.'

'I believe we've both done a bit of that this time,' Boyd replied. 'But it was an *exceptional* scenario.'

She eyed him over the rim of her glasses. 'That's the term for it, is it?'

He shrugged. 'Well, I'm assuming we're all done with Russian OCGs for now.'

She nodded. 'Let's hope.' She looked over his shoulder at the people spilling out of the building. 'Let's end this conversation here, shall we? I'm meant to be on sick leave, not standing around in gardens spilling national secrets.' She raised her brows, turned away from him and begin walking back along the path to her car.

'How long will you be off, ma'am?' he called after her.

She stopped, turned and looked back at him, her

demeanour business-like once again. 'Don't push your luck, Boyd.'

# 60

B oyd watched the four-carriage train come to rest just short of the bumper. A moment later the doors opened and several dozen passengers emerged.

He spotted Charlotte immediately, being pulled by Mia on her leash and struggling to get the handle of her suitcase to extend properly, then equally struggling to get the cantankerous thing to stay standing.

He hurried forward to give her a hand. Mia started to dance in circles as soon as she spotted him approaching, tangling her lead around Charlotte's legs and almost pulling her and the wheelie bag over.

'Here let me,' he said grabbing the leash and the extended handle at the same time.

'Oh, thank God,' she gasped. 'The flipping left wheel's fallen off,' she said as he approached. 'I had to drag the wretched thing across London from King's Cross with Mia being a complete pain. If it wasn't for a lovely lady called Marcie who stopped to help, we wouldn't have made it here.'

Boyd untangled Mia and extended an arm around Charlotte. 'Well I'm glad you made it, you're a sight for sore eyes,' he mumbled into her hair.

She was a little taken aback. 'Mr Boyd!' she replied into his chest, with a fair degree of theatrical indignation. 'This really is most forward.'

'Sod it. I've missed you,' he said softly.

She hugged him in return. 'I've missed you too.'

He released her and then took a step back. 'Too much, too soon?' he asked, suddenly worried.

She smiled, stretched up and parked a kiss on his cheek. 'Not at all.'

'Here, you have Mia, I'll take the bag.' He reached for the handle of her case, pushed it back down and picked it up. 'Christ, what have you got in here?'

'A dead body, naturally,' she replied, deadpan.

He led her out of the station; at some point, as they emerged from the building, he realised they were holding hands.

'How was it seeing your parents again?' he asked.

'Lovely,' she replied. 'And a little strange. I felt like I was eighteen again. Which is both comforting and suffocating in equal measure. But yes, it was lovely. We had so much to catch up on. It really had been too long.'

Boyd clicked his car fob and his Captur beeped and unlocked. 'Hop in, m'dear, and I'll just stow this thing in the back.'

She let Mia onto the backseat and climbed in while Boyd went to lift the boot open. It was then that he noticed a small parcel placed beside the left rear tyre. Curious, he bent down to take a closer look. He picked it up, then turned it over... and froze.

The untidy scrawl smeared across the side was the exact same handwriting as on the note in his safe.

He stood up straight, feeling a moment of light-headedness as he did so, the blood draining from his face. He tossed the parcel into the boot and pulled Ozzie's muddy drying towel over the top of it. He looked around the car park and caught a glimpse of an old man with cropped silver hair and a hoodie walking swiftly away from him.

He recognised the scrawny son-of-a-bitch's cocky swagger.

The man paused for a moment, glanced back and saw Boyd staring at him. He cocked his head and grinned, revealing a glint of grisly teeth. He lifted his hand in salute, swung round and carried on his way.

Boyd looked down at the lump under the towel in his boot. God knows what was going to be in the gift box this time. He really didn't want to know. Maybe he'd just dump it in his safe and forget it. Or, better still, just dump it.

He hefted Charlotte's suitcase into the boot and pulled the rear door down.

'Everything okay there, Bill?' Charlotte asked as he climbed into the car beside her. 'You look a little pale.'

'I'm fine,' he replied. 'It's all good.'

'Are you sure?' she asked.

He nodded. 'Have you eaten?'

'No. I'm starving,' she replied.

'How does fish and chips on the pier sound?'

She smiled. 'It sounds perfect.'

## THE END

# DCI BOYD RETURNS IN

ARGYLE HOUSE available to pre-order
here

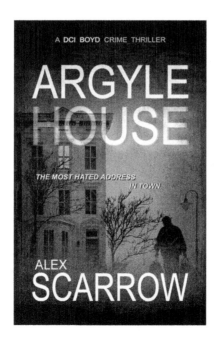

# ABOUT THE AUTHOR

Over the last sixteen years, award-winning author Alex Scarrow has published seventeen novels with Penguin Random House, Orion and Pan Macmillan. A number of these have been optioned for film/TV development, including his best-selling *Last Light*.

When he is not busy writing and painting, Alex spends most of his time trying to keep Ozzie away from the food bin. He lives in the wilds of East Anglia with his wife Deborah and five, permanently muddy, dogs.

Ozzie came to live with him in January 2017. He was adopted from Spaniel Aid UK and was believed to be seven at the time. Ozzie loves food, his mum, food, his ball, food, walks and more food...

He dreams of unrestricted access to the food bin.

For up-to-date information on the DCI BOYD series, visit: www.alexscarrow.com

# ALSO BY ALEX SCARROW

**DCI Boyd**

SILENT TIDE

OLD BONES NEW BONES

BURNING TRUTH

THE LAST TRAIN

THE SAFE PLACE

**Thrillers**

LAST LIGHT

AFTERLIGHT

OCTOBER SKIES

THE CANDLEMAN

A THOUSAND SUNS

**The TimeRiders series (in reading order)**

TIMERIDERS

TIMERIDERS: DAY OF THE PREDATOR

TIMERIDERS: THE DOOMSDAY CODE

TIMERIDERS: THE ETERNAL WAR

TIMERIDERS: THE CITY OF SHADOWS

TIMERIDERS: THE PIRATE KINGS

TIMERIDERS: THE MAYAN PROPHECY

TIMERIDERS: THE INFINITY CAGE

# ACKNOWLEDGMENTS

Here we are again with a big debt of gratitude owed to my wife, Deborah, who sanity-checks my pidgin english and incoherent plotting and Wendy Shakespeare who rigorously copy-edits and continuity-checks the series.

I also have to extend a big thank you to our team of beta-readers who once again have saved me from looking like an utter fool with various errata-'gotchas'. In no specific order they are; Maureen Webb, Donna Morfett, Susan Burns, Steve Dimmer, Paula Shaw, Pippa Cahill-Watson, Lynda Checkley, Andrew White, Lesley Lloyd and Marcie Whitecotton-Carroll - 'all dogs must be accounted for' - good save Marcie! :)

Once more, Boyd, Ozzie and I must thank the UKCBC group on Facebook for their continuing support for the series.

As always, my heartfelt thanks go to Spaniel Aid UK for allowing us to adopt our adorable boy Ozzie in 2017. He's loving being the most impawtant member of Team Boyd. If you would like to know more about Spaniel Aid UK and the work they do, please visit their website: www.spanielaid.co.uk

We share another of our dogs with Team Boyd. We adopted Charlotte's Mia from Brittany's Needing Homes in 2019. They work tirelessly to save dogs at risk in Spain and find them their forever homes in the UK. If you would like to know more, please look them up on Facebook.

Printed in Great Britain
by Amazon